Love's
MOUNTAIN QUEST

Books by Misty M. Beller

HEARTS OF MONTANA

Hope's Highest Mountain
Love's Mountain Quest

HEARTS
OF
MONTANA
BOOK TWO

MOUNTAIN QUEST

MISTY M.
BELLER

BETHANYHOUSE
a division of Baker Publishing Group
Minneapolis, Minnesota

© 2020 by Misty M. Beller

Published by Bethany House Publishers
11400 Hampshire Avenue South
Bloomington, Minnesota 55438
www.bethanyhouse.com

Bethany House Publishers is a division of
Baker Publishing Group, Grand Rapids, Michigan

Printed in the United States of America

Library of Congress Control Number: 2019055368

ISBN 978-0-7642-3347-0

Scripture quotations are from the King James Version of the Bible.

This is a work of fiction. Names, characters, incidents, and dialogues are products of the author's imagination and are not to be construed as real. Any resemblance to actual events or persons, living or dead, is entirely coincidental.

Cover design by Kirk DouPonce, DogEared Design

Author is represented by Books & Such Literary Agency.

20 21 22 23 24 25 26   7 6 5 4 3 2 1

To my agent, Cynthia.
I love your heart and passion,
and I continue to be amazed
at God's providence
when He brought us together.
I will ever be thankful for you!

Therefore if any man be in Christ, he is a new creature: old things are passed away; behold, all things are become new.

2 Corinthians 5:17

ONE

JUNE 25, 1867
SETTLER'S FORT, MONTANA TERRITORY

*T*he woman stood in the wind, skirts billowing, hair flying, as though the gusts swept away all her inhibitions. All her sorrows. The heavy weight of her losses. With the warm gale buffeting her, she seemed to revel in the freedom.

Isaac Bowen couldn't tear his eyes away.

Each time he visited Settler's Fort, he made a point to check on Joanna Watson. This time he'd been lucky enough to spot her on his way into town, in the grassy area beside the swimming hole. The little-boy laughter and splashes filling the air had to belong to her high-spirited son, Samuel.

Since she and her lad were in the party he helped rescue from the mountain wilderness several months before, he couldn't help but feel the need to make sure they fared well. Joanna had rented a house near the edge of town and taken on work as a washerwoman. She and her son seemed to have what they needed, but worry for her still ate at him. A woman without family in this rough territory faced a difficult existence, but every time he asked, she showed a capable front.

And now, seeing her unencumbered from worries, with the wind brushing her face . . . how could he have not realized the exhaustion she'd carried on their journey? In this moment, her face shone with a radiance that accentuated her beauty. Her pretty features had never been lost on him, but apparently he'd been too dense to see how much life weighed her down. Was it life in the little town of Settler's Fort that caused her weariness? Or simply the challenges of trying to feed and clothe herself and her boy since her husband had succumbed to an ax wound seven months before?

"Ma, come see what I can do," the little boy's voice called from the water.

Mrs. Watson turned toward the stream but stilled when her gaze passed over Isaac. His heart stilled, as well, but he nodded in greeting and nudged his gelding forward. The two packhorses trailed them dutifully, worn out from the week spent traveling the mountains while Isaac hunted and trapped. Once he spent a few minutes with Mrs. Watson, trying to ascertain the truth of how she fared, he'd take his furs and part of the elk meat to trade for supplies at the mercantile. Maybe he'd ride the hour home tonight. Or maybe he'd stop in at the café for a home-cooked meal. The thought raised a growl from his middle.

Mrs. Watson shielded her eyes with a hand as he approached, and Isaac offered a friendly smile.

"Afternoon, ma'am." He dismounted to greet her eye-to-eye.

"Mr. Bowen. This is a surprise." She lowered the hand shadowing her face, revealing a soft smile that lit her pretty brown eyes. "Samuel and I are enjoying the pleasant Sunday afternoon."

He sent a gaze toward the stream just as a red tousle of hair rose up from the water, droplets streaming down the boy's tan back. He shook the water away like a puppy would. "Mr. Bowen. When did you get here?"

Isaac couldn't help but match the boy's grin. "Hello, Samuel. I stopped to say howdy on my way into town."

"I'm glad. Watch what I can do. Mama, did you see me?" Samuel leaned sideways and popped one ear with his palm to dislodge liquid from the other ear.

Isaac glanced back at the boy's mother, who met his look with a sheepish smile. She raised her voice to answer her son. "I didn't see. Can you do it again?"

"Watch." Samuel didn't stop to ensure she watched, just dropped back under the water.

Isaac stepped closer to the bank's edge to see what feat the lad had learned, and he could feel the weight of Mrs. Watson's presence beside him.

Under the water's surface, Samuel twisted and darted like a tadpole, then rose up with a splash. He shook again, then grinned up at them both. "Did you see me? I can do a flip."

His smile was so infectious that it was impossible not to match it. "Good job. You're swimming better than I could when I was your age."

9

Samuel beamed, then turned and splashed back under the water, his five-year-old legs kicking for all he was worth.

Isaac chuckled as he turned back to the boy's mother. Being around Samuel made him want to settle in and enjoy life as much as the lad did. But he'd better get moving if he was going to reach the mercantile before they closed. "I'm back from a hunting trip and have extra meat I'd like to give you. Do you want me to leave it at your house?"

A shadow passed over her face, bringing with it the weariness that had been there in days past. "I can't take your food. Surely you need it yourself."

He forced as casual an air as he could manage and shook his head. "I bagged two big elk and a bunch of smaller game. It will go to waste if I keep it all." Which was true, although he'd be trading all the extra he and Pa couldn't take on. But first he'd give as much to Mrs. Watson and her boy as he could get her to take.

Without waiting for an answer, he turned back to Samuel, who'd splashed up to the water's surface again. "You're swimming like a fish." He raised a hand in farewell. "I'm headed on now, Samuel. Take care of your mama. See you soon."

"Bye, Mr. Bowen."

Isaac turned back toward his horses, and Mrs. Watson strolled beside him. "Is there anything I can do for you while I'm in town, ma'am?"

"Thank you for offering, but we're managing just fine." Her soft voice rolled out in a cadence so convincing, it had lulled him into belief the other times she'd responded such.

Yet she must have repairs that needed doing or heavy lifting she couldn't handle.

Unless other men in town saw to her needs. The thought sank in his gut like a stone.

Since he and Pa lived outside Settler's Fort, he didn't make it into town to check on her as often as he'd like. Of course the other men in town wouldn't let her rest, as starved for female attention as many of them were. Did they badger her? Maybe that was why she'd developed such a convincing rebuttal.

He glanced at her from the corner of his eye as he neared his horses. "I'll be in town overnight if there's anything you think of." He wouldn't be pushy, but he couldn't help the need to offer once more.

"Thank you, Mr. Bowen. It was good to see you again."

The only response he could think of was a nod, and then he took up the reins and mounted.

As he rode away, he couldn't help a quick glance back. Mrs. Watson stood in the same place, face tilted toward the sun. Her willowy figure looked so slight with the breeze whipping her skirts, brushing her feathery brown hair around her face.

If only there was more he could do to help her.

⊰⊱⊰⊱

Joanna Watson's shoulders sagged under the Monday evening strain. The weight of her worries seemed to wrench every muscle, every weary limb. And as she walked along the quiet main street of Settler's Fort, she let herself succumb to the ache. Just for a moment.

Life was simply too hard sometimes. Just yesterday she'd been watching Samuel dart through the water as they'd enjoyed their Sunday, her one day of rest.

But today's work had exhausted every renewed part of her. If only she hadn't chosen laundry as her line of work in Settler's Fort. But there weren't any other suitable ways to bring in enough wages for food and shelter.

This new life she was trying to create for herself and her son hadn't turned out the way she'd hoped for them. And she wasn't quite sure what to do about it.

The last time she'd had to create a new life—after her parents and sister died in the train crash—she'd married Robert. But he wasn't here to save her now.

She had to manage on her own.

She probably shouldn't have rushed to finish her work early today. Should have worked on the stack of washing she was saving for the next day, but her new friend Laura had taken Samuel swimming again to escape the heat of the late June afternoon. And Joanna hadn't been able to squelch the impulse to meet them with a picnic for an early evening meal.

Her young son had so few pleasures these days. She owed Laura a favor for offering to take him from the heat of their little home and allow Joanna an afternoon to work without having to keep him occupied, too. Swimming had quickly become Samuel's favorite pastime, so he'd jumped at Laura's invitation.

The younger woman had become a good friend over the past month since she'd come to town, almost like a sister.

Maybe they'd grown close because they were both new to town. Or perhaps because they'd both lost almost everyone they held dear. Lord willing, they'd both be able to create the new life they craved.

But now was the time to push away her worries and put on a smile for her son.

The satchel containing the small meal Joanna had scraped together grew heavier the farther she walked past the outskirts of town, along the tree-lined edge of the shallow creek. At last, she neared the section where the waters gathered into a deeper pool, perfect for swimming.

She strained to hear the little-boy laughter that was a trademark of her son's exuberant personality. Samuel had more energy—and could get into more trouble with it—than any child she knew. His liveliness never ceased to cause apprehension when she let him out of her sight—and her protection. But a boy needed an outlet to release his pent-up energy. She had to keep reminding herself that allowing him to enjoy this afternoon with Laura today had been the right choice.

Almost to the water now, she heard no splashing of swimmers. Joanna's pulse and pace quickened. She stepped through the trees around the edge of the swimming hole. "Samuel? Laura?"

Only the faint gurgle of running water answered.

She reached the bank's edge and scanned the stream in front of her. No heads bobbed in the water. No figures relaxed on the stretch of rocky beach. An inspection in both directions still showed nothing.

She pressed down the panic that bubbled up in her chest. There had to be a logical reason. They must have hiked down the creek.

Dropping her food satchel, she cupped both hands around her mouth and yelled, "Samuel! Laura!"

She strained to hear their replies over the pounding of her heart.

No high-pitched voice answered her. Nothing but the trickling current.

Alarm lashed her imagination, creating scenes of horror. What if Samuel had been caught in deep water, a root holding him under? Maybe he and Laura had both drowned trying to free him.

Or Indians. Though she'd rarely seen them, this country was still home to more tribes than she could name. What if a group of them had come along and taken her son for his curly red hair? *Oh, Lord, where is my baby?*

She scrambled through the trees and brush, moving farther and farther downstream as fast as she could weave through the branches.

Over and over, she called their names. How far would they have gone? Had something happened to make them pack up and return home early?

No. She would've seen them on the road. Unless Laura knew of a shortcut. The other woman had lived in Settler's Fort slightly longer than the half year Joanna and Samuel had resided here.

She paused for one final, desperate scream of their names. Only her own voice echoed back.

Dear God, let them be safe. She couldn't lose her son, too. Not after everything else she'd lost.

She had to stop jumping to conclusions. Laura was probably, even now, taking Samuel through a hidden trail on their way back to the little rented house Joanna could barely afford. Maybe they were already sitting at the small table, snacking on biscuits, waiting for her to return.

Joanna turned away from the creek, working her way back through the trees and brush to the road that followed the water. Without her load, she could move faster. Getting home to her boy was all that mattered.

Once she reached the road, she turned toward town and raised her skirts so she could sprint. Just past the swimming hole, a flash of white caught her eye. A sack. It looked like the one she'd seen Laura carry when she'd come to pick up Samuel earlier.

She veered toward the fabric, then paused in front of it, her breath coming in giant heaves. She opened the cloth bag to peer inside. An apple. A blanket. She riffled through the contents to see if anything was hidden underneath.

Nothing.

Turning to the ground around her, she scanned the area for something—anything—she'd missed. There were no clothes strewn around, although the grass was pressed down in this spot like people had recently spent time here.

Once more, she screamed her son's name into the air, tasting her desperation with the cry.

Still no answer.

Gathering her skirts, she ran toward town again. Every

few minutes she stopped to call for Laura and her boy, which gave her lungs a chance to gulp in air. Still, no response.

God, please let them be at home. They had to be. She would snatch her son into a giant hug and breathe in his boy scent—a combination of dirt and sunlight and creek water.

As she entered town, the streets seemed even more deserted than before. Settler's Fort was a quiet town, mostly occupied by miners, but a few families also resided here. People must still be hard at work for the afternoon, or otherwise hiding inside from the fierce sun. This was the warmest June she could remember in the mountain country.

Her side ached as though pierced by a knife, but she didn't slow her stride until she reached her door. It gave way beneath her push, and she almost fell inside. "Samuel? Laura?"

The dark interior tightened the knot in her belly.

"Laura!" She yelled loud enough to wake the neighbors, but only a thick silence answered her call.

"Oh, God, where are they?" She pressed a hand to her forehead, working to rein her thoughts into a semblance of order. Maybe they'd gone to the mercantile. Samuel always loved to look around there, and he usually wheedled for a sweet. Maybe he'd talked Laura into stopping.

She spun and charged back down the street toward the shop she'd already passed twice. This mercantile didn't have glass-front windows like those back in St. Louis, so she had no idea who was inside as she opened the solid wood door.

The bell jingled, and she scanned the interior, squinting to see in the dimness. "Laura? Samuel?" It might be poor manners to raise her voice in the store, but there were too many shelves and barrels they might be standing behind.

And the fear inside her couldn't be contained any longer.

TWO

*M*rs. Watson?" A voice to her right spun her that direction, and she stepped into the store and closed the door so her eyes could better adjust to the lighting.

Mr. Bowen stood beside a shelf of glass jars, and the sight of his familiar face eased the edge of her fear. "Mr. Bowen. Have you seen my son? Is he in here with Laura Hannon?"

There was another time this virile mountain man had come to her aid, when she and Samuel had been stranded while traveling with the Bradleys to Settler's Fort. She couldn't look at his face without remembering the strength and capability he'd shown during that arduous journey.

And the gentleness he'd offered her son. The memory brought a surge of the tears she'd been forcing down. Even after that journey, Mr. Bowen went out of his way to check on her when he came to town. Never pressing her like some of the other men did, just offering friendly help. And never going without leaving some type of food or other gift, like the parcel of elk meat he'd left at their house the night before.

"I haven't seen either of them." His sharp gaze scanned the mercantile. "I'm pretty sure I'd know if that boy was in here."

She bit back a sob. He was right. If Samuel wasn't moving his body, he settled for working his mouth, talking until the adults around him clamped their hands over their ears in exasperation.

If she could just hear his sweet voice now, she'd never be exasperated again.

"Laura took Samuel to the swimming hole while I finished my work. But they've disappeared. I searched down the creek and back at my house. They're not anywhere." Her voice broke. "Something's very wrong."

Mr. Bowen stepped toward her. "Did you check both sides of the water? How far down did you go?"

She pressed both hands to her temples. "Not both sides. I went as far down the creek as I thought they would walk, and I yelled for them the entire time." Had she not searched hard enough?

"Let's go have another look. I know a back way we can check, too."

Joanna nearly wilted from relief. Having someone help with the search—someone who knew more about the area than she did—removed a layer of strain from her shoulders.

As they traveled down the quiet street, Mr. Bowen's long stride ate up the ground, but she was glad to run along beside him. Even though her body protested against another sprint, her nerves craved to move even faster.

Near the edge of town, he veered to the right before they

reached the water, then led her down an overgrown path through the woods. Before long, they reached the swimming hole.

Her hungry eyes scanned the area, and she cupped her hands around her mouth to call them again. Once more, no response.

"Let's go downstream to where the crossing is shallow. Did they leave any sign they'd been here?" Mr. Bowen was already moving.

She lengthened her stride to keep up while her chest struggled to inflate. "Laura's sack is in the grass on the other side. I dropped mine somewhere, too."

He slowed to help her across the rocky streambed, but she motioned him on. "Go. See what you can find."

He hesitated but must have seen something in her eyes that convinced him, for he turned and leapt up the steep dirt bank in two long steps.

By the time she reached the open area where she'd left Laura's bag, Mr. Bowen had ventured farther into the woods than she had during her own sweep of the area. He was crouched down low, examining something partially hidden in the grass behind a cluster of trees.

"What is it?" But as she neared, the lump of clothing took shape. Her feet slowed as her eyes struggled to make sense of what she was seeing.

A person lying in the grass? Her heart surged. *Not Samuel. Lord, no!*

Mr. Bowen looked up at her approach, his gaze turning wary. He stood and stepped toward her, his hand outstretched as though trying to stay her. His body blocked most of the figure lying prone on the ground. A numbness sank through her, taking over her mouth so she couldn't force words out. Taking over her mind so she couldn't think straight. *Not my son. Surely God wouldn't take the only person I have left.*

"It's the sheriff." Mr. Bowen's words buzzed in her ears. "He's been shot."

The word *shot* finally broke through the haze locking her mind, and she replayed his explanation to make sense of it. *Not* her son? She leaned around Mr. Bowen to see for sure, her body moving before her mind knew what she was doing.

A swollen face glared up at her, eyes rolled back in his head. The bruises disfigured him so much she could barely see the scars from pockmarks that usually glared a bright red, remnants of the smallpox outbreak that had surged through the community only months before.

Blood trickled from his lip, and more from one ear. She bit her lip and turned away, her stomach threatening to spill what little was left.

She'd seen plenty of gruesome images living in this mountain wilderness, including the mangled arm of her late husband. But just now, her nerves were in too much turmoil to be strong.

She took a step backward, dropping her gaze to the ground beside her. "What happened to him? Was it a hunting accident?" And did this have anything to do with why Samuel and Laura were missing? Maybe they'd found the dead man and hurried back to town to report the news. But wouldn't they have gone to the mercantile? Everyone knew Mr. Lanton served as acting deputy whenever the sheriff wasn't around.

And with this new turn of events, it looked like Mr. Lanton would have his hands full.

Mr. Bowen knelt again beside the body for several minutes, then stood and studied the ground around them. He walked several paces across the clearing, studying the grass with an intensity that seemed to mean he saw something of interest.

Keeping herself from asking what he saw was no easy feat, but he would tell her when he was ready. Men hated pushy women. At least Robert had.

At last, he looked up at her, his brow furrowed. "It wasn't a hunting accident. The bullet went through his chest at an angle he couldn't have accomplished himself. There are horse tracks, too. Were Miss Hannon and your son on horseback?"

She jerked back, trying to process the odd question. "We don't own a horse. Are the prints recent?" She'd lived in the wilderness long enough to be able to read some signs, but probably nothing like the abilities of this sage mountain man.

He turned back to examine the ground, and Joanna neared to see what had captured his attention. Deep hoofprints marred the grass, much more than one horse could create, unless that horse rode back and forth through the area several times. Gooseflesh tickled her arms. "How many do you think were here? Indians, do you think? Why would they shoot Sheriff Zander?" And where was her son? Maybe she should go look for Laura and her boy while Mr. Bowen investigated the sheriff's death. But what if the two events were connected?

"I don't think these tracks are from Indian ponies. The horses were shod." Mr. Bowen stood, then turned back toward the creek, his gaze still focused on the grass.

As relief sank through her from his words, she looked again at the ground, but nothing jumped out at her. The early summer grass was a mixture of green and brown, and still thick enough that it didn't show human footprints. Only those deep tracks from horses.

Mr. Bowen straightened from examining the grass, then turned with a determined expression as he marched toward the road. "I need to see where these tracks are headed."

The knot in her middle tightened at the sight of his squared shoulders. Joanna focused on clamping down her imagination as she waited for Mr. Bowen to return. And when he did finally turn and come back to her, the dark foreboding in his eyes was almost her undoing.

She met him partway. "What is it? Where are they?"

"Four sets of horse tracks, all shod. One looked like it was running loose, maybe the sheriff's mount. Two men dismounted and moved toward the river, then four people walked back to the horses." He paused and worked his jaw, as if tempering his words. "The two additional tracks were smaller, one narrow like a woman's boots, and the other small like a child."

Breath wouldn't fill Joanna's chest as his statements tumbled through her mind. His words hinted at something too awful to accept. Too horrible to fathom. "What are you saying, Mr. Bowen? Just tell me." She grabbed his arm, willing him to produce her son right then and there.

He placed his hand over hers, but she was too focused on his face and the sorrow creasing his features to trouble over anything else. "I think it's possible that whoever killed the sheriff kidnapped Miss Hannon and your son."

THREE

*B*ut why would they take them? What would they want with a woman and boy?" But she knew what they would want from a lovely young woman like Laura. Joanna's knees nearly buckled, but she held herself up by sheer force of will and her grip on Mr. Bowen's firm arm.

His Adam's apple bobbed under the scruff of newly grown beard at his throat. "Maybe the two saw the shooting. The men might've gotten scared and scooped them up so they couldn't be witnesses. Killing a lawman is a hanging offense, no doubt about it. I'll round up some menfolk from town and we'll set out after them."

She gripped his arm tighter. "I'm coming, too. I'll get a horse from the livery." She tripped over her skirts as she ran to gather Laura's bag and her own satchel of food. With a stumble, she barely kept herself from tumbling down in the grass beside the swimming hole.

"Mrs. Watson. It's not safe for a woman to go after them, and we can move faster without you."

She ignored his words. There was no time to quibble, especially when nothing he said would change her mind. With the satchels in one hand and the hem of her cotton work dress in the other, she sprinted along the dusty road toward town.

Halfway there, she registered the deep breaths and pounding feet of the man running beside her and glanced at him. A sheen of sweat coated his forehead, but his expression seemed equally set on rounding up the help they needed. For that she was thankful, despite the panic urging her forward. Dare she hope they could find Laura and Samuel before it was too late? She could well imagine what they would do to Laura, but what would the evil men expose her son to?

The streets of town remained empty and deserted. Why had she brought Samuel to this tiny settlement in the middle of nowhere? If only she'd gone back to St. Louis, such a travesty would never have happened, or at least there would be other lawmen around to help.

The livery stood near the edge of town, and Mr. Bowen stopped at the doorway. "I'll have Sam get the horses ready, then go tell Lanton the news."

But as she followed him inside the livery, the place seemed devoid of human presence. All the men must still be in the mines, or maybe there was some kind of town meeting she didn't know about. Horses nickered from the stalls as they entered, and the high-pitched bray of a mule sounded from far down the aisle.

"Anyone here?" Mr. Bowen called as he strode in.

No answer sounded, so he called again. At last he turned to her. "Sam must be off for dinner. See if there's a bay mare in one of the end stalls. She's gentle and will work well for you. I'll run down to the mercantile, then come back and ready my animals so we can get going."

She'd never been in this barn, had never met Sam, but she wasn't about to question Mr. Bowen when he was helping her find her boy. She'd deal with the cost of renting the horse later.

Even though she moved as quickly as her shaking hands would allow, by the time she found a saddle and readied the bay mare with the kind eyes, Mr. Bowen had returned and was saddling the chestnut gelding he'd been riding the day before. Within minutes, he had another horse lined up in the hallway and was fastening a packsaddle on its back.

Her throat tightened. "You think we'll be gone overnight?"

He pulled a strap tight to fasten down one of the packs. "After we find your boy and Miss Hannon, I'll ride home from there, so I'd like to have my things with me. Besides, something in here might come in handy."

He thought they'd find Samuel and Laura within a few hours? She wanted to cling to the hope. But they'd been gone for so long already. Hours, probably.

"What did Mr. Lanton say?"

Mr. Bowen pulled the cinch strap on the packsaddle. "He's gathering men to bring in the sheriff's body, then to help us catch up to the people who have your son. I told him we'd ride on ahead and follow the tracks."

Good. At least they wouldn't have to wait for others to saddle their horses.

After Mr. Bowen scribbled a note for Sam explaining why

they'd taken the horses, they mounted and rode out of the barn.

Her heart cried a desperate prayer with every beat of her horse's hooves. *God, save my boy.*

<hr>

They rode as fast as Isaac could track on the rough wagon ruts that passed for a road through this mountain valley. The hoofprints led away from town, which made sense if the men who shot the sheriff were running. Maybe they were ne'er-do-wells living up in one of the ravines where miners congregated. But their trail wasn't going in the direction of any communities he was aware of.

Lord, let us find them before dark. They would. They had to. If he lost the tracks, there was no telling how far ahead the despoilers would get. Maybe all the way back to the rock they crawled out from under.

But as the tracks left the main path, heading southwest instead of north toward the mining camps, his chest squeezed tighter. Just traveling this direction brought back memories he never allowed himself to relive.

For ten years he'd avoided this trail—and for good reason. He still fought against the dark, hollow places that catastrophe had etched in his heart.

He had no choice now but to go on. Mrs. Watson needed him. So he swallowed the bile churning inside and rode forward.

The one good thing about being familiar with this land

was his ability to move fast through the mountain passes, finding the hidden ravines he used to travel back in his lawless days.

Yet, the fact that the men they pursued also rode through those ravines didn't sit well in his gut. Those men must be just as familiar with this hidden path that would keep them far from any form of law, just as at home in the treacherous gorges and gullies.

Please, Lord, let this not be the gang I started all those years ago. Just because this was the trail to the hideout they'd used didn't mean the three horsemen they followed were part of that band.

No. He thrust the menacing thought aside. He'd long ago stopped letting his past rise up to haunt him.

For her part, Mrs. Watson kept up remarkably well, her horse following close behind his pack gelding. But as daylight faded to dusk, then to night, the tightness in Isaac's chest gripped harder. There was enough moon that he could see the tracks as long as they were out in open areas. If they moved into tree cover, he'd probably lose the trail.

Should he keep going? With this woman? He'd hoped to overtake the men before nightfall, but that had turned into a foolish wish. Were the other men from town following close behind him and Mrs. Watson? The posse would have to stop for the night, too.

Since it looked like this chase wouldn't be over tonight, should he return Mrs. Watson to town where she'd be out of danger? He should at least try.

He reined in his horse and turned to her.

"What is it? What's wrong?" Her voice held a thick edge of panic, but she hadn't fallen into hysterics on him yet, proving once again that she was a strong woman. The only kind who could survive in this mountain wilderness, if any could.

He chose his words carefully. "It doesn't look like we'll catch them tonight. You'd better go back to town. I'll stay on their trail, and when the men Lanton sends catch up, we'll free your son and Miss Hannon."

The moonlight shone in patches on her face, casting her eyes in deep shadows. "I'm not leaving my son out there without searching for him. He's all I have left. I'd rather die than risk his life in someone else's hands."

God, what do I do? If he allowed this woman to accompany him, keeping her safe may be the hardest part of the journey—especially if it turned out the kidnappers were the ghosts from his past. Or men like them. Or worse. Perspiration coated his palms at the thought.

"We have to ride on. Every moment we're not moving, those men are getting farther away with my boy." She moved her horse up beside him. "We should keep going. Both of us. Now."

The hard set of her chin made her resolve unmistakable.

Will you keep us safe, Lord? But he knew the answer deep in his bones. He'd placed his life in God's hands, and the Almighty would guard them. The quiet whisper in his spirit only confirmed it.

Breathing out his pent-up nerves, he nudged his horse forward. "We'll ride until we can't see the trail any longer."

"This is where we get a few hours' sleep." Mr. Bowen's voice broke the silence between them.

Joanna stared up at the crags and angles of the mountain rising above them. Her spirit fought against the idea of stopping before she had her boy in her arms, but Mr. Bowen was right. They couldn't traverse this peak in the dark of night without endangering them both.

And right now they were Samuel and Laura's best hope.

In fact, it didn't look very likely they could scale those cliffs in the daytime, but she had to trust Mr. Bowen's leading. What choice did she have? And if a group of despicable men could find a way over them with her son and her friend in tow, she and this seasoned mountain man definitely could.

"How far ahead do you think they are?" She leaned forward to dismount, her body aching with the movement.

"I'm hoping only an hour or two, but it's hard to tell how old the tracks are in the dark. We'll know more come morning." His voice drifted through the night air, guarded and weary. He'd already slid from his horse's back and was working at the pack behind his saddle.

She led her mount toward a spot of ground that seemed more level than the rest. "I guess this is the best place for sleeping." Except she'd brought nothing with her to use for bedding. She'd only had the satchel of food she'd intended as a picnic, and she'd shared half of that with Mr. Bowen while they rode.

Maybe between her saddle blanket and the sack, she would

have enough to cushion her head. Thank the Lord the weather was warm enough she wouldn't need a cover.

"Here. There's food and blankets in this pack." He handed over the bundle from behind his saddle. "If you're hungry, eat. Then divide up the bedding between us. I'm going to stake the horses out so they can graze."

A breath of relief slipped from her. At least he'd come prepared. Perhaps she should feel guilty for using his things, but as she laid the blankets and furs in two stacks, a breath of thanks was all she could summon.

She had biscuits remaining in her satchel, but maybe he had roasted meat in his pack to accompany her meager fare and fill her protesting belly. Several leather-wrapped bundles looked to be the foodstuffs, and in the second one she checked, she found what she was looking for. Chunks of cooked meat.

As she tucked the other bundles back in the pack, the feel of something hard at the bottom caught her notice. The stiff leather felt almost like a book. Her fingers slid along the surface until they slipped over the edge, brushing the feather-like pages of a thick volume.

She shouldn't look any further, but she was too exhausted to fight her curiosity. Slipping her fingers around the edge of the book, she eased it out. In the glimmer of moonlight, faded gold lettering on the worn cover read *Holy Bible*. A glance inside revealed tattered pages and tiny handwriting in some of the margins. A well-used guide, which explained some of the reason why this man seemed so solid.

Closing the book, she slipped it back in the pack, but her

34

fingers brushed another volume as she replaced the Bible. Two more, actually.

She couldn't help but pull them out. What more would they tell her about this man in whose care she'd placed her life—and the well-being of her son and friend? The first was *The Scarlet Letter* by Nathaniel Hawthorne. Not as worn as the Bible, but the spine definitely showed wear. The second, Charles Dickens's *A Tale of Two Cities*, looked to have journeyed with him longer than Hawthorne, with dog-eared corners and finger smudges throughout its pages.

What kind of man traveled with his own library? Especially out here, where books were hard to come by. She knew that well, as she'd not had more to read than her own Bible and a couple of well-worn novels by Jane Austen and Charlotte Brontë. She'd brought them when she'd first come west with Robert. Samuel had only been a year old then.

It seemed like another lifetime.

The sound of quiet footsteps on stone brought her back to the present, and she quickly tucked the books back in the pack, then set to work assembling the meat and biscuits for a quick meal.

Mr. Bowen eased down on one of the stacks of blankets, then took the food she handed him.

"I didn't look for plates." This was hardly the table her mother had taught her to set. She'd be appalled at her eating food with her hands, no serviette or any other form of civility. Still, it was all she had the energy to muster after the long day. She sank down on her own bedding and took a bite of her biscuit.

"No need. Anyway, I'm afraid I only have one set of tin dishes. Hope you don't mind sharing when we need them."

"Of course not." As she chewed, she glanced up at the few remaining stars in the sky. "What time do you think it is?"

"Maybe an hour past midnight." As long as her day had been, his had probably been just as trying.

A blanket of remorse slipped over her. "I'm sorry I kept you from going home tonight. How long did you say you've been gone?"

"A couple weeks." His voice held that relaxed quality that made her wish she could have so few troubles. "And no worries about the delay. Doesn't matter much if the trip is extended a day or two—and we switch to hunting weasel."

The last words caught her off guard, and if she wasn't so exhausted, they might have summoned a smile. Just now, that felt like too much effort, but she did manage a long overdue offering. "I want you to know how grateful I am for your help." She looked over at the man so the scant remaining moonlight would show the earnestness on her face.

He nodded. "Lord willing, this will all be over tomorrow." Then he shifted to pull the blankets from underneath himself. "Best get to sleep. Dawn won't be far off."

As she lay on her own bed pallet, she gazed up into the cloudy sky. This seemed so strange, lying only a short distance from a man she barely knew. When she'd risen that morning, her primary concerns were how quickly she could escape the drudgery of the boiling washpot.

Now, she'd give anything to wake tomorrow with only those same worries. With her son tucked in close beside her in their little bed. His mouth usually hung open as he dreamed, often accompanied by a circle of moisture on the pillow, giving evidence of how deeply he slept.

Bring my boy back, Lord. You know I couldn't bear it if I lost him, too.

FOUR

*E*verything hurt.

As Joanna forced herself to rise the next morning, the act of standing took every bit of her willpower. The pain in her neck felt like a knife each time she tried to turn her head, and every part from her waist down protested her ability to walk. She reached for a nearby boulder to steady herself before she attempted the feat.

At least Mr. Bowen had already risen, so her weakness wasn't being flaunted before him. He was already doing so much to help her; she would *not* become a burden to him.

Which meant she'd best take care of morning matters, then put together a quick meal that they could eat in a hurry. Maybe he'd even agree to break their fast in the saddle as they continued the journey.

By the time she returned from her morning ministrations and refilling their canteens at the creek, Mr. Bowen was already back at their little camp, refastening his bedroll.

She dropped to her knees beside the food pack. "How are the horses?" That must be where he'd been when she woke.

"Fine. I hiked up a ways to see what path the tracks took over the mountain."

How early had this man arisen? There was just now enough light to say dawn had officially arrived. Perhaps the tension pulled as tightly through him as it did her own exhausted body. They had to catch up with the kidnappers today. Her son and friend may not last much longer with those blackguards.

She handed Isaac several cherries, then a piece of roasted meat. "I haven't gone through all the food bundles to see what's here, but can we eat the rest on the trail?"

He pushed to his feet with a faint groan. "That's best. I'll go saddle the horses."

She made quick work of pulling out food and repacking the bundle, then shuffled down the slope to where he'd tied the horses. The least she could do was saddle her own mount, despite the ache in every part of her body.

Within a few minutes they were on the trail, and her backside threatened to mutiny as her mare settled into the same rocking gait she'd used the day before. How long since Joanna had spent so much time in the saddle? Too long.

Not since she'd been mounted on a mule, riding behind this same man as he and his father led their little group through the snowy mountains to Settler's Fort over six months before.

Even that seemed like a lifetime ago.

Her son had ridden with Mr. Bowen on that journey. And

now, once again, she was trusting Samuel into this man's care.

Except not exactly. First they had to find those horrid kidnappers, then get Samuel and Laura away from them. She hunched low over the saddle but couldn't seem to block out the spinning in her mind. What were they doing to her boy? Had they taken him and Laura because the two had witnessed the murder of Sheriff Zander? She could imagine they might have kidnapped Laura for *another* reason—and was trying hard not to think of what her friend might be enduring.

But a five-year-old boy? It wasn't as if Joanna had a great deal of money to pay a high ransom. And they were taking the pair away from Settler's Fort without demanding anything.

"Mr. Bowen?" Her voice broke the silence that had settled between them this first half hour. Maybe she shouldn't ask, but she had to.

He glanced back at her. "Call me Isaac."

His unexpected response jolted her, and she let out a breath. "All right."

He turned back to the trail, guiding his horse in a route that wound around the side of the mountain.

Now she had to reassemble her thoughts so they'd come out in a coherent question. "Isaac?"

He didn't turn this time. "Yes, ma'am?"

"Why would they want my boy?" Her voice probably broadcast her fear, but she couldn't seem to control it.

For a long moment he didn't answer. Maybe it wasn't

fair to ask such a question of him. The answer couldn't be pleasant.

But if he had any idea, she needed to know. Knowing would be better than this awful twist in her belly that sent her imagination down horrible paths.

At last, he spoke. "I suspect Miss Hannon and your son saw something they shouldn't have, and the men are trying to cover their tracks."

His words did nothing to calm the roiling in her middle. "Do you think they're hurting him?"

He looked back at her again, and the compassion in his eyes only made her feel worse. "Mrs. Watson."

The way he spoke her name was like a gentle chiding mixed with a warm hug. And he was right. She'd best not dwell on what she couldn't control.

But the quicker they moved, the sooner they'd free her son. She leaned forward and nudged her mare faster over the mountain.

⋯⊷◦⊶⋯

A thick layer of clouds covered much of the sky that night as Isaac reined in his mount and packhorse. "We'll stop here. This footing is too treacherous for the horses to pick their way in the dark."

Tracking in the thick blackness was no longer a problem, because he was fairly certain where the men were going. This trail was so remote, so hard to travel, there was really only one way through, and he knew it well enough to follow with his eyes closed. He'd traveled the same path to their hideout during those early wayward days, riding through here more times than he could count, chasing the demons he thought would make him happy.

Now, the occasional fresh horse droppings confirmed this was the trail the kidnappers had taken. When he and Mrs. Watson reached the cave mid-morning tomorrow, if he found signs the men had slept there, he'd be fairly certain they were part of the gang as he'd suspected. The one he'd started with his two closest friends over a decade before. That hole in the mountainside was so well hidden that only he, Aaron, and Nate could know about it, aside from a mountain lion or two. Probably also aware of it were those two good-for-nothings whom the brothers had joined on with after Isaac had finally washed his hands of that life. The thought churned hard in his gut.

A heavy sigh drifted from the woman behind him as he dismounted. She'd been quiet much of the day, not voicing a single complaint. The least he could do was acknowledge her unspoken desire.

He turned to her. "I know you'd rather keep moving, but the men who have your boy will have to stop, too. We'll be ready to ride out at first light."

She offered a weak smile and a nod, then leaned forward to dismount. Each of her movements was slow and made his body hurt just to watch. This journey couldn't be easy for her, a woman not accustomed to riding all day. Add in the lack of sleep the night before and fear for her son and friend, and she must feel like all the worries in the world weighed her down.

There wasn't much he could do to help her, other than take care of as many chores as he could. After untying the pack behind his saddle, he carried it to the flat spot where they would sleep. Mrs. Watson followed him.

"I'd say it's too risky to light a fire. There should be some fruit tucked down in the bottom, though. That, along with meat and corn bread, will have to do for our meal."

Too bad he'd not had time to finish purchasing his supplies at the mercantile. They could have had fresh bread and preserves instead of his dry skillet corn bread.

She sank down to the hard ground, her shoulders slumped, not reaching for the pack. "I'll take care of it."

He patted one of those shoulders to offer encouragement. The womanly softness of her nearly snatched his breath. He'd forgotten how different a woman felt from his own hard lines. So rarely had he ever let himself touch a female, and only in the most innocent contact. At least, for the last ten years.

Maybe he'd kept himself too far from women, for this one simple touch shouldn't affect him so strongly. He'd best put some space between them. "I'll settle the horses, then be back to help."

While he watered and fed the animals, his mind had too much time to wander. If the gang moved to the old hideout after stopping at the cave, it'd be another six days before they reached it. Certainly he could catch them before that.

The men were moving fast, though. As hard as he'd pushed today, it didn't seem like he and Mrs. Watson were gaining on them by even a minute.

In some ways, that was good news. If they kept riding every minute they could, they weren't taking time to *enjoy* their female prisoner. His stomach churned at the thought, but he had to be honest about it. At least to himself.

He couldn't imagine Nate or Aaron doing something so vile to an innocent young woman, especially not Nate. Perhaps Aaron had been hardened by the two men they'd added to the gang when Isaac dropped out.

He'd heard stories of some of the gang's actions in recent years that made his blood boil. And heaped on another layer of guilt for his part in starting the group.

But that was behind him. He'd been forgiven by his father—both his heavenly and earthly fathers. And the last thing he wanted now was for his past misdeeds to be brought to life.

Especially in the presence of a proper woman like Mrs. Watson. Hardworking and strong, yet with a grace about her that caught his notice time and again. Not a woman who would ever pay heed to a man like him, forgiven or not.

How shameful he'd feel if she came to know his past. His connection with the men who'd taken a young woman. And her son.

Was it possible to face down this gang without making his past known? Only time would tell.

✧⊶══◯══⊷✦

Laura Hannon huddled low in the saddle against the rain falling in steady rivulets down her face. Not only did she not have a bonnet, but the hat of the man riding behind her regularly dumped its load of water down the back of her neck.

If only that were the worst of her troubles.

This was their third morning in the saddle, and she had no idea where these men were taking her and Samuel. By that first night, she'd established they were some kind of outlaw gang, and from the off-color comments and looks that made her want to shrink underneath a heavy blanket, she was quite certain what they wanted from her.

Yet none of them had made advances. Not even Aaron, even though she'd been riding for two days with him, pressed much closer than she liked.

The two men riding in the lead were the ruffians who worried her. The taller brute had been the one to attack the poor sheriff with such savage blows while the other sat nearby on his horse, rifle pointed and face a stoic mask. Until he pulled the trigger.

Her eyes had been glued to the beaten man. The sound of his cries still haunted her ears, the image of his body jerking as the bullet slammed into him at such close range pulsing through her mind. She didn't remember crying out, but she must have. How else would the men have known she and Samuel were hiding below the edge of the riverbank?

Remnants of fear clutched her chest again as her mind brought back the memory of the massive brute charging down the embankment faster than she'd thought possible for someone his size. His grip around her arm had stopped all blood flowing to her hand, and Samuel's cry had stilled her heart the same way.

She hated that the boy had to ride with that beast of a man. Maybe she should ask to switch places with the lad. Samuel was being so brave, although he still talked and wiggled enough to keep himself always in their awareness. He'd only cried once as they'd bedded down the night before, his oversized tears sliding down freckled cheeks as he pleaded for his mother. Her own tears had joined his, but she couldn't let that happen again. She couldn't show weakness, even in the dark of night.

She shifted in the saddle as they rode down a muddy incline. It took all her strength not to lean back against the man behind her while they descended the steep hill, but she wouldn't give him the satisfaction. Yet her lower body ached with a fierceness that would take a long time to overcome. The day before she'd finally gone numb from the pain of sitting against the saddle horn for so many hours. If only that numbness would come again now.

Please save us, Lord. Get us away from these men somehow.

Out here in the middle of the mountain wilderness, with rain streaming down her face and saturating all her clothing, she struggled to believe the Almighty heard her tiny cry.

If only she could find a way for her and Samuel to escape these ogres tonight. Before something worse happened.

<hr/>

"We'll stop here for the night."

Joanna had been expecting those words, and as desperate

as she was to push on and find her son, relief slipped through her, stealing a bit of her strength. The rain had drenched them for hours—all day really—only slowing to a misty drizzle a little while ago.

Isaac dismounted from his gelding, moving with an easy grace that must mean he didn't ache everywhere from the long day in the saddle. Must be nice.

"It should be safe to start a fire if we can find any dry wood. With that mountain between us and the men we're chasing, and the clouds blocking out all the starlight, I don't think they'll see our smoke."

"Good." She leaned forward and let her weary body slide from the horse's back. Isaac may have expected more enthusiasm from his announcement, but this was all she could muster. Her ankles nearly buckled when her feet hit the ground, and she clutched the saddle to keep herself upright.

"We'll need to dry out some things in the packs once we get the blaze going. It'll be nice to have something warm to eat, too." Isaac approached, leading his two horses, and took her mare's reins.

In the darkness, she couldn't see much of his face. "Might help to walk a little and look for dry wood in those trees."

Walking sounded too painful just now, but she had to let go of the saddle so he could take her horse.

Maybe her posture gave away too much of her thoughts, for he added, "Or you can sit and rest for a minute."

She gathered her strength and stepped away from the horse, squaring her shoulders as she moved. "I'll look for wood." Joanna Watson did *not* shirk her responsibilities, no matter how exhausted and worried she was.

As she scrambled along the base of the mountain toward the trees, she gathered every stick and log that seemed to have a chance of burning. She didn't find much wood dry enough to start the fire, but there was plenty they could set out around the blaze to dry for use later in the night.

She could appreciate Isaac's caution from the night before, especially if it helped them sneak up on the kidnappers. But the idea of a fire to stop her shivering and dry out the twenty pounds of water weighing her skirts sounded too wonderful. Isaac had no idea how much easier the day had been for him in his waterproof buckskins.

There were several times during the worst of the deluge that she'd almost asked if he had an extra pair of the leathers. If it rained again tomorrow, she very well might.

What a sight she'd be then. Mama would swoon with one glance.

But her mother wasn't around to chide her. She would never be. Not since the train accident that took both her parents and her sister—her entire family—in the space of a single hour. That had been the end of the happy life she'd first known. The beginning of a new life of hard work and struggle.

And it seemed like the losses just kept coming. But she couldn't let herself get bogged down in those miring thoughts.

She had work to do.

When she'd finally gathered enough wood to start a decent blaze, she traipsed back to camp, her skirt dragging in the mud. It didn't take long to find the flint, steel, and tinder Isaac kept in his pack—she'd become quite familiar with the contents of that case. Maybe tonight she'd ask him about the selection of books her fingers kept rubbing against. Did he carry those specific titles for a reason, or did he have an entire library he rotated through?

Her mind had spent more time than it should imagining details about this man's life. But at least those wonderings kept her thoughts from drifting to Samuel and Laura, a harrowing topic she couldn't seem to stay away from for long. But she had to distract herself. If she didn't, if she allowed her imagination to walk those paths, she'd go mad.

"The horses are liking all the grass in that valley." Isaac's strong voice made her jump as he stepped from the darkness and dropped to his haunches beside her where she was laying out the tinder. "I can start this fire if you have something else that needs doing."

"I have it." There was a great deal that needed doing, but she'd begun this task and she'd see it through to completion. "If you'd like, you can gather a load of wood to dry beside the fire's heat. I think I've found enough to get a good blaze started."

Without a word, he rose and disappeared into the darkness again.

He was a quiet man, Isaac Bowen, but that was something she appreciated about him. He honed in on his work and noticed details most people would miss. She'd seen all this when they'd first met on that other journey, but spending so much time with him now—just the two of them—gave her a much closer look at his character. She could only be thankful he was the one God had laid in her frantic path as she first sought her son.

By the time Isaac returned, she had a small flame devouring the kindling, with a few bigger logs encircling it, ready to catch fire. Now for something warm to eat. Stew would take a while, but they both desperately needed the hot broth to thaw their insides. Scooping up the pot, she marched down to the creek.

While Isaac tended the fire, she put together the stew, then set to work laying out their wet things. The leather pack had done a remarkable job keeping their bedding dry, but there were still a number of items that had been saturated by the continuous downpour. Unfortunately, the clothes she wore would have to dry on her person, for she had nothing to change into.

She was just hanging out the last few items when Isaac's voice rose over the crackling fire. "Joanna, come and sit. Your stew's ready and you need to rest."

He'd used her given name several times that day, but the sound of it in his warm voice gave her pause every time.

"Just let me finish hanging these." She should probably gather another load of firewood before she sat, too. As she worked, her mind wandered to the new worry that had taken up residence in her exhausted mind. "Do you think the men Mr. Lanton sent will find us tonight?"

"Maybe." His tone didn't sound any too confident.

She shot a glance over her shoulder to check the expression on his face. Weary lines were cast in shadows as he stared into the firelight. Surely the men were coming. They wouldn't leave her and Isaac to take down the kidnappers alone, would they?

When she turned to head back down the mountain for another load of firewood, Isaac snagged her skirts. "Sit, woman. You're running yourself ragged for no reason." She might have been affronted by the way he addressed her were it not for the gentle teasing in his tone.

She paused and turned to him. "I'm going to bring one more load of wood so it can be drying."

He rose to his feet, standing at least a head above her, and close enough that her chest ceased drawing breath. His hand settled around her elbow, and she wished she could see more than the glimmer of firelight reflecting in his eyes.

"Joanna, sit and eat. Let yourself rest." The low gravel in his voice slipped around her shoulders like a warm blanket. "I've brought in enough wood to last half the night, and I'll gather more before we turn in. Wearing yourself out isn't going to bring us to your son any quicker. If you get sick, it'll only make you more miserable. Slow us down, even."

She eased out a long breath, forcing out as much of her pent-up angst as she could muster. He was right. She made herself meet his gaze. "I have a bad habit of keeping myself needlessly busy when I'm worried."

He chuckled, a sound that eased her nerves even more. "I'm not sure that's a bad habit all the time, but we'd best keep a check on it tonight." With a gentle pressure, he turned her toward the fire. "Let me scoop you out a cup of stew. You'll feel better with something warm inside you."

She had to sit on her hands to keep from helping as he spooned out a generous portion. She couldn't remember the last time someone else had served her. Robert had been gone these seven months. And even when he still lived, she'd been the caretaker in the family.

Although it was hard for her to accept, the fact that Isaac cared enough to help warmed her insides as much as the stew.

FIVE

*T*he night hung thick and muggy around Laura, laden with the remnants of rain as she listened once again for the sounds of breathing from the men. It was a wonder they couldn't hear her heart ramming against her chest. Tonight was her chance to get free. To escape with Samuel before something awful happened.

The scoundrels had tied her and Samuel both to a tree—as they'd been doing every night—but she'd been working for hours with the somewhat-sharp edge of a rock to cut the leather strap binding her. Though her arms ached and no doubt her wrists bled, only a few fibers still held. She scraped the leather across the rock once more. Then again.

With a jerk, her hands broke loose.

She wiped her bloody wrists against her skirt. The pain would be worth it if only she could finally get Samuel and herself free. Hopefully the thick cloud cover would help with her escape plans. She had no idea how they'd get back to Settler's Fort, but hiding would be the first order of business.

Somewhere so discreet not even these seasoned mountain men could find them.

Then each night, she and Samuel could cover as much distance back to town as they could manage in the dark. She could probably form some sort of map in her mind from watching where the sun set and rose, along with the patterns of the stars. And Joanna must have summoned help from town to look for them. It might take a day or two—or four—to find the search party, but she *would* make it back to town with this boy. She wouldn't let anything happen to him. Or to her own honor.

This wasn't the first hopeless situation she'd pushed through, not after the downfall of her family. Losing her mother when she was only seven. Having to practically raise little Henry and keep house for Pa and Will. Of course, Will wasn't any trouble. If anything, her older brother had been the one light in all those dark days. Without his teasing, the times he'd stolen her away from the heavy weight of responsibility to go exploring, she may not have survived those days.

The knife of grief pierced sharply, straight in through her ribs. *Will.* Never again would she see his lopsided grin. Henry's passing had been hard, and Pa's a shameful waste, but the grieving would have been much harder if she hadn't still been numb over losing Will. The long-familiar burn crept up her throat, threatening her eyes. Threatening her control.

She clenched her teeth and forced herself from the memories. This was to be her new life. Her fresh start. And if it took her dying breath to accomplish it, she'd get Samuel away from these beasts.

The first step required escaping from camp without waking her captors. Listening once more for the breathing of all three men, she checked off each in her mind. The light snore came from the man named Aaron, who'd shared a saddle with her. Rex, the man whose lecherous glances made her want to cover herself, snored like a drunk. But Bill, the one who was liberal with his fists, barely made a sound at all.

She honed in on the light breaths that had to be coming from Bill, breathing so steady, he must be sleeping. And the volume hadn't grown or lessened in the hours she'd been listening.

Easing herself upright, she tucked her still-damp skirt into her waistband. Not decent by any stretch, but she'd have to do some crawling to free Samuel, and this was better than letting the fabric slow her down.

Aaron slept nearest her, and she knew from experience he wore his knife at his side, whether waking or sleeping. The bruise on the inside of her elbow could well attest to hitting the bone hilt too many times as she was forced to lean backward going down mountain slopes.

Every contact with the man required her to lock her jaw to keep from squirming, but soon she wouldn't have to worry about him again. Or any of them.

Creeping toward Aaron, one tiny breath at a time, she shifted her focus between the man's face hardened in sleep and the knife stored at his waist. He was a big man, with broad shoulders and a chiseled profile. Thankfully, he wasn't as large as the oaf, Bill.

But as she stole toward Aaron now, her gaze lingered on

those large hands. And thick muscular arms. One hard blow from him could knock her out. *God, don't let me wake him. Please don't let me wake him.*

When she was just close enough to reach the knife, she extended her hand and closed two fingers around the hilt. The handle was cold, and the blade would likely be even colder. She'd seen that blade flash in the sunlight, then glimmer in the firelight as he wiped it clean after a meal. That very night, he'd even sharpened the metal to a wicked point.

Perfect timing if her plan succeeded. A deadly coincidence if she failed.

She withdrew the blade one fingertip at a time and didn't breathe until the knife was fully extracted. The man's low snores never changed. *Good work, Hannon.*

Now for some food. She had to be prepared for her and Samuel to travel through the mountain wilderness for several days. She'd never hunted with only a knife, and she wasn't sure she could keep them both alive without bringing along something to eat.

Unfortunately, tonight's evening fare had been stew, the remnants of which still sat in the pot by the barely glowing embers. Not something she could easily carry. But she'd seen the pack where they kept their food supplies. It was near Rex, so hopefully his snoring would cover any sound the rustle of the bag made.

She crawled toward the man, forcing herself to take as much time as she needed to keep quiet. When she'd closed half the distance to him, his snoring ceased.

Her heart ceased its beating, too.

Then, with a snort, the sound started up again, with just as much gusto as before. She waited a full minute to make sure the rhythm stayed even, in case he was faking.

He was definitely asleep.

She started forward again. When she reached the pack, a decision faced her. She could either pull out the smaller satchel that contained food supplies, which would risk waking the men with the sounds of the bags brushing. Or she could take the entire outer pack, which would make it harder to crawl back to Samuel and sneak away from the camp.

Better to chance removing the smaller satchel under cover of Rex's snores.

She reached into the pack and only had to fumble for a moment before her hand closed around the smaller leather bag that she'd seen the men handle. It was heavier than she expected. She opened the larger bag wider to extract the food satchel.

So far, so good.

Turning back toward Samuel, she attempted to crawl his way. But that was impossible to do silently while holding both the sack and the knife. She'd have to walk. And maybe that would be quieter anyway.

As she pushed up to her feet, she stepped on a piece of her skirt that had come untucked from her waistband. Throwing her free hand out for balance, she barely kept herself upright. She inhaled a deep breath to steady herself, then released it in a slow stream.

Now to cut Samuel loose, then get him out of here. Should she wake him so he could walk? Or try to carry him quietly?

He was such a big boy for his five years; she'd probably do best with the former option. Besides, the last thing she needed was for him to wake in her arms and start asking questions aloud. The child did love to talk and had no concept of a whisper.

She focused on watching every place she stepped to keep from crackling a branch or leaf or kicking a stone. How horrible it would be to wake one of the men now, when she'd almost achieved her—

A blow slammed into her temple. The force knocked her sideways, sending her to the ground as light exploded in her head.

She clutched at her skull, trying to hold in a scream as a boot struck hard in her side. Pain blasted through her body, and she curled her legs up, trying to shield herself from another hit.

Voices sounded above her, but with the pain radiating through her head, she could barely make sense of them.

Samuel. Where was the boy? She had to protect him from the brutal attack that could potentially strike him next.

She forced her eyes open. Dirt and rocks skittered against her legs from the activity around her. She had to know what was going on. Had to get to the boy.

The way she was curled, seeing anything required lifting her head. The movement launched a fresh wave of light flashes behind her eyes, and she pressed her lids shut until they stilled.

By now, rough voices were penetrating the fog of pain. First Aaron, then Rex.

"Hands off, Carlton. We'll restrain her, but there's nothing to be done to her or the boy until we get home. No force. No hands. Nothing." Aaron spat the last word as though he couldn't stand the man he spoke to.

A few mumbled curses filled the air, and it took her a moment to find the source. The man she'd thought was named Bill lay on his back, glaring at Aaron, who stood over them.

She slid her glance to Samuel, who lay by the tree where he was still tied, the whites of his eyes wide even in the darkness. Did she dare scoot over to him to ease his fears? Her side felt like a fire licked it with every breath she took. Had she broken a rib? Maybe more than one. If something happened to her, who would look after Samuel? She clenched her teeth, then crawled to the boy.

"Miz Laura?" Samuel inched as close as he could and put his hand on her arm.

"I'm all right, honey. Nothing to worry about."

"Did he hurt you?" She could hear the fear in his little voice.

She squeezed the boy's leg. "I'm not hurt. We'd best be quiet and try to go back to sleep."

As one of the men bound her hands with a fresh cord, she let her eyes drift shut and willed the pounding in her head to cease.

Tomorrow she'd be stronger. She'd be smarter and more observant. She had to be. Samuel's life and her own depended on it.

SIX

Joanna's spirit churned under the burning sun the next afternoon. The rock-strewn incline they traveled down only made the air seem hotter, devoid of any breeze to cool her sweat-dampened neck.

Even the birds seemed far away, with the only trees around way off in the distance. Only the clatter of the horses' hooves against the rocks echoed in her ears, melding with the squeak of saddle leather. The same sounds she'd heard for days, and she'd be happy if she never heard them again. At least not under these conditions.

She should be more content now since it wasn't pouring rain today, but how could she feel anything except misery while her son was in the hands of those kidnappers?

Three days now and they still hadn't caught up. When would they reach them? And the men from town hadn't appeared yet, either. Maybe Mr. Lanton hadn't sent anyone. Or maybe the rescuers had turned back after the first day or two. In truth, she couldn't blame them. Being away from work and responsibilities for days on end, not knowing if they'd even find the kidnappers, was more than she could expect from mere acquaintances.

Which made her even more grateful to the man riding in front of her. It may be just the two of them left, but at least Isaac Bowen showed no signs of deserting her.

That morning, he'd said he thought they were still a couple of hours behind the outlaws. Did she dare ask him again? His strong profile, those broad shoulders tapering to a trim waist and the way he carried himself tall and capable in the saddle, bespoke a man not accustomed to his authority being questioned. She didn't want to anger or frustrate him, but she had to know. So yes, she would ask, but maybe she would wait until they reached the bottom of this mountain and he could hear her better.

Her mount stumbled, sending Joanna's heart into her throat. She jerked upward on the reins to help the horse keep her head up. "Easy, girl." The mare scrambled, and—for a heartbeat—it felt as though they were both about to tumble headfirst down the rocky mountainside.

God, help. If she died in this fall, what would happen to her son?

But then the mare regained her footing, taking one more stumbling step forward before finally skidding to a stop. Both of them were breathing hard, and Joanna reached down to pat the horse's shoulder as she willed her heart to return to normal beating. "Thank you, Lord." When she pulled her hand from the mare's neck, the sticky warmth of the horse's exertions left her palm damp.

"You all right?" Isaac had reined in his horse farther down the hill, and even over the distance, the worry on his face was hard to miss.

"I think so." The pounding in her chest made the words shakier than she would have wanted, but she was still working to bring her breathing back to a normal rhythm.

Her mare stepped forward, as though the horse was ready to keep moving, but Joanna kept a tight grip on the reins as they maneuvered the rest of the incline. Most of the rocks ranged between the size of Joanna's fist and that of her head, and she did her best to guide the horse around the worst of them. She was pretty sure the animal hadn't gone down on a knee, so hopefully there weren't injuries to tend.

When they finally reached the bottom, Isaac halted his horses to wait for her to ride alongside. The intensity of his gaze burned almost hotter than the sun. "Are either of you hurt?"

She pulled her mare to a stop beside him. "I don't think so. Her legs aren't scraped, are they?"

He leaned forward to see beneath the horse. "Doesn't look like it." Then he straightened and studied her again with that penetrating gaze that seemed to see everything she tried to hide. "And you? Are you hurt?"

The intensity of his care, the breadth of it, was almost more than she could take. Over and over, he made her feel as though she didn't have to carry the weight of their struggles. Like she didn't have to be the backbone holding everything together.

As much as she wanted to sink into that feeling, she couldn't let herself relinquish control. Not when her son's safety depended on them reaching him soon.

Still, the least she could do was be grateful for Isaac's kindness. His care. So she nodded. "I'm fine."

The mare blew out a long breath, and they stood still for a minute, letting the animals rest. But she couldn't waste this chance to ask her question. "Do you think we're getting any closer to them?"

He glanced over at her, the relaxed lines on his face tightening. "It's hard to tell for sure, but it seems like we're staying even. They're moving fast, and it's hard to push the horses much more in this terrain."

The knot in her middle pulled tighter, pressing desperation up to her chest. "Then how will we ever catch them?"

Working his strong, shadowed jaw, he didn't answer right away but shifted his dark green gaze to the great majestic peaks that rose up to meet the clouds. Then he closed his eyes for a moment. "I think I know where they're going. We should reach it in about four days if we don't catch them before that."

"Four days?" She couldn't bite back the words. Her son and her friend were at the mercy of what had to be a despicable group of kidnappers. How could they last another four days without rescue?

"Isaac, they can't wait that long. We *have* to catch them. Now. *Today.*" She couldn't keep the desperation from her tone. Not anymore.

He nodded, still not looking at her, but she couldn't miss the hard set of his jaw. "Let's ride, then."

He kicked his horses into a canter, and she did the same.

After only a few strides, her mare's gait jerked. A knife of frustration stabbed Joanna's chest, but she pulled up again. "Isaac, wait!"

He must have heard her, for he slowed his horses and reined them back to her as she dismounted.

"What is it, girl?" She stroked her mare's neck. The limp had felt like it was in the front, maybe on the left side, so she ran her hand down that leg, feeling for warmth or swelling.

The limb was a little warm from the horse's exertion, but nothing excessive that she could feel. When she picked up the hoof, a few small pebbles fell out with the mud. Not anything that should have caused the extreme limp, though.

"Feel anything off in that one?" Isaac had moved to the mare's other front leg and was running his hands down it the way she had.

"Not that I can tell." She lowered her hoof to the ground so he could raise his.

"Ah, here's the problem." He held the hoof in his large, work-roughened hand. "She's thrown a shoe."

Her chest tightened as the words sank in.

Not this, Lord. Not now.

Her deceased husband had always been able to fix lost shoes easily, but that was back in their barn with all their tools and supplies. "Do you have what you need to repair it?"

He lowered the hoof and straightened to look at her across the mare's back. "If we can find the shoe and it has a few nails left in it, I may be able to rig something until we get back. Maybe. But it'll be tricky to keep moving fast without losing it again."

Everything seemed to be working against them. Frustration welled in her chest, pricking hot tears in her eyes.

"Hopefully, she lost it when she stumbled, not far back." Isaac started hiking up the mountain they'd just come down. "I'll go see."

Joanna held all three animals while he searched. This was going to delay them further. Her throat tightened, but she whispered a prayer aloud. "Please help, Lord."

Moments later, Isaac bent to pick something up from the ground, then straightened with a horseshoe in his hand. "Got it. Looks like there are a couple nails here, too."

Thank you.

He jogged back down the slope, then moved to his pack-horse and fished inside the bundles.

It seemed to take forever as Isaac used a rock to pound the shoe and nails straighter, then raised the mare's hoof and set to work there. He moved methodically, and his lack of urgency made her skin itch.

"Is there anything I can do to help?" she asked, desperate to rush this process along.

"Nope." He lowered the mare's hoof and moved back to his pack to retrieve something else. "This has to be done right. If not, it'll make her sore, and we'll have an even bigger problem on our hands."

He turned back to her, a piece of rolled leather in his grip. His gaze found hers, the intensity in his eyes slowing the rapid beat in her chest. "Just keep praying, as I'm sure you're doing."

A check pressed on her spirit. She'd been praying, yes, but had she really been trusting that God would answer her prayers? Or were they merely an outlet for her anxiety?

Father, guide Isaac as he fastens the shoe back on. Keep the animals safe and healthy. And most of all, Lord, help me reach my boy. Protect him and Laura from those men. She imagined sealing the words in a letter, then the paper soaring up to the heavens where her Father's hand grasped it.

She'd shared her concerns. Prayed her desperation. Now she had to trust that God would answer in His time.

He was—after all—the only one who could control this situation.

⋅⟩⟨⋅

Isaac should have been more prepared. If only he'd known.

Worry knotted his gut as they set out again, and he slipped a glance over his shoulder to see how the mare was doing with her refastened shoe. He'd switched her with his packhorse, which Joanna was now riding. Hopefully the lesser weight would be easier for the sensitive hoof.

Of course, Joanna probably didn't weigh more than a sprite. As hardworking as she was, she looked to be all lean muscle. Yet his body still remembered the softness of her shoulder when he'd touched her two days before. He could only imagine how womanly the rest of her would feel, were he ever to get close enough. He imagined all that pretty long hair draped around her probably felt as soft as a new baby's.

But he'd never know for sure. He couldn't. No matter how

much his respect for her grew with every hour. No matter how being around her made his body crave her nearness.

She didn't deserve a man like him. Though he'd changed from the Isaac of a decade before, Joanna deserved better. He'd thought he'd buried that past and become someone respectable. But it turned out the past could creep up and catch a man. Make him regret those mistakes a hundred times over.

The ground they traveled leveled off, and Joanna rode up beside him. He glanced her way for just a second, but it was enough to see the strain on her face. She wanted to move faster. He could feel it in the tension that tightened the air between them.

He didn't dare push the mare any harder with the makeshift wrap he'd put on the shoe. As it was, he'd probably have to change the leather a couple times each day.

Darkness would be on them soon, and he'd have even more reason to slow their progress over this rough terrain. His own spirit chafed at moving so slowly. Images of what might be happening to that innocent little boy kept slipping into his thoughts, kindling the flames of anger. And the woman . . . If he let himself think of it, he'd do something foolish.

And he didn't do foolish anymore. Joanna was relying on him. Relying on his wisdom and his tracking skills. And he couldn't let her down.

God, help me to not let her down any more than I already have.

⊹⊱═◊═⊰⊹

Hunger gnawed at Laura's insides as their fourth morning in the saddle dragged on.

"Mr. Bill, I'm hungry." Samuel's whine from the horse behind them tightened the tension in her shoulders.

Would Bill strike him again or simply ignore him? As much as she'd coached the boy to be silent, it simply wasn't possible for a hungry five-year-old to hold his tongue all day. Especially this particular five-year-old.

She didn't dare turn in the saddle to talk to Samuel. The pain in her side wouldn't allow it, nor the pounding in her head. And Aaron's bulk sat right behind her. He didn't seem as ruthless as the other two, but she still didn't trust him.

She'd heard the men talking about a fourth member of the group who would be meeting up with them soon—Aaron's brother, if she understood correctly. But he hadn't appeared yet. And for that, she should be thankful. Adding another brute would only make it harder for her to escape when she found another opportunity.

An angry growl emanated from her middle, and she pressed her eyes shut as she willed her body into quiet submission. They'd likely stop for a noon break within the next hour or so. Food seemed to be getting scarce among the group, and she and Samuel were given less than a quarter of the rations the men ate.

How much farther until they reached their destination? One more day of straddling the saddle horn through every possible hour of daylight might just push her over the edge of insanity. Her raw blisters felt like they were spreading with each jolt and jostle. And the heat of the day didn't help, making her dress cling to her in a sweaty, foul-smelling mess.

The thought of what was to come once they reached their final destination loomed over her, and there were moments she almost wished Bill hadn't been stopped from his merciless blows the night before. Ending her misery now might be—

A gunshot exploded, splitting the air. Two birds took flight from a scrappy bush beside the trail, and Laura snapped from her self-pity, heart pounding.

In front of her, Rex kicked his horse forward and grabbed the rifle in Bill's hand. "What'd you do that for, you half-wit?"

Bill pulled the gun back, yanking it from the other man. He held Samuel and his reins in one paw, and must have shot with his one free hand. "What'd you expect me to do when we're starving and a deer waltzes across the trail in front of me?"

"You're dumber than you look." Rex's voice dropped a notch as his lips formed an ominous sneer. "Don't you think those two following us heard you? If they had any question about where we are and how close, you answered it with fireworks. Wouldn't surprise me if we have a gunfight on our hands in the next hour."

Two following them? Laura worked not to flinch or turn around to look. Were they men Joanna had sent?

Bill shrugged, his mouth twisting in a snarl. "Then we'll get 'em out of our way once and for all. That's not a worry. Or . . ." One side of his mouth pulled up in a grin that sent a shiver down her spine. "We can put an end to the boy right here an' now. Give those folks somethin' to slow 'em down when they find his carcass. We don't need him anyway."

"We're not killing him yet." Rex's tone turned to a growl. "We'll get back to the cabin first, then figure out a quiet way to dispose of him. And the woman, too, once we're done with her."

Rex spit into the grass. "We wouldn't be in this place if you and Aaron hadn't messed up that robbery and put the sheriff on our trail." The hard expression on Rex's face as he glared at Aaron almost made her shrink back. He turned back to Bill. "Now bleed that thing, then let's get moving. There's not good cover out here."

The bigger man dismounted, leaving Samuel alone in the saddle. But he handed his reins to Rex, leaving the boy no way to spur the horse and escape. Samuel looked so young and helpless alone in the saddle.

Rex parked the horses where he could watch their back trail, then stood sentry while Bill made quick work of the deer he'd brought down.

Someone is coming for us. Just the thought of it sent Laura's heart into a gallop, making it easy to distract herself from the gruesome work being done just in front of her.

If only she could turn and watch for whoever was following them . . . Maybe she'd have a chance to send them a signal. Warn them. But Aaron kept his horse focused forward, and she didn't dare draw attention to herself by looking back. That never seemed to work in her favor with these men. Nothing did.

Aaron and Bill exchanged a few testy words as Bill strapped the carcass to his horse. All the men seemed more irritable than they'd been the first days.

Lord willing, they'd eat fresh food tonight and all would be more genial.

Bill swung aboard his horse and turned to snarl at Rex. "What are you waiting for? Get a move on." His gaze slid to Laura and she forced herself not to flinch under the wrath in his glare.

Who was she kidding? That man would never be genial.

She *had* to find a way to communicate with the rescue party. Before it was too late for them all.

SEVEN

If their situation weren't so dire, Joanna would love the mountains they were traveling through. Isaac seemed to know all the shortcuts and hidden passes between the peaks, and twice so far they'd come upon waterfalls that nearly took her breath away. Every rise, every view was so majestic; the land tried its best to pull her mind from the possibilities of what Samuel might be enduring.

Someday she'd like to bring her boy back to this inspiring country. The two of them didn't have to stay holed up in town the way they had since arriving in Settler's Fort. A camping excursion here and there would be a welcome adventure for them both.

As long as she had her son in her arms.

Maybe it wouldn't be the same without Isaac. The journey would certainly be harder without this capable man to help. Without his wisdom. She was coming to appreciate his presence more with each hour.

But she and Samuel could manage. As long as she had her son, she could overcome anything.

From ahead, Isaac raised his hand to signal a halt. He focused on the ground, and she nudged her gelding forward to see what had caught his attention.

The moment her mind registered the crimson stain in the grass, a weight pressed hard on her chest. She slid from her mount and stumbled forward to get a closer look.

"Joanna."

She ignored the warning in Isaac's voice as she struggled to take in the sight before her. Blood spread through the grass in a wide circle.

A lot of blood. "Oh, God." It was the closest she could come to a prayer, her heart nearly rupturing as her mind spun with images of how this could have happened.

Strong hands closed around her shoulders. "Joanna."

She gave in to their tug, turning away from the sight. She pressed her hands over her mouth, holding in the sobs that churned up in her throat.

"Shh . . ." Isaac pulled her into his chest, and she let herself hide there, feeling the strength of his arms wrapped around her.

Yet it was impossible to suppress the pictures sliding through her thoughts. Had there been a knife involved? There must have been for so much blood to be spilled. Did this mean her son had been killed? Or was he brutally injured and suffering in agony somewhere?

But maybe this wasn't from Samuel. Had they done those awful things to Laura? Even as her chest squeezed so hard she couldn't draw breath, she turned back to see if there were any other clues.

"Joanna, I think this is only from a hunting kill." Isaac's words jerked her focus up to his face. He motioned toward the ground. "See all the bits of fur? That must have been the shot we heard a while back. They didn't want to take the time to fully skin the animal, so they just bled it out here and moved on."

He stepped forward for a closer look, and she did the same but kept one hand clinging to his firm arm, the other pressed over her mouth. Her swinging emotions had taken all the strength from her legs. Could Samuel truly be unhurt? She didn't know that for sure, but if Isaac was right . . .

He turned back to her, then placed his hand on hers where she clutched his arm. His gaze locked into hers even as his smoky green eyes softened. "It's just an animal kill. We can still assume they're not hurt, and hopefully this slowed the men down enough that we can make up for a little lost time."

He studied her face as though he was reading her. She was sure he could see every bit of her emotional struggle. Her eyes must be rimmed with red, even though she hadn't let tears fall. "Are we ready to keep riding?"

She swallowed, straightening her shoulders. "Yes." Whether or not her son and Laura were hurt, every minute mattered as she and Isaac tried to catch up with them.

For a shadow of a moment, a different kind of expression crossed Isaac's face, and she thought he might step closer.

But he didn't. Instead, he turned away with a final pat on

her hand. "I'll just check the mare's shoe before we mount up."

She released him, daring one more glance at the bloody ground before she turned back to the gelding she now rode. Slipping her boot into the stirrup, she pulled herself upright. The effort seemed harder than usual as weariness weighted her bones and stole the strength from her muscles.

Just as she settled in the saddle, a squeal erupted from the mare Isaac was checking. The horse crow-hopped, sending her back legs high in the air and jerking her front hoof from Isaac's hand.

He stumbled backward, but something tripped him, and he landed on his backside.

Joanna screamed as the mare half-reared, then crow-hopped again. Isaac's legs were still practically under the horse, and she couldn't tell if he was being trampled or not.

She slid from her mount and sprinted toward the frantic mare, who was still tethered to Isaac's gelding. The front horse was shifting dangerously, and a squeal erupted from his nose. She had to get them separated before a kicking match started.

Isaac was already scooting backward as she reached the mare's head.

"Easy, girl." Joanna grabbed the halter and reached to untie the tether strap. The mare stamped hard with her right back leg but didn't kick out again.

The gelding in front, however, was still fully riled. The mare's antics had been enough to frustrate him, and as much as Joanna tried to keep the mare quiet, the animal stomped again, and the movement caused her to bump against the gelding's hindquarters.

He struck out with a hard backward kick, and Joanna jerked away just in time to miss the blow. The mare squealed in rage, and for a second, it looked like the two would have a fierce kicking match—all while tethered not more than an arm's length apart.

"Quit," Isaac barked as he limped toward the mare. With a quick motion, he pulled out his hunting knife and sliced the leather holding the two together.

The mare jerked away, and Joanna reached for her halter, catching it with two fingers. "There we go, girl. Settle down now." She led the horse away from the others, then rubbed down the length of the mare's neck and chest to calm her, checking for wounds as she worked. "What's bothering you?" There had to be a problem with that back leg—maybe a horsefly or beesting—for this girl was usually so laid back. Maybe Isaac had seen the cause.

She glanced over to see if he was coming to check the mare, or maybe he still had his hands full with the gelding.

Neither was the case.

He was seated on the ground again, his right leg extended in front of him as he pulled up the hem of his buckskin trousers. Fear pressed anew in her chest. She'd never seen Isaac shirk responsibility to tend to his own needs.

"What is it? What's wrong?" Her voice came out reedier than she meant it.

His mouth formed a thin line as he examined the whitened flesh above his boot. He didn't answer her question.

Lord, please don't let him be hurt. She moved toward him, keeping a tight hold on the mare. As she neared, the swelling on the side of his calf became clear. Was it broken? Or merely sprained?

The mare had finally settled, so Joanna released her to graze. She needed to focus on Isaac just now.

She dropped to her knees beside him. "Did she step on you?"

"Yep." The word was terse, no more than a grunt. "Not sure if it's a break or just a hard bruise. The leg doesn't wanna hold my weight though."

She exhaled. *God, not this, too.* Tears sprang to her eyes, but she pushed them back. All she wanted was to wrap her arms around her son, but one obstacle after another kept delaying them, widening the chasm between her and her baby, a divide that was splitting her heart in two.

Isaac's breathing had taken on a rough quality, sawing through the air as she peered at the leg. The swelling definitely seemed focused in one area and was growing with each second. She couldn't tell for sure if the bone was straight or not.

She glanced up at his face. The strain lines at the corners of his eyes had deepened. "It's probably a break, isn't it?"

He nodded. "I've had broken bones before, and this hurts like it."

She sat back on her heels, willing her mind to focus on what should be done next. It needed to be splinted. The position of the sun marked midafternoon. By the time they had the leg secure, would it be late enough that they should camp for the night? Would Isaac even be able to ride a horse? *Why, God?* If she could scream to release her frustration, she would.

"If you can find a straight stick the size of my lower leg, and also the roll of leather strips in the rear pack on the mare, I'll wrap this up and we can get going again." Isaac's breathing was still rough, but the determination marking his face gave her a bit of hope.

She pushed to her feet and strode off into the woods. She'd never actually set a broken bone before, although she'd seen it done a couple of times. *Lord, give me strength. And wisdom.*

Within a few minutes, she'd found both the leather and a stick she hoped would work. She also grabbed a cotton tunic from the pack, because he'd need some padding between his skin and the rough wood. A glance at the sweat beading on his face made her veer toward the gelding he'd been riding to retrieve his water flask.

"All right." She dropped to her knees beside his leg and handed him the drink. "Have you ever set a broken bone?"

He nodded, uncorking the canteen and taking a long guzzle. His Adam's apple bobbed as he lowered the flask and returned his focus to his leg. "I think it might be just a partial break, so that won't require a true setting. Just need to strap the wood to the leg to help support it."

As she set to work, positioning the shirt to protect his leg, then wrapping the leather strips around and around the pole and his calf, she couldn't help but feel the warmth of his skin as her fingers brushed it. This man was pure, virile male, with a strength she'd only guessed at before.

Something fluttered in her midsection. Something she'd rather not acknowledge, and she was careful not to glance at his face again. Was he aware of each sweep of her fingers the way she was? Surely not, given the pain he must be suffering. She tightened her jaw and focused on finishing up the task. There was too much at stake on this journey to let herself fall for him. Even though he'd proven himself a friend these past months, he'd come along on this trip merely to help her recover her son and friend—which was one more reason he seemed to embody everything she could respect in a man.

At last, she sat back and examined her work. That was the best job she knew how to do. She chanced a peek at Isaac's face. "Anything else you need now?" What she really wanted to ask was whether he was ready to ride, but she didn't want to sound completely heartless. The man had just broken his leg, after all.

He shook his head. "Better check the mare and make sure she's not hurt. I'm hoping it was only a beesting that upset her. Then, if you can bring my gelding down here, I should be able to pull myself up. Probably best to tether the mare to your mount for now."

She rose and followed his instructions. The horse who'd been upset enough to break Isaac's leg a half hour before now grazed a short way down the hillside, as calm as could be. Joanna grasped her halter and pulled the mare back up to the others. "You'd best not give any more trouble, missy. You've caused enough the last few days for an entire lifetime." It wasn't the horse's fault she'd thrown a shoe, but blaming her for the frustration roiling in Joanna's chest helped a little.

She glanced at Isaac. "Were you able to check the shoe before she lost her composure?"

He nodded. "It should last till tonight."

Good. She tied her own mount and tethered the mare to the saddle, then turned her focus on Isaac's horse. The gelding raised his head from grazing when she approached. "Hey, boy. You're gonna have to be extra good now that Isaac's hurt. I'm not sure how we'll get him mounted. By chance, do you lie down on command?"

When she led the horse to Isaac, he was trying to stand. But on the incline and without anything to help him balance, he teetered like a blade of grass in a windstorm.

"Wait, Isaac. I'll help you." She stopped the horse beside him, holding the animal's head as she studied the best way for Isaac to mount.

He gripped the saddle, hopped on his left foot a couple times, then tried to pull himself up on the horse. His first attempt didn't raise him high enough to fit his good foot in the stirrup, and he slid back down to the ground.

A grunt issued from him as he landed, his grip on the saddle turning white.

"Isaac." She stepped closer, the ache of seeing him in pain pushing her into action. "Please don't hurt yourself worse. Maybe we should just stop for the night."

He shook his head even as he eyed the saddle. "I can do it." Tightening his hold on the leather, he bent his good knee and jumped up to lean as far over the saddle as he could.

This time the grunt came from the horse.

Isaac groaned, his face contorting as he used all his strength to pull himself up. Joanna propped a hand under his elbow and pushed. Working together, they finally heaved him into the saddle. As he straightened, she caught her first view of his face, which was bright red from the exertion. Or was it something else?

His breath rasped as he struggled to draw in air. The pain must be radiating through his leg.

Maybe she shouldn't have let him climb in the saddle so soon. Yet if they didn't push on, the kidnappers would get so far ahead they'd be out of reach.

As if he could read her mind, Isaac turned to her, releasing a long breath. "I'm ready when you are."

Was he truly? The solid, steady man she'd come to rely on—the man who made her feel cared for—was no more. For the rest of the journey, she'd need to be the strong one. She'd be the one tending the horses and carrying wood and seeing to all the other chores.

All she could hope was that the pain didn't gain a hold on his mind in a way that would affect his ability to track the kidnappers. Just the thought of losing his tracking skills filled her with a hopelessness that increased with every step she took toward her horse.

But no matter what happened, she'd find her son. She had to.

EIGHT

*L*aura might have fallen asleep from the rocking of the horse if it weren't for the piercing pain in her side every time she slouched. She'd also acquired a cough, which had kept her awake much of the night. Each rough hack was like a bullet in her ribs. Probably why she couldn't keep from yawning now.

But she wasn't the only one miserable. An incessant stream of sneezes, sniffs, and coughs flowed from little Samuel, who still rode with Bill in the rear of the group. She could do nothing for the boy except pray that he healed and that his captor didn't grow annoyed with the mess.

She'd caught quick conversations among their captors about "jobs" they'd completed and a "heist" they were planning, and also something about Aaron's brother Nate. Those were the words they'd used, and they hushed quickly when she made the mistake of shifting under her blanket as she listened in the darkness.

A curse drifted from Rex at the front of the group, pulling

her from the memory. Then he raised his hand to signal a halt. "Hold up. Something's wrong with my horse."

She would have sighed in relief if it didn't hurt so much to breathe. Maybe this meant they'd get a break. And it would give whoever was following them more of a chance to catch up.

Rex dismounted and bent to lift the horse's hoof, a steady stream of profanities flowing from his filthy mouth. She could only hope Samuel didn't hear the man. What awful effects would this journey have on the boy? Lord willing, nothing permanent. Nothing more than a few nightmares that would fade after they escaped.

Rex spent several minutes working on the horse, lifting its hooves and pulling it along the side of the mountain. He wasn't a gentle man under the best of conditions, but the way he vented his frustrations by jerking the poor animal around made Laura cringe. That horse hadn't planned to injure itself, as the extreme limp proved to be the case.

At last, Rex stomped toward the rest of their group. "I don't think she'll go any farther today. Better find cover to camp."

Would the horse be well enough tomorrow to travel? Something about the fierce expression on his face made her think things wouldn't go well for the animal if it still limped when morning came.

But as much as she didn't want the horse to be abused, her focus had to be on her and Samuel. As she dismounted from her horribly uncomfortable seat next to the saddle horn, stabs of pain shot up through her lower regions. Could day after day of this ride be causing permanent damage? She could only pray not. The steady bouncing certainly wasn't helping her ribs heal.

Another round of thick, wet coughs sounded from behind, and she forced her weary body to turn. Deep circles shadowed Samuel's eyes as he finished coughing, then ran his sleeve across his nose. He looked up at her, sniffling again, and the exhaustion on his face made all the pain she was feeling seem paltry.

She moved toward him, and he met her partway. He pressed his head into her side as she held him close. "I'm so sorry you're not feeling well." She kept her voice low and soothing while the men moved around them. Was there anything she could do to help the boy?

He needed warm food and lots of water. Shelter from the elements. The only one of those she could actually provide was the water.

She bit down hard against the sting of tears. She hated this helplessness.

⊸⊷◦⊷⊸

He was slowing them down.

Isaac gritted his teeth as he crawled toward a cluster of small trees the next morning. His leg ached something powerful, but that wasn't the worst of things. He'd watched Joanna march around the camp for the last half hour tending to *his* work. Bringing in water from the creek. Seeing to the horses. He'd pulled a little food out of the packs for their early meal, but that'd been the only thing he'd done all morning to lighten her load.

It was well past time they should have been on the trail, but Joanna was just now saddling the horses and loading the packs. If he could find a good strong sapling in these trees, maybe he'd be able to get on his feet again. It would likely help him mount his horse, too.

Trying to climb into the saddle yesterday had been a pitifully embarrassing fiasco, and he wouldn't let himself repeat it, if there was any way he could help it.

He found a young tree that was reasonably straight, but by the time he cut it down with his knife blade, Joanna approached with the horses. He'd have to smooth the end later so he could fit it under his arm to lean on while he walked.

As he crawled out from the little patch of woods, she turned to him with surprise marking her face. "There you are."

He gritted his teeth. He hated having to crawl over to her like an invalid, but there was no other way.

"Ready to mount up?" Her voice held a cheery tone that was probably forced. His injury was making her life harder.

Maybe he should tell her to ride on ahead and let him catch up later. That way he wouldn't slow her down and she could get her boy back faster. But he couldn't send her deeper into the mountain country defenseless. She didn't have the experience in this land to foresee the dangers.

And there was no way he'd allow her to face the gang on her own. This evil, one he'd had a part in creating, was something he had to face.

He had to destroy this wickedness once and for all.

Joanna held his gelding next to a low rock embedded in the dirt. When he reached her, she held out her hand to help him stand. "I thought this might be easier, but we can try a different spot if you prefer."

"This is fine." He reached for the stirrup, ignoring her hand. He could do this without making her bear his weight. Surely.

He managed to stand by clutching the saddle, but even just resting his injured leg to help him balance shot fire through the limb. If he had to endure a full day of the pain he'd worked through the afternoon before, he might not make it.

But he had to.

He positioned his grip on the saddle to mount, then bent and forced every bit of strength he had into the jump.

The attempt was almost as pitiful as yesterday's.

Joanna's hand came around to grip his upper arm, helping to push him up into his saddle. As much as he'd craved her touch before, he hated that she was forced to reach out to him now. He didn't want to be a burden to her. He wanted to be someone she could respect. A help to lighten her load, not add to it.

At last he was in the saddle and he straightened, doing his best not to let the strain of the ordeal show on his face.

But the way she studied him, she seemed to see all the way inside. Reading his thoughts. Seeing his darkest parts. The past he'd long since covered over.

He cleared his throat, lifting his eyes to the other two horses. "Ready to ride?"

She didn't move. Didn't walk toward her mount. The burn of her gaze almost broke through his resolve. "Are you sure you're up to this?"

He tightened his grip on the reins, sealing his jaw against a response he'd regret. His condition wasn't her fault, and he couldn't let himself vent his frustration on her. So he only allowed one word to slip out. "Yes."

She heaved out a long sigh and turned away. Without another word, she mounted her horse and turned both animals toward him. "Lead the way."

⋄⟶⊙⟵⋄

Laura eyed the flushed circles on the cheeks of the sleeping boy in the faint dawning light. If she didn't wake him soon, the men would grow angry. They were already moving about camp, preparing to pack and head out for the day.

That must mean Rex's horse no longer limped. Or maybe he planned to push the mount regardless of injury. She could well imagine that callous, unfeeling man ignoring his animal's pain.

She brushed a hand down Samuel's forehead. "Wake up, honey." His skin nearly burned her fingers. *Not this, too, Lord.*

Was a fever merely a side effect of his stuffy nose and cough? Or was his sickness turning into something more? She was no nurse, and had no experience raising a child of her own. She did know the boy needed rest. And water. Warm broth would probably be best for him to eat. But that wasn't to be had this morning, for the men certainly wouldn't allow her time to cook it.

Samuel's eyes drifted open, and he looked at her with that sleepy bewilderment that always reminded her how young and innocent he was. Even though his incessant talking and squirming could be a trial, Samuel was still a young boy who needed kindness and compassion and a mother's love.

As he sat upright, looking lost and weary, she pulled him into her arms. His mother couldn't be here with him, but God had given Joanna's place to Laura for this journey. This wasn't the first time she'd been forced to play a mother's role to a young, grieving boy. She would be a refuge to this dear child through the days of darkness and misery.

"How is he today?" Aaron's voice sounded behind her, and she turned to see him holding out two bowls of corn gruel.

She glanced down at her charge, who'd snuggled into her side. His stillness was a sure sign he didn't feel well. Normally he would stand only a quick hug, then he was ready to unleash his energy on the day. "He's feverish this morning. Seems to feel worse than yesterday."

She took one of the bowls and looked up at the man. "How is the injured horse?"

Aaron's mouth formed a halfhearted smile that held no mirth. "Better, I think. At least, well enough to move on." His sarcastic tone told her exactly what she'd suspected. Rex would have no sympathy for man or beast.

She glanced down at Samuel, then back up to Aaron. She hated to ask a favor of any of these blackguards, but the boy needed every bit of help she could offer. "Is there water for Samuel?"

He nodded. "I'll fill a canteen he can carry in the saddle today."

As the man stood and moved away, she exhaled a long breath, forcing her tension out with the spent air. At least this was one kindness she could be thankful for.

⊰⊱

Joanna was already exhausted, and they'd just started on the trail for the day. She didn't mind the extra chores, truly. Staying busy kept her from fretting about her son. At least . . . not as much.

But worrying about Isaac's broken leg added a whole new layer of strain that had kept her checking on him all through the night. His sleep had been uneasy, and maybe that was why he seemed to wear grumpiness like battle armor this morning.

And the pain had to be gnawing at his strength. Few people could break a leg and climb right back into the saddle for hours of riding on these rocky, uneven trails.

Maybe she should have insisted they rest this morning. But every moment mattered with two innocents held hostage at the hands of ruthless men.

She'd have to trust that Isaac would speak up if he couldn't go on.

Lord, am I making the right choice? Please hide Laura and my son under the shadow of your wing. Give Isaac strength. And, Lord, I could use an extra dose of wisdom. And strength.

The morning dragged slower than molasses in winter. They weren't riding as fast as before, but she couldn't begrudge the lack of speed. Not with Isaac in so much pain and the mare still limping on her loose shoe.

At least they were moving.

The trail wound around the side of a mountain peak, down into a crevice, then up another steep incline. Staying astride her gelding took work on such terrain, and she kept an eye on Isaac to make sure he wasn't having trouble.

He still sat tall and straight in the saddle, showing no sign of his injury. Isaac was strong, no doubt about it. The kind of man who could be trusted. Depended on.

They were descending the hillside when her gelding's ears perked up. The animal arched its neck toward a grove of trees near the base of the mountain.

Something must be down there. She glanced at Isaac to see if his horse was giving the same signal. It was.

Isaac's gaze was narrowed on the small patch of woods, and he'd already laid his rifle across his lap. How had he drawn it from its scabbard so quickly?

She shifted her focus back to the trees as a man on horseback appeared from their depths. Her heart raced into her throat. Was he friend or foe?

NINE

*J*oanna only needed a second to process the long black braids with interwoven feathers that proclaimed the stranger an Indian. Then, a second man rode from the woods. His braids and buckskins were much the same as the first, although his horse bore flashy brown-and-white markings that drew her eye much more than the plain sorrel coloring of the first man's mount.

The Indians rode toward them, no surprise in their expressions. They must have seen her and Isaac from the trees.

A glance at Isaac showed no fear on his face, and he kept his horse moving toward the men. She could only pray her own countenance reflected such calm. *Lord, keep us safe.*

Living on a homestead in the mountain country for the last four years of her husband's life, she'd seen a few Indians traveling through. Robert had always treated them with an apprehensive respect, knowing that keeping peace with the natives could very well help the three of them stay alive.

Yet he'd never exuded the same level of confidence the man riding just in front of her showed as he reined his horse to a stop a short distance from them.

Isaac raised his hand in greeting, and the men responded with the same.

Joanna breathed out a tiny sigh of relief. Though the braves' stoic faces were impossible to read, the greeting must be a good sign.

"We're looking for three men, a woman, and a boy. Have you seen them?" Isaac's hands shifted in a flurry of motions, giving signals of some kind.

The brave who'd been leading the way looked at the other, then back to Isaac. He spoke a string of sounds Joanna couldn't identify, but his hands moved in wide gestures, pointing toward the northeast.

Isaac nodded. "All right." Then he raised a palm to the Indians and nudged his horse forward. With his other hand, he motioned her to come along with him.

Was that it, then? She kept her horse close to Isaac's as they rode past the Indians and forced herself to maintain a pleasant expression. She knew she didn't look as relaxed as Isaac seemed to be around these strangers. But at least she'd made the effort.

As soon as they were out of hearing, she leaned close to him. "Could you understand what they said?"

He nodded. "Not their spoken words, but the sign language is pretty much the same between the tribes in this area. I could read what they were saying."

"What did they say?" A beat of anticipation stalled in her chest.

"They haven't seen the group we're after. But those two came from the northeast, so it's not likely they would have crossed paths with the men we're looking for."

A new weight slumped her shoulders. That's what she'd assumed when Isaac bade them farewell so quickly, but the seed of hope she'd briefly allowed to grow made the disappointment stronger than it should have been.

The next few hours passed quietly, which gave her more time with her thoughts than she would have liked. Thankfully, she found some relief from constant imaginings about what might be happening to Samuel and Laura—relief in the form of the man riding just in front of her.

He must have been around Indians a great deal to be so comfortable in their presence, and to learn the sign language those braves had used. Some of the gestures were obvious, but not all. Not enough that she could follow the conversation.

She could understand how Isaac's excellent skills in the wilderness could have been developed by time spent among these majestic peaks. Not to mention his impressive ability to find and follow tracks, too.

But what she'd just witnessed had to come from more than just years of mountain living. Had he lived with the Indians? Had he always resided in this territory, or had he and his father come from somewhere back east? She knew both the older and younger Bowen men lived together in a cabin about an hour's ride outside of town. They'd passed it when Isaac and his father had rescued her and the Bradleys on their way to Settler's Fort.

Which brought up another question she should have asked days ago. "Isaac?"

"Yep." His voice held a tension that probably came from his pain. Hopefully not from anger with her.

"Is your father worried about you, do you think?"

He cut his gaze to her, but she couldn't read the expression in his eyes.

As she replayed her words in her mind, she realized how they must have sounded. "I mean, did he expect you home already? Do you think he would come looking for you?"

Isaac was silent for a long minute. "He knew I'd be hunting for a while. And he knows things happen in these mountains that'll slow a man down. If he gets worried enough, he'll probably head to town, and someone there can tell him where I've gone."

He turned to look at her, and the pain lines at his eyes squeezed her chest. "Joanna, I'll do everything I can to bring your boy and Miss Hannon home safely. My father wouldn't want me to do anything else."

The pressure that had kept mounting on her all morning slipped from her shoulders. This was the Isaac she'd been coming to care about. The one who made her feel like she had a partner in this journey. Someone capable of taking charge. Of bearing some of the load.

Most of the load.

<hr>

Isaac was beginning to regret his choice to dismount for their noon break. But the horses needed a rest, and his leg needed to be propped up for a few minutes. The swelling had grown the limb to nearly twice its usual size.

Joanna was probably appreciating the chance to stretch her legs, too, although he suspected she'd never volunteer that information. She wasn't one to complain. His respect for that trait grew more each day, especially as her burdens increased.

Just now she sat in the grass near him, enjoying the warmth of the sun as she ate the dried meat he'd pulled from the pack. This high in the mountains, the air was still cool enough for the sun to be a welcome relief.

A glimpse at her relaxed face tilted toward the sky made him a little jealous of the sun's rays. If only *he* could be the one to take away her cares, even for a minute. If only his past didn't haunt his present and future still. But the sins of bygone days wouldn't remain buried much longer.

He struggled for something to say, to be part of her happiness while he still could, but he was never good with finding the right words.

Joanna didn't seem to mind the silence, which was another thing he liked about her. She seemed comfortable in her own skin—and a beautiful skin she possessed, no doubt about it. But she didn't seem to feel the need to be someone she wasn't. He'd never met a woman quite like her.

At last, she turned her attention on him. "Have you always lived in these mountains?"

They hadn't talked much about life before this journey,

but her question made him want to open up. To share a little more of himself with her. As long as he steered clear of that year when his good sense had been overridden by his desire for an easier life.

He nodded. "Since I was seven. We lived in Indiana before that, but when my ma died, Pa moved us west to see if all the commotion about gold had any merit."

She tipped her chin as she studied him. "So he worked in the gold mines? What did you do all day?"

He shrugged one shoulder. "I worked along with him. We didn't have the big mines back then, the kind where a bunch of men are employed by the owner. Each man—or boy, in my case—staked out his claim and worked a gold pan and a sluice box. I got to be pretty good at sorting through the mud and rocks."

"Did you have any schooling?"

Did she think him uneducated? She must have seen the books in his pack by now. "Pa brought books along and taught me in the evenings. When I got a little older, a new miner and his wife moved in up the creek from us. Mrs. Travers had been a schoolteacher, so she took me under her wing. Taught me advanced arithmetic. Latin. Things I've had little need to use since." He shot her a sideways smile.

Her brows rose. "Latin? I hated those lessons."

He couldn't help a chuckle at her honesty. "Me too. The declensions are awful, and it was hard to make myself learn, knowing I'd probably never need it."

"You still like to read?" A soft smile spread over her pretty mouth. "English, I mean."

He nodded again. "I do. Sanford at the mercantile orders me a book with most of his shipments. I pay dear for them, but the cost is worth the entertainment."

"A book with every shipment? You must have quite the library."

Heat crept up his neck, stronger than the sun was producing, and he shrugged with both shoulders this time. Hopefully he didn't sound extravagant. "They fill up one corner of the bedchamber. Pa enjoys 'em, too, so the space and the money are worth it to us."

She settled into quiet for a moment. Maybe this was a chance for him to ask a little about her. He knew she'd been married and they'd homesteaded somewhere in the mountains south of Settler's Fort. Knew her husband had died of an ax wound. Maybe asking about him would be too hard for her, but did he dare inquire about life before that?

Before he could find the words, she spoke again. "Have you ever thought of setting up a library? Either in Settler's Fort, or maybe even at your home? I'd think folks would be willing to ride out to your place every week or two for the chance to read such a collection of wonderful books. They're so hard to come by for most people."

He eyed her. "Never thought of it."

In this country, where survival could require every bit of a person's energies, it didn't seem like there'd be a lot of interest in books—at least not enough for him to go through the effort of setting up a system to loan them out. But maybe there were others like him who enjoyed a good story but didn't have the means to pay for both the books and the shipment.

Joanna's sweet smile deepened with a blush of excitement. "Think about it. I'd be happy to help you get set up." Her eyes twinkled. "Especially if I get to borrow them, too."

More warmth burned across his neck. An excuse to see her more often would be nice. He motioned toward the pack. "Start with the two in there. The Bible also, if you've a mind. Take anything you like."

A root of yearning caught her expression, but she only nodded. "Thank you."

He'd have to make sure she took him up on the offer when they were back in Settler's Fort. But now it was his turn to ask the questions.

His leg throbbed, so he adjusted his buckskins around the bulky splint, holding in a groan. "What of you? I know you homesteaded a few years, but what before that?" He stole a glance at her to see if his words raised pleasant or sad memories. He didn't want to push if she wasn't ready to talk about them. She certainly had enough sorrow along this journey to find her son; he didn't want to add more.

"St. Louis. That's where I grew up, where I met Robert, and where we were married." Something like a sigh drifted from her, and he could feel the sadness in it, although her face didn't reflect the emotion.

"You still have family there?"

She shook her head, her lips pinching. "Not anymore. Neither of my parents had siblings. They and my sister died in a train accident when I was eighteen."

He sucked in a breath. Her entire world had been stolen in one fell swoop. What did he say to that? Offering his condolences seemed too shallow, too easy, when the words wouldn't actually help her.

"I had met Robert several years before that, but we renewed our acquaintance during the time I was settling my father's business affairs. Not long after that we married. Then Samuel came a year later. Robert had traveled to the Montana gold fields before we married, and he fell in love with the mountain country." She inhaled a breath. "So when Samuel was almost a year old, we sold most of our belongings and moved west."

She offered a sad smile. "It was a good life on our homestead. Lots of hard work, but peaceful living."

Quite a story that. And he couldn't help the interest that nudged his insides about the man she'd married. The man who'd captured her heart enough to leave civilization and all she knew to come to this wild country. But how could he ask without sounding as though he was trespassing into territory where he didn't belong?

Maybe a subtler approach would work. He summoned a picture of Samuel in his mind. "Your son's red hair and freckles fit his personality just right. Did those come from his father?" He watched her face for signs he'd pushed into painful memories.

Instead, her expression turned soft, some of the sadness fading. "They did. Robert's hair was a bit darker red, and most of his freckles had faded by the time I knew him, but they both had the same rambunctious spirit." She grinned.

"The first time Robert let Samuel ride the horses as he plowed for crops in our bottomland, our son was three years old. I expected them back by midday, thinking Samuel wouldn't last any longer than that. They didn't come back until the middle of the afternoon, though—both of them covered in scratches, with blue fingers and their faces tinted green from all the huckleberries they'd eaten. Seems they'd found quite a patch and ate the berries instead of food I'd sent with them. Neither man nor boy could bring himself to stop eating until they couldn't stand another bite."

Isaac pictured a larger version of Samuel, the man gripping the boy's hand as they offered Joanna matching sheepish grins. The image brought an instant smile. "Sounds like he enjoyed life."

She nodded, her eyes taking on a look that was . . . wistful? "He was a good friend." Her voice softened. "Life wasn't always easy, but Robert . . ." Her brow knit, as though she was searching for the right words.

Isaac's gut tightened. Why, he couldn't have said. Was he jealous of a dead man? Or maybe it was the life together he and Joanna had shared. But that was the last thing Isaac needed to worry over just now.

A sigh leaked from Joanna, stealing the stiffness from her shoulders. "I suppose I wasn't always the best wife. We were both human, with all our flaws. But he kept us sheltered and fed, and we worked through the challenges as they came."

And then she'd had to leave the home she and Robert had built. Did she miss the quiet of living so far in the hills? Settler's Fort was a good town, filled with hardworking people. But probably not the peaceful living she was describing.

"And what now? You're taking in washing in town, right? Are you settled comfortably?" During these past months, it bit deep in his gut every time he'd thought that she might not have everything she needed. And even the idea of her slaving over a washtub and hot fire all day didn't sit right. She was meant to do more with her life than that kind of drudgery. Deserved so much better.

She nodded, and her shoulders sagged a little. "We're making do."

Making do. Those two words formed a knot in the pit of his stomach. When they finally arrived back in Settler's Fort, he'd make sure life changed for her and Samuel—for the better. Even if he had to build her a house himself and set her up with enough milk cows and chickens to live off the sales of their milk and butter. Maybe she could even manage that library she talked about.

The idea settled better than images of her slaving over boiling water, but there was still something that made his chest tug because he knew, deep down, that he wanted to be in that picture his mind formed, seeing her and Samuel's eager smiles each day.

But that would never happen.

He was content in his life, taking care of Pa. Satisfied each evening that he'd put in an honest day's work. Enjoyed being around to help a neighbor in need.

Like now. He was helping Joanna in what was probably

one of her darkest times. And once they accomplished their mission and she no longer needed his help, he'd walk away. By then, she'd know about his past and any trust he'd gained would be destroyed.

He needed to remind himself of that truth more often.

TEN

*N*ight had settled in earnest when the men finally finished setting up camp. After Laura and Samuel ate the meager pittance they were given, there was nothing left for her to do except to hold the weary lad close to her.

She ran a hand through his matted curls. In the darkness, they shone a rich auburn, and even though they were as desperate for a washing as the rest of him, the strands still possessed a silky feel that she loved.

Yet his labored breathing made her heart ache.

She pressed a kiss to his hair. "I'm sorry you don't feel well, love. If there was any way I could take it from you, I would."

A whimper sounded, and he pushed deeper into her lap. "Mommy."

The word sprang tears to her eyes. "I know, honey. I wish she were here, too." Actually she wished them both far away, back in Settler's Fort with Joanna. But she had to keep the child's spirits up. She pressed another kiss to his hot temple.

"At least we're together, though. And we'll see your mommy again soon." *Lord, please let that be true.* Where were the people who'd been following them? They should have caught up by now. *Lord, don't let them give up. Lead them to us.*

A figure stepped toward them, and she stiffened as she strained to make out the form with the firelight behind him. She couldn't bear any more of Bill's rough handling. Not tonight.

When the approaching man dropped to his haunches beside her, she eased out a breath. Aaron.

He laid something on the ground. "Here's a little extra I was able to save for you two. Do you have enough water for the night?"

She could smell the roasted venison wafting up from the plate. "Yes, thank you."

Her middle gurgled at just the thought of more to eat, and she had to stop herself from raising a chunk to her mouth right then. She couldn't remember ever being this hungry, and her clothes had grown looser each day of the journey. The lack of food might be contributing to Samuel's sickness, too.

"Is there anything else you need?" Aaron's voice sounded so earnest, as though he truly wanted to help.

She almost asked if he could set them free, but that would be a silly request. He was one of the men holding them captive.

So she shook her head. "Thank you for the food."

"Aaron, you over there trying to earn her good graces again? It won't help you. I get first dibs, no matter what you do." Rex's voice sounded too loud in the still of the night, his whiskey-laden tone grating on her last tightly strung nerve.

Aaron's mouth pinched. "Sorry about him." Then he rose

and turned away. The flicker in his eyes looked almost like remorse. Was there a chance he'd help them escape? Maybe she could find a chance to ask him.

She was too tired to sort through the fears and questions in her mind. For now, she and Samuel had a little extra food to soften the ache in their bellies. Then she'd best get them to sleep.

As they ate, a stirring among the men pulled her attention to the fire. Bill settled his rifle in his lap, aiming it in the direction they were all staring. She peered into the darkness where they were looking, but the night was so thick she could see nothing.

Birdsong sounded nearby—unusual at this time of night—and all three men visibly relaxed. Someone they knew must be coming.

Moments later, the crunch of footsteps sounded. "It's Nate," a voice called just before he stepped into the circle of firelight, leading a horse behind him.

Rex raised his cup in greeting. "It's about time you showed up."

Aaron rose and clapped his brother on the shoulder. "I'll settle your horse while you fill your belly. We've fresh venison."

Aaron took his horse's reins, and Nate moved toward the fire. But as he was about to sit, he caught sight of her and Samuel. He stilled as he took them in, then swung around to face Rex and Bill. "Who are they?" His voice rang with alarm. Maybe even suspicion.

Rex took another gulp from his flask before answering. "We had more trouble than expected with the sheriff in Settler's

Fort. They were the unfortunate witnesses to his demise, so we brought them with us until we decide what to do with them." Even with a hint of a slur, his voice contained a lecherous quality that made her skin crawl.

"You killed the sheriff?" Nate's hands fisted, then released. "Then you made the problem so much worse by kidnapping? How could you think that was a good idea?"

"It was the only choice we had." Bill's tone was more than a little defensive.

Nate whirled away from them, marching toward her and Samuel. She shrank back from him before she could stop herself. His face was shadowed with the firelight behind him, but the angry set of his shoulders and the stomp of his boots was impossible to miss. "Did they hurt you?"

Before she could answer, another voice sounded. "Nate." Aaron's voice held a low warning as he stepped into view.

"Get your brother under control, Aaron." Rex's casual tone barely covered a clear warning.

"You went along with this?" Nate sent an accusing glance to Aaron.

The other man shrugged. "It was the only choice we had," he repeated.

Nate stood for a long moment, the rise and fall of his shoulders his only movement. Then his chin came up. "This is it. I won't be party to murder and kidnapping. I haven't felt right about everything else for a while now, but I stayed because of Aaron. But I refuse to stand by for this."

He looked to his brother. "We're leaving, Aaron. And we'll take the woman and boy with us. Go saddle the horses."

"You're not leaving." Rex's growl was low and frightening enough to raise gooseflesh on her arms. "You know as well as I do you'd be recognized in any town you entered. You're an outlaw, Long. That'll never change."

Bill lifted the rifle and aimed it squarely at Nate. "Sit yourself down and eat a bite."

Nate ignored them and strode back toward her and Samuel. He reached for the knife fastened at his waistband.

"Nate. Stop." Aaron's sharp voice cut through the night.

Nate paused, then turned back to him.

"We're not going anywhere tonight." Aaron spoke with the same measured, easygoing manner that seemed to be his trademark. "When we get back to the cabin, we can decide our next move, but splitting out in the middle of the wilderness in the middle of the night isn't a good idea."

Long moments passed as the two brothers stared at each other. She couldn't read either expression, but the turmoil churning inside Nate seemed to radiate from him.

At last, the stiff line of his shoulders eased. "All right. We'll talk more when we get back to the hideout." His quiet tone made the words sound like they were meant for his brother only. He trudged back to the fire and sank to the ground near the roasted meat, still hanging from the stick they'd used for a spit.

Laura eased out a long breath, trying to relax her own tension. Part of her had thrilled at the thought of Nate taking them away from Bill and Rex. But she knew nothing about this fiery stranger, except that he was Aaron's brother. The two didn't seem very similar in personality, although their looks were almost identical the more she studied them. Could she trust Nate more than these other men?

It didn't really matter, though. He'd given in to their resistance and abandoned his plan to free her and Samuel. Maybe he'd been all bluster from the beginning.

Sleep came easy at the beginning of the night, but then Samuel woke frequently during the darkest hours, keeping her awake more often than not. Sometimes the fever made him restless, sometimes he struggled to breathe through the congestion. Poor lad.

When the men began to stir at first light, she had to force her groggy eyes open. The skin on her face pulled tight like it was swollen, and every part of her felt as though she were attempting to swim in a lake fully dressed with her winter coat on. Each movement took effort.

Aaron came to untie them and walk her to a tree where she'd have a minimum of privacy to relieve herself. She was getting used to the humiliation, but the anger it stirred wasn't a good way to start each morning. When he brought her back to camp, he took Samuel to do the same.

As she unplaited her braid and refastened it for the day, Nate approached with two steaming bowls and a cup. He squatted down in front of her and lowered the bowls to the ground. He cradled both hands around the cup as he spoke in a low voice. "I didn't have a chance to introduce myself last night, but you probably figured out I'm Nate Long, Aaron's brother." His mouth formed a thin line, but his eyes seemed to offer an apology. Or maybe that was only hopeful thinking on her part.

She nodded, but he must have been expecting more, for he raised his brows. "You are . . . ?"

"Laura Hannon."

"This is your son?" He motioned toward Samuel, who stood near the tree with Aaron.

She shook her head. "I'd taken him for an afternoon at the swimming hole when we met your . . . friends." She couldn't help the bitterness that crept into her tone.

"I'm sorry. So very sorry." His eyes spoke the same message as his words as he gazed at her. Then he pulled his focus down to the cup he still held. He lowered it to the ground, slipped something from his hand, and placed it underneath the tin. As he did so, he raised his eyes to her with a penetrating look.

Then his face changed to a relaxed expression and he stood. "I think we'll be ready to leave in a half hour or so. Call if you need me, but otherwise best to stay put."

She nodded, her gaze trailing him as he walked away. But her mind strayed to the slip of white he'd placed under the cup. A paper?

Her fingers longed to reach for it, but Aaron was approaching with Samuel. Nate had taken pains to hide the object, so she'd best wait until she was alone to look at it.

As the man and boy approached, her heart pounded loud enough in her chest that Aaron had to hear it. But he simply motioned for Samuel to sit, then turned and walked away.

She forced herself to breathe.

Samuel reached for his bowl and began slurping corn mush. He seemed focused on his food, so she reached for the cup with both hands, trying to scoop the paper into her palm as she took up the mug. Anyone paying close attention to her would see the act, but the men seemed busy, and Samuel didn't look her way.

She needed to look at the missive now, for once Aaron retrieved them to mount up, she wouldn't have another moment alone until at least noon.

Tucking the paper into the cradle of her crossed legs, she used the pretense of drinking as an excuse to look down. The slip of paper had been folded so it was no bigger than her palm. Once she opened it, small neat words spread across several lines. Her eyes took a moment to make sense of the markings, but as they sank in, a bit of cautious hope bubbled up in her chest.

Camp tonight will be in thick woods. I'll cut you both loose before bedding down. Sneak away after midnight and climb trees to hide. After we leave the area, go to the town west of here two mountains over. Get help.

If her heart had been pounding before, it galloped in her chest now with the thunder of stampeding horses.

Nate was helping them escape? Against her better judgment, she shot a glance his way. He was saddling his horse, as was Rex. Bill and Aaron were still loading camp supplies in their packs.

None looked at her, yet it seemed as if all were aware of her and the paper tucked in her hand. She turned back, her stomach roiling with the thought of what all this might mean.

"Aren't you gonna eat, Miz Laura?" Samuel's words jerked her focus to him. The lad was eyeing her bowl of gruel, and he certainly did need more to fill his belly. But she also needed sustenance, especially if they were to escape that night.

"I can share a little." She scooped two large bites into the boy's dish, then worked to finish the rest herself. When she was pretty sure no one was looking, she tucked the paper down in her bodice.

If she and Samuel could only make it through the long hours of riding ahead, freedom would be theirs by this time tomorrow.

⋯⊙⊙⋯

Joanna studied the sagging line of Isaac's shoulders as evening brought a pink blush to outline the peaks on the western horizon. The pain must be wearing him down. His horse's pace had been slower than usual through the afternoon, probably because Isaac wasn't able to prod him with only one good leg.

She rode up alongside him. "Is there a good place to camp around here?"

His head drooped, and he looked over at her without actually lifting his chin, as if the effort was too much. "I was going to push on another hour or two until full dark."

She shook her head. "Let's stop as soon as we find a suitable place." As much as she wanted to ride on, he didn't look like he'd make it much farther. Perhaps after a few extra hours of sleep he'd be stronger.

"Those trees will give good shelter. I think there's a stream running through them." He nodded toward a small grove of aspen and pine in the valley just below.

"Good." The trees were surrounded by a grassy area, which would be helpful for the horses. And stopping early would allow her to tend the animals and gather wood before dark fell in earnest. Her weary bones would be ready when she finally fell into her blankets later.

They reined in the horses at the edge of the trees, and she slipped to the ground quickly so she could help Isaac down. Dismounting seemed a great deal easier for him than climbing up on his gelding, but she still liked to be close. If the horse stepped forward or if Isaac landed wrong, he could do a great deal more damage to his injured leg. She pulled the walking stick from the packhorse's load and moved to Isaac's side.

As she gathered the reins at his gelding's head, the horse seemed fixed on something in the trees. She stroked her hand down his neck. "It's all right, boy. Only shadows in there."

Isaac gripped the saddle and leaned forward as he hauled his splinted right leg over the horse's back.

"Careful." The word slipped out before she could stop it.

He didn't make a sound as he eased down to the ground, but when she finally saw his face, every tendon in his neck bulged from the strain.

She handed over the walking stick, which seemed like a paltry offering when he needed so much more. Twin sticks would probably make it easier for him to maneuver, but they hadn't had time to find and fashion a second.

With the walking stick positioned under his arm, he let out a long breath and looked over at her. She worked to conjure up a smile on her tired face, then stepped beside him and slipped herself under the arm on his good side.

The warmth of him wrapped around her caught her off guard every time she helped him from his horse. The strength obvious in the arm draped over her shoulders, the touch of another human, was something she hadn't realized she missed. Other than Samuel, of course, and his sweet little-boy hugs. But the child always moved so quickly, wrapping his small arms around her neck, then darting away to his next distraction.

This connection with Isaac was different in every way.

They hobbled forward into the trees, and she could tell he was trying not to put the force of his weight on her. She wouldn't have minded, though. Helping him like this filled her with purpose and a tingly sensation in her middle.

The trees were interspersed with underbrush, quite thick in some places, but the sound of bubbling water drifted from up ahead. Maybe they'd be blessed with a cool, clear spring.

"Do you want to go all the way to the water?" She guided him to the right, around the trunk of a large tree.

"Yep." His grunt gave evidence of his strain, and maybe his pain, too.

"All—" Her toe hit a root, and Isaac's weight pressed harder on her, knocking her balance askew. She scrambled to get her foot back under her, but she was already tumbling forward. She landed hard on her knee.

Isaac was falling, too, and she braced herself for the impact of his body hitting hers. But he twisted to tumble forward, landing hard on his knee and elbows, missing her completely. A cry slipped from his mouth as his broken leg thrust out behind him.

She scrambled to his side, ignoring her own aching knees. "Where are you hurt?" She pressed a hand to his shoulder and almost rolled him over, but stopped herself just in time. She didn't dare move him until she knew the extent of any new injuries.

"Not . . . hurt." But the way his eyes squeezed shut and the bite of the words through clenched teeth proved he must be. Had her fall snapped the bone even more? *Oh, God.*

He worked himself up to his elbows and one knee, then eased around to sit upright. His face contorted into a grimace and his breath came in rough gasps as he reached to straighten his splinted leg.

She scooted toward his foot and adjusted it to lie naturally, then shot a glance at his face. "Is that better?"

His eyes were still closed but more relaxed. "Yeah." The word came out on an exhale, and she forced herself to breathe out her own spent air.

"I'm sorry, Isaac. So sorry."

He opened his eyes, and his dark green gaze seemed to see deeper into her than usual. Deeper than she wanted. He reached out a hand and, for a second, she stared at it. Did he want her to give him something? Or to place her hand in his?

Another glance at the soft expression on his face meant the latter, she was almost certain. So she obliged, slipping her palm into his, brushing against the calluses that came from a lifetime of honest labor.

With a gentle strength, he tugged her forward. She scooted toward him, coming to rest on her knees just in front of him.

He took her hands in each of his, and the earnestness in his gaze—the intensity—raised a burn to her eyes. She swallowed to keep the tears at bay. Why did they come now, of all times?

"Joanna." His thumbs stroked the backs of her hands. "I'm all right. No damage done. And it wasn't your fault anyway."

The words, spoken so gently, were her undoing. A tear slipped past her defenses. "I'm so sorry." Though she'd said it before, that phrase seemed to be all she could summon.

"Aw, Joanna." He released one of her hands and reached up to cup her cheek, his thumb stroking away the errant drop.

The way he spoke her name, so much affection in his tone, only made it worse. Another tear followed the first. Then a drop leaked down her other cheek. She reached up to wipe it while he thumbed away the other.

She couldn't help but lean in to the warmth of his hand. The forgiveness it offered. Nay, more than forgiveness. Did she dare explore how much more?

She'd come to respect this man more than she'd thought possible over the months she'd known him. And his nearness made her heart speed up. Even now, her body was aware of every part of him.

His eyes drew her, called her in deeper, until she was lost in their depths. And in them was safety. A secure place she could lose herself.

Then those eyes lowered to her lips. Her chest ached as a longing spread through her. She hadn't felt this desire in so long. Had never thought she'd experience it again. Yet with Isaac, the yearning felt different. New and stronger than anything she'd wanted before.

With everything in her, she craved his kiss.

ELEVEN

*J*oanna's body drew toward Isaac without her bidding. And as he lowered his mouth toward hers, she couldn't help but notice how perfect his lips were. Not too full. Not too thin. Just . . . right.

His breath brushed her chin before his mouth touched hers, a warm precedent to a luxury that stole her breath. His lips were gentle, tender, but with an underlying strength that both called to her and made her feel safe.

She responded to his kiss, and he drew her nearer, pulling her in even as her desire grew. This was so much more than she'd imagined.

He was so much more than she'd let herself hope.

With a groan he pulled himself away, but not far. He rested his forehead on hers, his breaths coming in deep drafts. For that matter, her own chest struggled to inflate fully.

"Joanna." His voice held an ache, as though drawing from the deepest part of him. He raised her hand to his lips and placed a gentle kiss on her knuckles.

She should say something. Somehow communicate how deeply his kiss had affected her. Yet her mind couldn't summon a single word. She closed her hand around his.

Her other hand had already found his cheek, but she slipped it back to cup his neck, her fingers sliding into his hair. The thick deliciousness of it drew her, and her fingers explored deeper.

With another groan, he pulled himself back, adding another handbreadth of space between them. "Joanna." He pressed her hand to his lips again, then eased backward farther, his hand slipping from her cheek. Her own hand slid out of his hair, finding its resting place in her lap.

With a long exhale, he studied her face. Then one corner of his mouth tipped up. "I don't feel a bit of pain now. You must have healed me."

A laugh slipped from her chest, completely unbidden. Her nerves were a jangled mess.

A new awareness now tightened the air between them, and she couldn't quite meet his eyes. She had to say something. Now. "I-I suppose we need to get you to the water, then I should get back to the horses."

"I can make it the rest of the way. Do what you need to with the animals." His voice had lost a bit of its intimacy.

She shot a look at him. His eyes still held the sweet intensity of their kiss, but a bit of pleasure had dimmed from them. Not being able to walk on his own was hard for his pride, she had no doubt. He could crawl to the creek from here, so it would be best if she left him with his dignity.

"All right, then." She pushed to her feet and turned back the direction they'd come.

⋯⊰❈⊱⋯

Laura cradled Samuel in her arms, stroking his hair from his face and willing her heart to stop pounding so loudly in her ears. Darkness was closing around them in earnest as the men moved back and forth through the camp, settling the horses, pulling out food, and going through their usual evening routine. Just like any other night.

But this wasn't a normal night at all.

Tonight, under the thick cover of darkness, she and Samuel would escape. *Lord, let him be well enough for what lies ahead.* The boy had slept in Nate's arms most of the afternoon and now lay remarkably still in hers. His breathing was still hoarse, as the air had to fight through the thickness in his nose and throat.

"Miz Laura, I'm hungry," Samuel whined, but she no longer had the heart to correct his tone.

Her own stomach ached for food, feeling as though she hadn't eaten in days. The meager strips of meat they were given at noon hadn't sufficed to still her belly's cry, not after so many meals of these slim rations.

"I know, honey." She ran her fingers through his copper curls again. "They'll bring our food soon."

"When is my mama coming?"

It was the question she dreaded the most, and he still

123

asked every time they had a few moments together. Again, she couldn't blame him.

A fresh sprout of anger burst in her chest. Soon they'd be away from these scoundrels. Then somehow they'd find their way to the town that Nate's note had spoken of. The note that now lay tucked in her bodice. Hidden, yet its presence so strong her skin had burned from its touch all day.

Lord willing, the people in the town would help them back to Settler's Fort. Had the search party Joanna would have sent given up on finding them yet? Maybe she would meet up with the group on the way back home.

"All right." Rex's voice sent a jolt through her, jerking her from the hopeful thoughts. He strode to her and loomed almost directly overhead.

She cringed away from him before she could stop herself. But he grabbed her arm, hauling her upright and rolling Samuel off her lap in a swift motion.

"Let's take a walk to the trees." The man's slimy voice didn't have as much energy as usual, like he was weary from the long day, too. That usually meant his manner would be even less patient than normal.

She stumbled forward to keep up with his iron grip on her arm, chancing a quick glance back to make sure Samuel had recovered from his tumble out of her lap. The boy was propping himself up with his arms, but the red rims around his eyes looked like the start of tears. *Oh, Samuel. Just a few hours more.*

Keeping pace with Rex was no easy feat, but she did her best not to anger him. She'd learned early on that, of all their kidnappers, Rex was the one to be feared most. Bill might be free with his fists, but this knave had an evilness about him that sent fear all the way to her core.

Especially when he looked at her with as much lust as he did now. He practically threw her behind the first tree they reached outside of camp. She grabbed the coarse bark to keep herself upright and chanced a quick glance at him to see if he would turn a little to give her at least a pretense of modesty like the others did.

His leer slid down her filthy dress, then back up to her face.

She crossed her arms in front of her chest, hoping the look showed that she wouldn't cower to him. But in truth, she was desperate for any barrier she could place between his hungry eyes and her body. And no matter how badly she needed to relieve herself, she'd combust before she did so while this man watched.

But then his gaze dropped to the ground, and a wash of relief slipped through her. He leaned forward, and she stepped back, even as her heart climbed into her throat again. What was he doing?

He didn't reach for her, though. His hand shot out to swipe a slip of white from the ground.

Horror sank through her as she realized what he grabbed. The note—it must have slipped from her bodice when she struggled to right herself.

And now, what had been the ticket to her and Samuel's freedom would be their death sentence.

TWELVE

*S*hould she run?

Every instinct in Laura screamed for her to sprint through the woods. But she couldn't leave Samuel behind.

Still, as red crept up this crazed man's neck, her frantic mind told her she couldn't stay here. Even though they were only strides from the camp, his icy stare and the steel set of his jaw left her little doubt he'd snap her neck in a second if he so desired.

She took a step backward, but she couldn't force herself to turn and run. Something about his inhuman calm—the gleam in his glacial blue eyes—seemed almost unholy. Like she'd always imagined Satan would look.

And she couldn't pull her gaze from him.

The cock of a gun made her jump. Her gaze dropped to where the sound had come from. A pistol in Rex's hand. She'd not even seen him draw the weapon.

"Bill." His voice held the same level cadence as normal, even as he called out. Yet the sound possessed an undertone so powerful, it might crush her in a single blow.

"Yeah?" Thank goodness Bill came striding quickly, for she didn't want to see what Rex would do if he had to call twice. Maybe Bill had picked up on the odd tone in this Satan-man's voice.

Without a word Rex handed him the note.

Bill's reaction was very different from Rex's. Anger seared up to his face in a red-hot fury, erupting in a single yell. "Nate!" He spun toward the camp, crinkling the paper in a meaty fist as his long strides covered the distance.

Nate was standing by Samuel, his hand on the boy's shoulder. But after one look at the bully marching toward him, he motioned for the child to sit. Then he stepped forward to face whatever onslaught approached. He didn't slip a glance toward Laura, which was probably best for him.

As Bill neared, Aaron stepped in front of his brother, his own pistol drawn. "What's your complaint, Carlton?"

"Your brother"—he spat the word like it tasted of dung— "is planning to set our prisoners free tonight."

She couldn't see Bill's face, but it wasn't hard to glimpse the flash of surprise that crossed Aaron's. Nor the leveling of his gun.

"Nate, is that true?" Aaron didn't shift his gaze from the bear of a man in front of him.

Nate stepped up beside his brother. "I told you I won't be party to kidnapping. Let the woman and boy go free."

A low growl emanated from Rex's throat, jerking Laura's focus back to him. The sound was so menacing, she took a tiny step away before she could stop herself.

From the corner of her eye, she saw Bill look their way,

too. Then he turned back to the brothers. "You two weren't more than pickpockets before we picked you up. We've made you rich, and this is how you thank us?" Bill's burly hands squeezed into fists the size of her own head.

Tension hung so thick in the air, she could barely breathe. She could almost smell the acrid odor of death. And fear. Like a soap-making gone horribly wrong, with the lye bubbling up just seconds before it exploded, spraying the landscape with a scalding mass that would incinerate everything it touched.

Her gaze slipped to Samuel. The boy huddled in a tiny ball. She couldn't see his eyes but could well imagine how round they were. Stricken by more terror than any child should know.

"Put your gun away, Aaron. Or the woman dies here and now." Rex's low voice still held that almost otherworldly quality.

"I'll put my gun away if you swear not to touch her or the boy until we reach the cabin. Just like we agreed." Aaron's voice held a remarkable amount of steadiness—and a disinterestedness that had to be forced. She could only pray he wouldn't back down on that demand.

"And why would I make a promise like that? Our deal ended when your brother turned traitor." Rex's voice picked up the leer that she hated as his gaze raked over her again. It made her skin crawl.

"Because we don't have time for this." Aaron's tone was growing impatient. "You know the rules. We all do our part. We all split the profits. The sooner we get there, the sooner we enjoy our reward."

Oh, God. No. An image of what they planned for her flashed through her mind, and bile rose in her throat. She gulped a draft of air to keep it down. Surely God would save her before they reached that point. If He didn't, she'd find a way to save herself.

Rex reached for her and gripped her arm tight enough to stop the blood flowing, then kept the gun pointing at her as he propelled her beside him and marched back to camp. He hadn't answered Aaron but seemed to be taking her back to the tree where Samuel waited.

Aaron and Nate watched them pass by, and their distraction must have been the diversion Bill was looking for. He lunged for Aaron's gun, landing partly on the man and rolling them both.

Nate spun to the commotion, about to dive into the fray to side with his brother.

"Don't move." Rex's sharp command pulled a sideways glance from Nate. Enough to see the gun pressed to Laura's own temple.

She didn't dare breathe. Couldn't draw in air with Rex's arm wrapped around her throat. This may well be the end of her. She had no doubt this rapscallion wouldn't hesitate to pull the trigger.

Poor Samuel. What would it do to him to witness another death? *God, be with him. Save the boy.*

Nate's jaw hardened, but he eased his hands out in front of him. "You hurt her, you're dead."

Bill sprang to his feet and backed a few steps, Aaron's rifle in his hand. He was breathing hard, as was Aaron, who still sat on the ground. A trickle of blood leaked from Aaron's mouth, or maybe from a gash on his lip. The gaze he nailed Bill with would have felled a smaller man.

"Keep them both still while I tie up the chit." Rex finally loosened his viselike hold around her neck, then gripped her arm again and jerked her toward the tree.

Within minutes, they were all tied—Nate, Aaron, Samuel, and her. And with the binding of her hands, the hope she'd let grow was trussed up, too.

Joanna worked the pot back into one of the packs. With the cold spring beside them, Isaac had taken the chance to soak his broken leg the night before, and again that morning. She'd used the opportunity to make a nourishing meat stew and fry corn bread they could eat that morning and later on the trail. The respite had been much needed for them both, but now he was crawling out of the pool, and they'd best move on.

When she had the animals saddled and all the packs loaded, she brought them into the camp so Isaac wouldn't have to walk far to mount.

He stood waiting for her, his walking stick under one arm and his opposite hand braced against a tree. His face looked fresher than the day before, and every bit as handsome.

Memories of their kiss flooded through her, stirring her insides with an intensity so strong that she could almost still feel his hand cradling her cheek. Still feel the warmth of his lips against hers. If only she could step into his arms and see if the sensations were as strong as she remembered.

One corner of his mouth tipped up, as though he could read her thoughts. And of course that sent a surge of heat to her face that gave away anything he hadn't guessed already.

She focused on his horse and adjusted the animal's reins. "Ready?"

"Yep." His voice sounded so near that a tingle ran down her back. Against her better judgment, she turned back to face him.

He stood close, and she could feel the warmth of his breath on her face. With just a slight movement, either of them could close the distance. She could fulfill her wish from a moment before. A wish that had quickly turned to a craving.

But he stepped back, breaking the link between them.

His foot must have caught on something, or maybe he didn't have the walking stick positioned right for the action. He stumbled backward, his upper body falling much faster than his feet could right himself.

She grabbed for his arm, and her fingers grasped his shirt just before he would have fallen out of reach. She wasn't strong enough to stop him, but her tug at least slowed his fall. He landed hard on his hip, and it took all her balance not to fall on top of him.

She kept her feet underneath her, though, then dropped to her haunches to check on his injuries. "Are you hurt? I'm so sorry, Isaac." She should have reached for him in time to help him stay upright. Of course he couldn't walk backward with only that stick for a crutch. He could barely hobble forward.

He waved her away, rolling to his side, then shifting to his good knee. She'd seen him perform this maneuver before, and it always tightened her nerves as he kept his injured leg extended, then pushed off with the toes of his good foot and did a hop that brought him upright.

She moved in closer so he could lean on her if he needed to.

But he didn't touch her. Just hopped forward on one foot so he could reach the horse's saddle. Why wasn't he letting her help? Men and their silly pride.

She'd learned with Robert not to get in his way when he was feeling the sting of a bruised ego. She'd worked hard to be Robert's helpmate and was always hurt when he pushed her aside to nurse his wounded pride. As though her efforts meant so little to him. But one day she'd realized those times of sulking truly had nothing to do with her. The slight was to himself, not to her. As was the case now.

She held the horse's head while Isaac pulled himself up into the saddle. The task seemed to be a little easier for him now than those first few times. She could only imagine how muscled his strong arms would feel wrapped around her.

Although she shouldn't imagine it. Especially not after he'd just stepped back from their almost-kiss moments before.

She turned to her own horse and mounted, then reined the animal toward the trail. Samuel needed them. And they'd lost too much time already.

They'd moved her to Bill's saddle. Samuel rode with Aaron, perched in between the man's bound arms. Aaron's horse was tethered to Rex's mount, and Nate's gelding had been tied to Bill's. Nate, of course, was trussed up tight, a hard set to his jaw every time she caught sight of him.

Which wasn't often, though, for riding with Bill kept her every nerve on end. She'd sat with Aaron for so many days now, she'd become immune to his touch. Or maybe he'd simply lost interest in her. Either way, she didn't feel his hands slide upward along her side the way Bill's did. Moving much higher than they should.

She'd tried to pull away, to put more space between them. But his bear-like grip around her tightened, squeezing her injured ribs until light flashed through her eyes. When he finally released her, she struggled to draw shallow breaths. Her lungs craved air, but her chest burned like fire.

The next time his hands roamed, the moment she tensed, his grip tightened. Not as much as before, but enough that she knew the pain would only increase.

She bit hard into her lower lip, forcing her mind onto other things.

By the time they stopped at midday, the first raindrops had begun to fall—the first of many, if the low gray clouds were any indication. The mountain that loomed ahead of them was mostly barren cliffside, with only a few scrappy plants clinging to the crags. Laura hoped they wouldn't try to cross such a peak on wet rocks. The horses had enough trouble finding secure footing in dry weather.

As they started up the rocky incline, the horses moved into

a single line. Loose rocks littered the path they traveled, and the horses stumbled more than once. There was nothing of a trail that she could see, just random switchbacks as the hill grew ever steeper.

She clung to the front of the saddle, leaning as far forward as her painful ribs would allow. Bill's thick chest still pressed on her, no matter how far she leaned.

Their horse stumbled over stones that tumbled down from the animals ahead, but Bill seemed to know how to help the gelding stay upright. For that, at least, she could be grateful.

By halfway up the mountain, their horse was drawing in great drafts of air, and she could feel its strain in every step. Every reach of its hooves seemed to take more effort. This incline was too steep for it to carry two riders, especially one as mammoth as the man at her back.

The animal grunted as it struggled to haul them up onto the jut of a rock, and for a second, the horse teetered halfway up. With a groan, it pulled its rear legs the rest of the way, then stopped. Its sides heaved with each breath. She couldn't blame the horse. Her heart ached for it.

Turning her head so the man behind her could hear, she raised her voice over the wind and rain. "This is too much weight for him to carry up the mountain. I'll walk alongside."

The grip around her waist tightened. "You're not getting off."

Did he think she meant to escape? "You can tie me beside the horse if you want, but he can't carry us both up this incline. Especially with the wet rocks."

"Get on." This time Bill's bark was aimed at the gelding and accompanied by a heavy jab of both his heels.

The animal grunted and lunged forward, stiff-legged from its resting position. Laura clutched the saddle and sent another prayer upward. If they made it over this peak, she would drop to her knees on solid ground and speak a heartfelt thanksgiving.

A yell sounded behind. Nay—more like a scream.

She spun to look but couldn't see anything around Bill's massive frame. He turned, also, and for a second, it felt as if they were falling. The horse scrambled sideways to catch its footing.

Laura jerked the other direction to help balance their weight, anything to keep from toppling down the rocky cliff they'd just climbed. Their horse stumbled, and Bill clutched tighter around Laura. He now leaned the other way, as though he realized they had to do everything possible to keep the animal from tumbling down the mountain.

But the cliff was too steep. The rocks too slippery. The horse's balance too far gone.

She felt herself falling backward, clutching tight to the saddle, unable to dismount or move at all for the viselike grip around her waist. Then something pushed her forward, as though a mighty hand shoved Bill from behind. Together they rolled to the right, away from the falling horse.

THIRTEEN

*L*aura's shoulder hit the ground hard, but then she was hauled backward as the giant clutching her rolled onto his back. She couldn't breathe, especially lying faceup with the bear-man's giant paw pressing down on her broken ribs.

She clawed at his arm, fighting to turn to her side. Any position where her chest could draw breath.

At last, the clutch around her loosened. She scrambled onto her hands and knees, pebbles pressing into her palms. She inhaled deeply, but the pain that plunged like a knife in her side nearly jerked her arms out from under her.

A shallower breath this time. Then another. Her chest finally filled one gasp at a time, releasing the awful pressure that had almost strangled her. Rain ran down her face, pasting wet tendrils of hair to her face. She pressed her eyes closed against the water.

At last she raised her head. She didn't dare lift a hand to wipe the rain from her eyes, for she needed every bit of stability her shaking arms could offer.

With the rain still pelting down and the sound of her own breathing loud in her ears, she almost missed the groaning coming from behind her and the clattering of boots and hooves against rock.

She glanced up the mountain, the easiest place to look from her current position. Nate stood on the ground, holding his and Aaron's horses, even though his wrists were still tied. Samuel pressed against his leg. Safe, thank the Lord. That was probably fear in Samuel's eyes, but she couldn't see well with rain blurring her vision.

She worked herself up to sit on her heels, brushing her hands against her skirts to clear the dirt pressed in her skin.

A cry from below grabbed her attention. Not that of a man, but high pitched. Like a horse in distress.

She spun, but the quick movement sent a shot of dizziness through her head. She reached out to steady herself on a rock that jutted up beside her. As the world stopped whirling, she was able to focus on the sight below.

Bill bent over a figure on the mountainside. Rex, from the dark color of his hair. The cad was propped up on an elbow, which meant he hadn't died. As much as she wanted him out of the way, the thought of any human losing their life on this mountainside made her roiling midsection churn harder.

Rex's horse shuffled uneasily on the incline, and at first that was all she could see. But then Aaron appeared behind the animal, walking backward. Pulling something.

That cry of distress sounded again, and in that instant, a wash of understanding sank through her.

Bill's horse.

The animal had been struggling to keep its footing when she and Bill fell off on the uphill side. Had their tumble knocked the horse in the opposite direction? *Oh, God, help it.*

With one hand gripping the rock beside her, she pushed up to her feet. That poor horse had struggled so hard to carry them up the mountain. She couldn't let it die for its efforts.

Dizziness spun her vision, but not as much as before. Only a few seconds passed before she could see clearly enough to start down the hill.

She passed by Bill and Rex, who seemed to be examining Rex's leg. Maybe he'd broken it. She couldn't summon too much sympathy for his pain.

Aaron's voice sounded even before she slipped past Rex's horse, which had blocked her view of the injured mount.

When she saw the animal, lying beside a boulder almost as tall as she was, her chest squeezed tight. The horse's legs straddled the base of the massive stone, making it impossible for the gelding to rise.

Aaron pulled on the reins and the horse gave an admirable effort, scrambling and pawing at the stone, but its hooves couldn't find purchase with its legs bent like that. *Oh, Lord, don't let any of its limbs be broken.*

The animal's movement revealed blood covering the boulder where the horse's belly pressed against it. Bile pressed against the back of her throat, and she had to look away to settle the contents of her stomach. This was no time to be weak. That horse needed help.

She stumbled forward. "He can't get up on his own. Help me slide him away from that boulder."

She'd spent most of her growing-up years around horses, and had helped rescue more than one animal who'd been cast against the wall of a stall. The horses would fight until they did permanent damage to themselves unless they were rescued first.

She moved to the gelding's hindquarters and leveraged her bound hands beneath him. With everything in her she pushed the horse, clenching her teeth against the shooting pain in her ribs. Her boots slipped on the wet rocks and she couldn't find solid purchase, but she did manage to shift the horse a tiny bit.

When she eased up to catch her breath, the agony in her side made it almost impossible to draw air. She forced herself to take slow, shallow inhales. The animal scrambled again to stand, but she'd not been able to move it far enough away from the boulder.

She motioned for Aaron. "We can probably move him if we're both pushing." Two people could pull a horse away from a stall wall; but on this steep incline, their work would be so much harder. And her side may not let her put in the effort she needed to.

Aaron finally moved around to her, taking up the position she'd just used where he would have the best angle to push. He heaved against the horse, his face turning red with strain, the tendons in his neck bulging.

Laura scrambled to help, digging the heels of her hands into the horse's warm hide, pushing with everything she had, squeezing her eyes shut against the pain in her ribs. Her feet braced against a solid stone, and she could feel the gelding's body inch up as they heaved.

They were making progress, but she didn't dare let up to celebrate. Not until Aaron stopped.

At last, he eased back with a groan. The moment he stopped pushing, the horse scrambled again, trying to regain its footing. The back legs were free now, but a jut of the boulder pressed into the animal's belly, just behind its front legs. They'd have to work on its front end before the gelding would be able to rise.

Laura shifted around to the horse's head and lowered to her knees, holding her side to keep the pain from shooting through her body. "Easy, boy. We'll get you out." She stroked the animal's neck. Its wide eyes regarded her with fear as it lay flat against the hard stone. How much agony was the horse in?

They wouldn't know for sure if any legs were broken until the animal stood, and she could only pray the blood stemmed from a surface wound.

"Let me through." Aaron had moved up behind her to work on the horse's front end. There wasn't much room to move with the boulder looming behind them. Only enough for one person to push.

She shifted to the side, but that still didn't give Aaron enough access, so she scooted all the way around so she was above the horse on the mountain. Maybe she could help at least a little by pulling.

Aaron braced his feet and pushed again. His face turned as red as the blood coating the rock, and the thick cords in his neck rose up again. His mouth spread wide to reveal clenched teeth as every part of him strained.

The horse slid up the hill, away from the boulder. Maybe enough to allow room to stand. Or maybe not yet.

Aaron stopped for a breath and adjusted his position, the ties around his wrists making things awkward. Then he was back into the effort, heaving with everything he had.

The gelding scooted farther up the mountain. Definitely far enough this time.

"That's enough." She pushed to her feet as Aaron collapsed into an exhausted heap.

He was lying just behind the horse's front legs, and the animal was already trying to stand again.

"Get back. Watch out." She dropped back down to press a knee onto the horse's neck to still it as Aaron rolled his weary body away from the animal.

At last he was on his feet and far enough back. She stood and gave the horse's neck a pat. "All right, boy. Up now."

The horse struggled to get its legs underneath it, its efforts almost as if it still thought its belly was pressed against the boulder. Laura grabbed the reins and pulled the horse's head, drawing it onto its belly to get its legs underneath it.

That was what the animal needed, and it released a loud groan as it pulled itself up to standing.

"Good boy. Good fella." She rubbed the gelding's neck, using a vigorous stroke to bring the horse back to life. Her gaze slid to its belly, but she couldn't see the wound from the left side.

Aaron still stood by the boulder, leaning against it as his chest heaved.

She moved around to the horse's other side and had to

bend low to see the blood matting its coat, just behind the girth that held the saddle in place.

The strap had shifted farther forward than usual, and blood dripped from a raw patch of skin where the horse had struggled against the boulder.

"We need to get this saddle off." She stroked the horse's shoulder, then glanced around at the others. Nate still kept Samuel away from the danger, holding the two horses farther up the mountain.

Bill had risen from Rex's side and now held his rifle pointed at her. "Nate, bring those horses down the mountain. The boy, too."

Relief sank through her. She couldn't even see the peak of the mountain now that a low cloud covered the top. But this horse needed its saddle removed and the wound cleaned.

And maybe their captors were as miserable in the rain as she was. Maybe Rex's injuries had eased a bit of his wicked control.

That last thought filled her with a tiny bit of hope. Perhaps this night would give them a second chance to escape.

FOURTEEN

*R*ex wants you to tend his leg."

Laura jerked her gaze up from the bed she was making for Samuel. The steady patter of rain on the trees around them had drowned out Bill's approach. Having the man loom above her now made her want to cower.

But his request tightened the pressure inside her even more. Tend Rex's wound? She'd rather give him a few more injuries.

From the glances she'd snatched as they were setting up camp, the man was quite conscious. The thought of touching him made her want to spew what little she ate for lunch all over this oaf's boots.

"Just so we're clear . . . this is not a request." The growl in Bill's tone finished the thought for him. *It's an order.*

She inhaled a steadying breath. The pain piercing her side with the action only reminded her just how heavy-handed the brute standing over her could be.

Turning to Samuel, she patted the blanket she'd just laid out. "Lie down and rest, honey. I'll be back soon."

Without giving Bill the respect of acknowledgment, she rose and walked toward Rex, who'd stretched out with his upper body propped on a saddle and a blanket. With Bill's behemoth presence behind her and Rex's leering gaze watching her approach, she may as well be a lamb herded to the slaughter. *God, protect me.*

When she reached Rex, she intentionally ignored his icy stare, focusing instead on his leg as she stood over him. His trousers were ripped in a diagonal line spanning from the outside of his hip, across the top of the leg, to the inside of the knee. Through the tear, she could see a fair amount of bloody flesh.

She'd have to kneel beside him for a closer inspection, but she couldn't quite make herself drop to his side. That seemed too familiar. Maybe even subservient.

"Come closer. I'd much rather have you tend me than Bill." Even if the words had been innocent—which they weren't— the slimy tone and lustfulness in Rex's gaze would push her away.

She stepped back, but a hard poke in her side stilled her instantly. That round solidity could only be the business end of a gun. She'd have to do this.

Clamping her jaw to hold in something she shouldn't say, she dropped to her knees beside the man. Her wrists were still bound, but she used the tips of two fingers to pull aside a bloody edge of the torn trousers so she could peer at the wound.

"Bill thinks it needs stitched. I'm sure your handwork'll be prettier than his."

Yes, that gash was deep enough it would require a seam to heal correctly. She'd never sewn human flesh. Horses yes, but not a wound on a man.

Still, maybe jabbing a needle into his sorry hide would be a pleasure.

She straightened and leaned back on her heels, nodding without looking anywhere near the man's face. "It would heal best with stitches. I can't do them with my hands tied."

"Since we don't have needle and thread, that'll have to wait till we're at the cabin. For now, clean it good and doctor it up for me." If possible, the man's voice turned more slippery, lowering into almost a rasp. "Bill brought you some water and salve."

He reached for the buttons at his waist, and horror clutched at her chest as she realized what he was about to do. Not since she was ten years old had she seen a male in his underthings. And then, it had only been her half-grown brothers.

She would *not* attend to this man unless he was fully clothed.

"Do not undress, sir. I can do everything I need to through the hole in your trousers." She could only hope her voice came through with enough command, not like a frightened schoolgirl. Which was how she felt.

He chuckled, but his fingers never stopped working at the buttons. He'd already released the top two, and she forced her eyes away from the awful sight. The branches were mostly leafed out, so they kept much of the water from falling on the camp. But they also hid what little sun dared press through the thick clouds above. This copse should have been shelter in the storm, yet instead a smothering darkness pressed down on her.

"Rex." The bark of the man's name made her jump, but it was the fury in the voice that made her spin around.

Nate's expression had melted into full rage. "Cover yourself, you filthy lowlife. Have you no shame?" He jerked against the ties that held him to a sturdy pine like a bull buffalo rushing an attacking wolf.

Bill spun the gun in his direction, but he didn't spare it a glance. "Get away from him, Laura," Nate said through a steely jaw.

With the weapon no longer pressed into her back, she was already moving by the time he finished saying her name. Even as she darted away, she prepared herself for Rex or Bill to grab her.

But neither did. God's hand must have stopped them, for only the Almighty could control the evil inside these men.

One more thing to regret.

Isaac usually loved long hours in the saddle, extended time where the sounds of God's creation spoke to him, the majesty of this land quieting his spirit. He'd think back through the verses he'd memorized, talk to God about anything on his mind, and soak in the peacefulness of it all.

But these hours of silence had been steadily eating at his nerves, churning a knot in his belly. He had to apologize to

Joanna for his ill-mannered behavior back at the camp. Pa would be appalled at his rudeness, and Isaac had promised himself a long time ago he wouldn't do another thing to disappoint his father. Not if he could help it.

He'd have to be careful when he apologized, though. No matter how hard he tried to build a barrier between them, every time he was near her—nay, every time he looked at her across the camp—every part of him wanted to pull her close. Not just for another kiss, but to feel the connection between them.

He'd never known a woman like her. Not only was she one of the prettiest he'd ever met, but she was also so brave and kind and hardworking. Yet it was more than that that drew him. She seemed to see every part of him—and didn't appear disgusted by what she saw.

But even so, there was a part she couldn't see. Not yet. It would be impossible to hide the truth from her for long. If he wasn't forced to admit it when they sought help in town, it would most definitely come out when he confronted the gang.

And the last thing he wanted was for Joanna to learn about his past from the lips of someone else. He could only imagine the shock, the horror, the hurt that would fill her eyes.

He couldn't bear for her to look at him that way. He had to tell her himself. At least then he could give her all the details. Could try to explain how much he'd changed.

How much God had changed him.

If the rest of their travel went without mishap, they'd reach the little town of River Crossing tomorrow night. With any luck, they could gather men to help, then reach the old cabin hideout by midmorning the next day.

Which meant he had to find a time to tell Joanna before tomorrow night. Maybe when they camped soon, since the thick of night was just about on them. Or maybe she'd feel nervous sleeping by the same fire as him once she knew his past. Might be better to tell her on the trail tomorrow. That way, if she wanted to ride off and leave him in her dust, she could do so safely.

He'd still get her boy back, and Miss Hannon, too. But he didn't want her to feel tied to him for a single minute. Not when he knew she would hate the sight of him.

So tomorrow it would be.

For now, he needed to watch for a good spot to camp. He'd shifted their direction a little to the west, more of a straight shot toward town instead of following the gang's tracks.

He and Joanna had experienced so many delays that it wasn't likely they would catch Aaron and the others before they reached the cabin, but they could at least cut off a couple hours of the journey to town by taking this route.

A stand of trees ahead would be a good place to camp. Even if there wasn't a creek in the woods, the water they'd crossed an hour before would hold the horses overnight. And he and Joanna had refilled their water flasks, so they could make that last until morning, too.

As they neared the spot, he motioned for Joanna to slow. "We'll camp here for the night, but I'd like to take a look in the trees before we dismount." Something about them raised his instincts. This country felt vast and empty, but it wasn't.

"Think we'll have company in there?" Joanna had read his mind, as usual. Her voice held a hint of teasing that brought a lightness in his chest. But on its flank was an awful reminder that soon she'd never joke with him again.

"Better to check than be surprised."

Joanna halted her horse and the packhorse at the edge of the trees. He'd already pulled his rifle from the scabbard, but now rested it loosely against his shoulder.

The night was so dark that entering the trees felt like walking into a cave. Isaac strained to hear sounds of what other animals were waiting for him there. Maybe a bear, or a mountain lion. Perhaps only a herd of mountain goats.

But this wasn't a cave, as was clear by the steady chirp of crickets. The cry of a nightjar rang through the trees, answered by another bird closer to him. The hoot of an owl sounded in a different section. Isaac cocked his head. The nightjar calls could have possibly been the sounds of humans signaling each other, but that owl hoot was too natural to be feigned. He'd ride on to the end of the little copse to be sure, but none of his instincts alerted to the presence of other humans.

And he could almost always trust his instincts. Unless, of course, they'd been dulled by a kiss so powerful, he could still feel it through every part of him. He pushed the memory away before it could take hold.

He was partway through the trees when shadows began to swoop over his head. In the darkness, he couldn't get a good look at them, but he didn't have to. These types of trees made the perfect home for bats on a summer eve. His gelding tensed, but the horse had been through worse than a few winged creatures.

"Easy, boy." His words seemed to calm the horse, and they finally reached the other edge of the trees without further excitement.

He circled around the grove to reach Joanna instead of going back through. When he was halfway to her, the sound of her voice—a little reedy—drifted to him.

"Isaac?"

"I'm here." He should have alerted her of his presence instead of frightening her like this. When he reached her, the faint glow of the crescent moon shone around her, making her look even more like the angel she was.

His chest ached at the sight. Which was probably why he let his horse walk all the way up to hers before halting the animal. This close, he could see the way each of Joanna's pretty features worked together to form a face that nearly took his breath away.

"Did you find a place to camp?"

Her words took a moment to register, but they effectively pulled him from his wayward thoughts. He turned his gelding toward the trees. "Yep. Just a few crickets and some birds in there. Should be fine for a camp."

Too bad there wasn't another cold spring to dunk his head in. He needed something to bring him back to his senses.

FIFTEEN

*S*omething wasn't right.

Joanna couldn't tell what had her nerves so unsettled. Maybe it was the darkness that hovered close around them. They'd agreed that with the night so late and no water nearby, there wasn't much sense in building a fire.

Or maybe Isaac's own behavior was what had her on edge. One moment he'd watch her with a soft expression, as though he might pull her into his arms. Then, a breath later, he'd clamp his jaw and answer with single-word responses. Was she doing something that bothered him?

Maybe he regretted their kiss. Perhaps he didn't want any permanent ties with her, so he was doing his best to build a barrier between them. If she were truthful with herself, during the long hours in the saddle she'd imagined what it might look like for this connection they'd been building to continue after things settled down again. After she and Samuel were returned to their little home in Settler's Fort.

But Isaac clearly had no desire to go down that path. She'd best put it out of her own mind.

While she'd tied the horses out to graze for the night, he'd pulled a simple meal from the pack, along with their blankets. She settled onto the bedding and took the food he'd wordlessly offered. "Thank you. How are we doing with supplies?"

"We have enough until we reach town tomorrow. I'll need to restock everything before heading back to Settler's Fort."

What did he mean by the shift from *we* to *I* in his statements? Maybe he simply planned to handle finding and paying for the goods himself. She couldn't allow him to shoulder all the costs.

"I'll give you money for food once we're back in Settler's Fort." It would take every last penny she had until she was paid again, but she owed him so much more than a few coins and a small pouch of gold dust for everything he'd endured to find Samuel and Laura. The man had a broken leg, for Betsy's sake.

And who knew what would happen when they caught up with the kidnappers.

Lord, keep us all safe. Prepare the way for us, and keep my boy and Laura unharmed. Please.

She bit into a piece of roasted meat as a nicker drifted from where she'd staked the horses.

"Sounds like the mare." Isaac sat straighter.

The whinny hadn't sounded fearful. Maybe she was simply caught in her rope. Joanna pushed to her feet.

"I'm coming, too." Isaac turned onto his knees, then

struggled to stand. Everything was such an effort for him, and she could hear the frustration in his tone. Maybe that was contributing to his strange behavior.

"Let me walk to the edge of the woods and look out on them first. If there's any cause for concern, I'll come back and get you."

He did his single-footed hop to push himself up to standing, then gripped a tree branch to steady himself. "Take the rifle." His voice had a bit of a growl. Then he added, "But don't use it unless you have to. Come back and get me."

A warmth swept through her chest. It wasn't hard to see through that grouchy façade to the protectiveness underneath. It felt like forever since she'd had someone else worry about her.

She bent to retrieve the gun and shot bag. "I will." Then she stepped toward the edge of the woods. Even now that her eyes had adjusted to the thick darkness in these trees, she had to move slowly to keep from tripping over fallen branches and rocks.

Another whinny sounded from the clearing ahead. This one was deeper . . . maybe one of the geldings? *Lord, don't let there be people out there.* A group of Indians could have ridden up, or maybe even the kidnappers had circled back on them.

Her heart lurched at the thought. She and Isaac needed the upper hand. The element of surprise. How could they get Samuel and Laura back when Isaac could barely hobble and they only had one rifle between them? Her son and friend would be in greater danger if the attack wasn't handled right.

At the edge of the woods, she clung close to a tree while her eyes adjusted to the brighter moonlight.

Their horses hadn't moved from where she left them. Yet all three stood with heads raised, shifting restlessly. The animals weren't staring in the same direction like they would if a group of riders approached. No, each seemed to be facing different directions.

Then Isaac's gelding charged toward something, ears pinned back.

A yelp sounded. Then a bark. A growl so menacing, it raised gooseflesh on her arms, even at this distance.

Coyotes? Nay, wolves. No coyote would be foolish enough to attack three healthy horses. But hungry wolves might.

She cocked the rifle and charged forward. Going back for Isaac would waste precious time. And she was a decent shot at close range. She'd had plenty of practice these last four years living on the wilderness homestead with Robert.

Another yip sounded, then the squeal of a horse. She didn't slow to see what was happening, just ran as fast as her skirts would allow through the thick grass.

The barking turned ferocious, even as the ground underneath her dipped in a hidden gully. She tumbled forward, landing on her knees and fists as she struggled to keep her grip on the rifle. Her left wrist bent hard under the force of her weight.

She ignored the pain, struggling back to her feet. Another squeal sounded from the horses, this one louder than the other. A mixture of anger and pain.

God, help me get there in time. She was still twenty or so strides from the horses, and with the tall wheatgrass and other weeds, she couldn't see the wolves clearly enough to shoot.

Why had she tethered the horses so far away? This had seemed like the best grass that provided trees for all three to be tied. But the animals were too exposed.

Finally, the grass was low enough to present a clear view of the wolves. Less than a dozen steps ahead, three doglike creatures faced one of the horses, bared teeth glimmering in the faint moonlight. The horse had turned its hind end to the attackers, and stood hunched, its tail tucked in preparation to kick at a moment's notice.

One of the wolves charged the horse's flank. A second darted to the other side, moving up toward the shoulder. Probably trying to reach the horse's neck. The third wolf attacked the flank on that same side.

The horse jerked, spinning and kicking wildly to fight off the onslaught. It reared up, and the wolf at its neck leaped high into the air. In the darkness she couldn't tell if the animal was hanging from the horse's neck or still trying to strike there.

Oh, God, help!

She raised the rifle to her shoulder and sighted down the barrel. With the animals spinning and writhing, it was almost impossible to get a good shot. Especially with all of them only dark shadows.

Moving closer and to the side to get a better angle, she focused on one of the wolves who must have been kicked away. It crouched in the grass, licking at a wound.

She aimed and pulled the trigger, bracing herself for the hard kick of the gun. The wolf slumped into a heap, moving no more.

The explosion seemed to halt the other attacks, and the two remaining wolves slunk back a few strides away from the horse. She worked quickly to reload the rifle for another shot, her fingers finding the rhythm she'd once known so well. Thankfully, this Hawken worked much like her own gun.

The horse stood with its head down and tail tucked. Ears tipped backward to hear the next attack. She couldn't tell how bad its wounds were, but the wolves had to be dealt with before she could focus on the injured animal.

She raised the gun to her shoulder just as the wolves began pacing behind the horse again. She aimed for the larger of the two and squeezed the trigger.

Either her focus was off or the wolf darted away at the last second, because when the gunpowder cleared the air enough for her to see, both animals were charging the horse again. She scrambled to reload, her heart thundering in her throat. That missed shot could be the difference between life and death for the poor horse.

The mare's fight wasn't nearly as strong this time as one wolf went for the flank and the other the neck. The horse must be injured pretty badly.

Shooting would be too dangerous with the animals so entangled, but she had to do something. Screaming like a crazy woman, she ran toward the animals, swinging the rifle like a club. The wolf on her nearest side was jumping at the horse's throat, so she went for that enemy first.

The wolf had caught hold, and either didn't hear her scream-ing or didn't think the threat worth breaking its grasp for.

She slammed the butt of the rifle into the wolf's head with all her strength.

The beast yelped and jerked back, pulling the horse's flesh with him for a moment as the mare cried out in pain. At last the wolf released the frightened animal. The horse shook its head and turned its efforts to kicking the wolf half-entangled in its legs.

Joanna had her own battle to fight. The wolf she'd just struck had regained its faculties and crouched not two strides in front of her. This time, its menacing growl and bared teeth weren't aimed at a wounded horse.

She raised the rifle to her shoulder to aim at the animal. *Lord, don't let my wild swinging have dislodged the bullet and powder.* The last thing she needed was a misfire.

But she didn't have enough time to adjust the rear set trigger and squeeze the front trigger that would make the gun fire.

The wolf leapt at her face. She plunged the rifle barrel forward, defending herself as best she could against the mass of fur and teeth. The metal of the gun caught the animal in the throat, halting his momentum midair and tossing it backward.

But the force of the wolf's attack pushed her back, too, knocking her on her backside. She scrambled up to a sit-ting position, shifting her grip on the rifle as the wolf also struggled to its feet. She had to shoot the beast before it could attack again.

Tightening the rifle against her shoulder, she positioned the rear trigger, aimed the barrel at the wolf's snarling teeth, then braced herself as she pulled the front trigger.

A blast lit the night sky with a flash so brilliant, she squeezed her eyes shut. The acrid burn of gunpowder assaulted her nose. *Thank you, Lord, that the gun didn't backfire.*

She forced her eyes open to see what damage she'd done. To prepare in case the wolf still had any fight left in it.

Her own body was just about spent, but she couldn't stop until the danger was gone. A lump lay on the ground in front of her, almost within reach. Unmoving.

A sound drifted from her left. From the injured horse. A kind of straining noise.

The third wolf wasn't around the horse, but she had to find and destroy the beast before she could see the extent of the damage to the mare. She scanned the area behind the horse, her eyes seeking movement in the darkness. Nothing that she could see, but it was too much to hope that the wounded horse had killed the wolf on its own.

She scrambled to reload the rifle, her attention split between the task and searching for the wolf. Just as she finished the job and pushed to her feet, a motion behind the horse caught her focus.

Maybe it was just the wind waving the tall grass. No, that was a dark body, just the size of a wolf. Slinking away from them.

She raised the rifle and aimed down the barrel, but the grass had already closed over the wolf. The tops of the weeds swayed where the creature must be passing through, trotting away. The canine would be foolish to continue the battle with its companions dead, and it must have accepted the fact.

She inhaled a long breath, then released it, the gun weighing heavy in her hands. Was the danger really gone? After the fury of the attack, this quiet seemed too much to believe.

A rustle from the horses behind her pulled her focus back to the most urgent need. Lowering the rifle so she could hold it in one hand, she approached the injured horse. The sweet bay mare from the livery. Wolves usually attacked the weakest member of the herd, and they must have sensed this horse was already vulnerable from its sore hoof.

"Hey, girl." She extended a hand to the mare, stroking its mane. One ear flicked toward her, but otherwise, the horse didn't respond. Joanna could see bits of hanging skin on the underside of the neck, but in the shadows, she couldn't decipher the extent of the damage.

She moved around to the other side, where the sliver of moon would shed some light. The hair was matted dark with blood, and a section of pale flesh shone against the darkness around it. She'd need to get the mare back to camp where they could light a fire and better inspect the wound. At the very least, the area would need salve, but probably much more.

Joanna stepped back and scanned the rest of the horse. More shadowed areas around the haunches were probably bloody, but none of them showed the white of underflesh. Hopefully the mare could walk to the trees, at least.

Isaac must be stewing terribly since she'd not come back. Then he'd have heard the three rifle shots. She had to get back before he did something foolish like attempting to hobble out here.

"Come on, girl." She untied the rope, then sent another look to the geldings. "I'd better take you boys, too." She couldn't leave them out where they'd be so exposed again. They needed to graze, certainly, but if that wolf came back with more friends . . . They couldn't afford another injured horse. Not when they were so close to town.

So close to help.

SIXTEEN

The mare limped along beside Joanna, but at least the horse was able to walk. The two geldings trailed behind on their longer ropes.

When they neared the trees, Isaac's voice sounded across the open ground. "Joanna?" So many questions hung in the word. Anxiety so thick she could almost touch it.

"I'm not hurt. Three wolves attacked the mare, but I stopped them. I'm bringing her in so we can care for her wounds. The geldings, too." She could barely see him, only a shadow among the tree trunks, but she kept talking. Maybe knowledge of the situation would help him feel less out of control.

Or maybe she spoke to calm her own nerves.

"We need a fire or some way to get enough light to tend her injuries. She has a large gash on her neck, and I think some on her flanks. It's hard to see much out here."

"You're not hurt?" The rasp in his voice sank all the way through her. Drew her in.

Her feet stepped nearer without her consent. Close enough to reach out to him if she chose. "I'm not hurt."

She could see his face now. The lines across his brow, the solid lock of his jaw. Yet his eyes were still shadowed. Impossible to read the expression there.

She could feel his need. Feel his urgency to touch her. Feel his restraint. Even if he had no desire for something permanent between them, he needed to know with his own hands that she was unhurt.

Dropping the mare's rope, she reached out and pressed her palm to his chest. The muscles tensed under her skin and the intake of his breath was loud enough to hear.

Yet he didn't move. Didn't reach for her. Didn't even breathe again, as far as she could tell. The pounding of his heart under her fingers was the only sign that her nearness affected him half as much as it did her.

Every part of her wanted to draw closer, to press her lips to his. To force him to wrap his free hand around her.

Maybe touching him had been a bad idea.

But then he reached out. Gripped her arm and pulled her closer. Pressed his mouth to hers with a hunger so strong it ricocheted through her body. It would be impossible to deny him, even if she wanted to.

But she didn't.

As he wrapped an arm around her waist, pulling her closer, she dropped the rifle and the gelding's ropes, then slid both her hands up to cup his neck. Her fingers brushed against his hair, its silky curls drawing her in. She wove her hand through its thickness, relishing in the sensation as the power of his kiss drove all the way through her.

He was everything her heart craved. A protector. Someone to

carry the load when she couldn't. And she couldn't remember ever being so affected as this man made her feel at this moment.

His lips strayed to her jaw, and she tilted her chin up. A tiny moan slipped from her mouth. Pure pleasure.

But the sound seemed to still something inside him. His mouth pulled away. Not too far, just enough to rest his forehead on hers. His ragged breathing drifted over her like a warm mist.

Part of her regretted the end of that kiss. That powerful, all-consuming connection. Whether he wanted something permanent with her or not, they fit together like two sides of a magnet.

He drew back, putting more space between them. Breaking their physical connection completely. "I'm sorry. I shouldn't have done that, I just . . ." He didn't meet her eyes, but dropped his head and scrubbed a hand through his hair.

She knew exactly how soft those curls were. Her skin still tingled with the feel of them, ached to pull his hand aside and take its place. She clutched hers into a fist at her side. Just to make sure it stayed put.

"It's all right, Isaac." Since they were clearly both of the same mind—that pursuing any more physical connection would be ill-advised—she at least didn't want to make him feel bad about what had just happened. "Let's get a fire started so we can see about this mare."

⋯⟐⟐⋯

Oh, God, take these feelings away from me. Isaac tried to focus on the deep gashes in the mare's neck, but with Joanna so near, it was hard to think of anything but her. He wanted so badly to tell her how much she'd come to mean to him.

The attraction between them was impossible to deny. Yet there was so much more. She was unlike any woman he'd ever known. Way too special for the likes of him.

And he was going to have to tell her why. Tomorrow.

A part of him wanted to tell her now. Explain his actions. To share how much he truly respected her. That his esteem for her was why he'd pulled away. And, once again, to apologize for touching her in the first place. Just another mistake of many.

If he could work up the nerve, maybe he should tell her tonight. After he doctored the mare.

For now, this poor girl was in rough shape. He doused the wounds with water from one of their canteens. He couldn't remember how far it would be to the next creek tomorrow, so he didn't dare use much. Just enough to flush out the blood and any loose dirt.

"Here's the salve. What's in this exactly?" Joanna stepped up beside him, holding out the jar of healing cream he always carried with him.

He took the medicine, careful not to look at her face or touch her in the exchange. His gaze didn't miss her slender fingers, though. Beautiful, every bit of her.

Clearing his throat, he forced his mind onto her question. "Pa makes it from several different herbs. To be honest, I'm not sure what all he puts in there, but he keeps us stocked."

A pang hit his chest at the thought that had been rising too often of late. "I suppose I should ask him the ingredients. I might need to know someday." Because Pa wouldn't be around forever.

She was quiet as he scooped out a fingerful and rubbed the cream into the wound. At last she spoke, her words soft. "You're blessed to have him so near you."

With a jolt, her earlier disclosure came back to him. She'd lost both her parents and a sister—her entire family—in a train accident. And here he was bemoaning just the thought of losing his father, when no real possibility of that event loomed before him.

He looked over his shoulder to offer an apology in his smile. "You're right. I am blessed. I guess I should do a better job of enjoying his company now."

Her eyes were soft, shadowed as they were by the firelight brushing her cheek. "He seems like a good man."

Isaac nodded and had to swallow down the lump in his throat before he could manage to speak. "The best of men."

What was it about this night that had his emotions in such a stir? Turning back to the horse, he forced his mind to think about what should be done next. "I don't suppose we have any bandages left? This needs stitched, but it'll have to wait until I can buy needle and thread. A wrap will keep the skin together and clean until then."

"I'll find something." Her dress swished as she stepped away from him, withdrawing the power of her sweet presence.

He moved back to the mare's flank to clean the other wounds while Joanna looked for cloth. The sounds of her riffling through the packs rose over the crackling of the fire.

Then a ripping noise sliced through the air. He spun to see what she was doing, but her back was to him, hiding her actions.

She was bent over something. Her skirts?

"Joanna, I didn't mean for you to tear up your clothing. Any bit of leather or an extra shirt would be fine. Or I could tie the satchel around her."

"This will work best. Just . . . turn away, please."

He obeyed, but his unrest only grew. As much as she'd already given up on this journey, she shouldn't have to give what little else she had for this horse. He wanted to make things better for her, yet he was so helpless with this broken leg.

"Here you go." Her voice was nearer than he expected, and when he turned, she held out a bit of fabric unlike anything he'd seen on this trip. The soft cotton had probably started off closer to white, but now had more of a beige look. Both side edges were ragged. "The ruffle was too muddy, so I had to tear that part off."

He nodded, doing his best not to think about the fact that this was her *underskirt* as he wrapped the cloth around the horse's neck.

She was quiet as he worked, and he was more conscious of her presence than he should have been. Maybe he should say something to break the silence.

But before he could summon words, she spoke. "I think I left the shot bag out where the wolves attacked. I'm going out to get it."

Another spurt of frustration pressed his chest. He shouldn't be sending her back out there, not when a pack of wolves had just attacked in that very spot. The carcasses from the two she'd shot would bring all kinds of animals, from vultures to mountain lions to more wolves.

He could limp along to the edge of the trees, but going any farther than that would require him to lean on Joanna, which would only add to her load. And what could he do without a gun anyway?

He tied off the knot in the bandage and turned to her. "Take the rifle with you." His words came out in more of a bark than he meant them to, but she obliged, dipping to grab the gun before stepping into the darkness of the woods around them. The thick blackness seemed to swallow her, even with the sounds of her feet snapping twigs and crunching leaves.

He scrubbed a hand through his hair. *God, I hate this helplessness. Why take away my ability to keep her safe?*

A verse slipped into his mind, completely unbidden. One he hadn't read in several weeks. *My strength is made perfect in weakness.*

Was that why this was happening? Why he'd been brought on this journey, thinking his help, his strength would make the difference in finding Joanna's son and friend? Why he was now so helpless he couldn't walk on his own, couldn't tend his own horses, couldn't protect the woman whose care he'd thought he was being entrusted with?

Joanna possessed an inner strength greater than most people he'd known. But leaning on her went against his grain. Yet perhaps that's what God intended in all this. For him to learn how to rely more on others. And for that matter, more on his heavenly Father.

And was God trying to bring him all the way from his knees to his belly with the truth he'd have to tell Joanna tomorrow?

He squeezed his eyes shut. *It's too much, Lord. I thought you'd promised to forgive those sins. Why make me grovel now?*

My grace is sufficient for thee; for my strength is made perfect in weakness.

Isaac pinched the ends of his hair and pulled. Would his past failures follow him around forever, then? Always be there to torment him?

And lest I should be exalted above measure through the abundance of the revelations, there was given to me a thorn in the flesh . . .

A matter of pride, then. This he could do something about.

Resting his hands on the mare's withers, he bowed his head, letting his chin touch his chest. *I'm sorry, Father. Sorry for thinking I'm the only one to keep Joanna safe. The only one capable of bringing back her son and Miss Hannon. In truth, there's no way I can do any of it without you. Go before us, Lord. Make our way straight. Fight the battle before us.*

He remained in that posture, soaking in the peace and the forgiveness God offered freely.

Tomorrow he would have to tell Joanna of his past. And if she walked away from him, refused to let him help, at least she'd have God on her side.

Paired together, there was no way they could lose.

SEVENTEEN

*J*oanna awoke the next morning with a knot in her middle. Her tension had spread through every part of her, pressing aches into her shoulders and neck.

More aches than usual after sleeping on this hard ground for six nights now. She forced herself to sit up, her eyes still blurry from not enough rest.

"Morning." Isaac's sleep-roughened tenor pulled her attention to where he sat beside the fire.

She had to blink to clear the haze from her vision, but the sight was worth the effort.

His rugged features sent a shiver through her, that strong chin and chiseled cheekbones now covered by more than a week's worth of growth. And the way his buckskins outlined hard muscles in his shoulders and neck . . . She'd felt those muscles, just the night before. Knew the richness of them. The strength that made her feel treasured and protected.

But it was his smoky green eyes that drew her, that held her, like always. Yet something was different about them

171

this morning. Maybe their intensity soaked into her with a stronger grip.

Maybe she just needed coffee to pry her from this sleep-starved fog.

He turned back to the fire. "I warmed the meat to make it more tender, and I'm brewing coffee now."

Her mouth formed a smile of its own accord. "You must have read my mind." She crawled from her blanket and began to fold it. "I guess I shouldn't ask how you found enough water for an extravagance like that."

"We had enough in that last canteen for two cups. If memory serves, we'll reach another creek an hour or so down the trail. We can restock then."

She glanced toward the horses, all three of them dozing peacefully in the early morning light. "How's the mare?"

"Better than I'd hoped now that I can see the wounds better. She'll need some attention once we get to River Crossing tonight, but I think she'll be able to travel today without much trouble. She may need to move slower. We'll see."

His words drew her gaze back to him. "Sorry I slept so late. You could have woken me."

One corner of his mouth tipped up, but the sadness in his eyes kept the look from being anything like a smile. "You needed the rest. And I've only been up a half hour or so."

She reached for the pack and added her blanket on top of where Isaac had already folded and stored his. If the mare was well enough to travel, they needed to get on the trail soon.

After tending to her morning ministrations, she stopped

by the fire long enough to grab a handful of meat and a cup of coffee, then started toward the horses.

"Joanna." Isaac's tone held more than a hint of frustration. "Sit and let the coffee soak in a minute before you start working. You'll be better for it."

She didn't let his words slow her. Taking a deep sip of the scalding brew, she looked for a stump to place the cup while she worked. "I need to saddle the horses and get us loaded." With the weight of the work on her shoulders, she really didn't have time for a leisurely breakfast.

Something like a grunt sounded from Isaac's direction, but she focused on saddling his gelding. Hopefully the mare could still carry the packsaddle with a few light supplies. She was pretty sure none of it would rub the horse's injuries, and she would do her best to load the heavier things behind the geldings' saddles.

As she hoisted the saddle on the first horse, her eye caught movement from the direction of the fire. Isaac was up, hobbling toward her with only his walking stick for aid.

Which meant he had to put at least some pressure on the broken bone. His face was a mask of determination, almost enough to cover the pain from the effort.

She left the saddle and strode toward him. "What are you doing up?" When she reached him, she tried to duck her shoulder under his arm for support, as they'd done dozens of times.

But he shook her off. "I can do it. You don't have to worry over me."

A spurt of annoyance charged through her. "Isaac, let me

finish saddling them first, then I'll bring your gelding over so you can mount."

"I can help." His words were almost a growl, just like those wolves from the night before.

Stubborn man. This would go easier if he just let her do the work.

But maybe he needed to help. To feel useful. She could certainly relate to that. The Lord well knew how hard it was for her to sit on her own hands when she was worried and there was work to be done.

"All right." She stepped away, but just enough to give him a little space—not so far she couldn't grab him if he started to topple. She couldn't help adding, "Be careful."

He'd come to mean more to her than she'd ever expected. More than she should have allowed. And she wasn't quite sure her heart could manage seeing him hurt again, especially not with all the other worries stringing her nerves tight.

Once he made it to his gelding, he did seem to be steady on his feet as he tightened the cinch and readied the animal. She moved to the other gelding, the one she'd been riding, and did the same.

By the time she was finished, Isaac was speaking softly to the mare as he strapped on the packsaddle. Joanna brought the lighter pack for him to load, while she divided the other supplies and fastened them behind the riding saddles.

When she finished, she finally turned her attention to the cup of coffee that had been calling her name. Not that she needed the brew to wake her up anymore, but she had a feeling she'd need extra fortitude for what this day might bring.

They may not catch up with the kidnappers today, since she and Isaac were moving a different direction toward town now. But, Lord willing, they'd find help. Then tomorrow she would have her boy back in her arms.

Isaac's low voice still hummed from where he stood beside the mare, and she marched over to help him finish.

They had to get on the trail. Not even one moment could be wasted. Her son's safety hung in the balance.

⊰⊱⊰⊱⊰⊱

Today would be the day. She'd given up hoping that whoever Joanna sent to rescue them would come in time. She would have to find her own way for them to escape.

Laura tucked her legs tighter into her chest as she watched the men working through their morning chores around the camp. After Bill finished rekindling the fire, she'd seen Aaron motion him over. The two had spoken in low tones for a minute, then Bill shuffled over to Rex. A scowl on the injured man's face had finally given way to a nod. Moments later, Bill cut Aaron free, then shuffled toward where they'd staked out the horses. Aaron set to work on the morning meal.

Rex hadn't risen to help but instead sat sullenly with arms crossed and a rifle in his lap, watching the others work. She didn't let her gaze stray toward him often, but she could feel every time the burn of his glare seared through her filthy, tattered dress.

So many times the men had mentioned that none of them

175

were to touch her until they reached their destination, the cabin they sometimes called a hideout.

Now they expected to arrive there tonight. Her blanket of protection would be ripped off, leaving her at their mercy unless she could find a way to escape first.

Perhaps Rex would still be too injured to ride today. Maybe they'd put off traveling for another night, or go so slowly that they wouldn't reach the cabin until tomorrow. Every day she could delay them, the better.

But better for what? If she didn't find a way for her and Samuel to escape, a delay would only shift the inevitable. She couldn't rely on the men to have a sudden change of heart where she was concerned. Not with the lust swimming in Rex's eyes. Bill's, too.

She pulled her legs in tighter, wishing she could wrap her arms around herself, too. But she and Samuel were both still tied to a tree, as they were every night.

A half hour later, Bill moved toward them, two steaming bowls in his hands. He sank to his haunches in front of them and set the tin cups on the ground. Then he pulled his knife from its sheath and reached for the rope that fastened her to the tree. "You get a minute at the tree before you eat." He sliced easily through the ragged cord that had been cut and retied too many times.

Samuel lay curled like a groggy caterpillar as Bill pulled her to her feet. The boy's fever was mostly gone, although he seemed more tired than usual. But, Lord willing, the worst was over. Hopefully, the boy would be strong enough for whatever escape she could find.

And it had to happen today.

While they walked toward one of the wider trees, she used the opportunity to brave a question. "Will we be riding again today?"

He glanced at her before turning back to their path to maneuver over a thick root. "Looks like it. You'll be with me. Aaron will have the boy." Was his horse recovered enough to carry a saddle? The poor animal.

They reached the tree, and she quickly accomplished her morning ministrations. All the while, her mind worked through possibilities for escape. She could find a way if it was just herself—when they took her for a quiet moment at the noon stop, behind whatever tree or brush could be found—but she and the boy were never allowed that liberty at the same time. And she couldn't leave him behind.

Even if she snuck away and they weren't cruel to Samuel, they'd probably tighten their security around him. She'd never be able to sneak close enough to free him without being recaptured herself. And her lot would be ten times worse if that happened.

Maybe Aaron could help her get away with Samuel. He'd not shown willingness to aid them before, but then . . . she hadn't asked.

If she gave Aaron warning of her plans and asked for his help, would he try to stop her? *Lord, what do I do?* Did she dare take a chance? They were so closely guarded, she'd need help to create an opportunity.

There was no other way. Not without divine intervention.

EIGHTEEN

*T*he men started on the trail at least an hour later than usual. And while Laura was thankful for every extra minute of reprieve, anticipation for what she had to accomplish at their noon stop had her nerves so edgy she could barely keep herself still.

But she had to. She couldn't give any sign that today was different than the last seven she'd endured.

At last, the horses were saddled and all of them were mounted. Bill's hands seemed to wander even more today than before. His grip tighter.

Finally, he raised his hand for a halt. "We'll stop and eat a bite."

They were on the side of what must be a small mountain, with a gradual upward slope covered in grass. A few rocks poked through the weeds, and the occasional cluster of bushes and trees dotted the hillside. No woods near them, though, only a boulder just large enough for a man to sit on.

As they all dismounted, Rex headed straight for that stone,

easing himself down with a grimace. His hair had lost its neat, every-strand-in-place look, and pain lines around his eyes made him appear a dozen years older than before. In truth, she'd never seen him so disheveled.

Yet he'd not lost the hardness in his crystal blue eyes. As he sat on the boulder, legs extended in front of him, he had the perfect vantage point to study every move she made.

After the first couple times of meeting that icy gaze, she was careful not to look his way again. She stood with Samuel pressed against her side, watching as Aaron pulled the food pack from behind his saddle and secured the horses where they could graze. Bill walked a few strides away and relieved himself, barely even turning his back to them.

She looked away quickly. It wasn't anything she hadn't seen her brothers do as lads, but heat flamed to her face. Especially when she accidentally caught Rex's gaze. The twisted smile on his face told her he'd seen every bit of her reaction.

Vile man.

Aaron ambled back toward them after finishing with the horses. "Since the trees are a fair piece away, I can take you both at the same time for a bit of privacy." His words and demeanor were as laid back as she'd ever seen him, and it took everything in her not to jerk her gaze to his face. Instead, she sent her focus to the trees he must be talking about, trying to look as casual as he did.

"Let Bill do it." Rex's tone sounded as sharp as a knife blade, and as hard as the stone he sat on.

Aaron raised his brows at the man. "You think I'm not capable?"

"Capable maybe, but not trustworthy." Rex spat the words as Bill clomped toward her with his big bear-like feet.

"Maybe we should both take them." Aaron's voice had dropped now, losing all hint of calm. "They may overpower you, Bill, and I'll need to be there to protect you."

What was he doing? Was he trying to help them? Or merely causing a stir? Surely he didn't plan to take Bill down himself. And with all these comments about them possibly getting away, the burly man would be on his keenest guard.

Bill shrugged. "I can take on all four of you if I need to."

"Aaron, you get the food ready. Bill, take them and be quick about it." Rex's tone brooked no argument.

"Start walkin'." Bill jabbed a massive finger in her back, pushing her forward.

With Samuel pressed close to her, they walked around the hillside toward a cluster of five or six trees, mostly pine and aspen, with a few bushes interspersed around the base. She couldn't see much beyond the foliage. Would there be a place she and Samuel could run to? Did Nate have a plan in mind? Unless he intended to run with them—which seemed unlikely—she couldn't imagine how he could help without risking his own life.

When they reached the trees, Bill pulled a pistol from his waistband and used it to motion her toward a thick bush growing at the base of a tree. "Go behind that one, but keep your head where I can see ya. Boy, you just take care of your business here." He motioned in the general area where they stood.

Laura bit down the humiliation of what she was being forced to do in front of men who were no relation. She'd managed to keep from exposing herself so far, but just the fact that they knew what she was doing was enough to send heat into her cheeks every time.

The hatred simmering in her chest was unlike any she'd ever felt before, and each insult and injury and lustful gaze added another log to her internal fire.

As she stepped around behind the bush, a glimmer of metal shone up at her. She blinked. That couldn't be what it looked like.

A quick glance up at the men showed Nate looking at her intensely. Had he planted a pistol back here? How?

She didn't have time to worry about that now. Dropping to her knees, she grabbed the gun and checked the chamber. Growing up on a farm, she was familiar with most mechanisms, and this looked to be a simple revolver. One of her brothers would have known what model, but she didn't care as long as its aim was true.

"I said keep your head up." Bill's harsh command made her jump.

Settle down, Hannon. He'll know you're up to something. She gave him a quick nod, then rustled her skirts loud enough that he could hear the fabric. She'd have to point the gun at Bill. Be willing to actually kill him should he advance. *God, help me.*

And from what she'd seen of this man, he probably would charge toward her, thinking she didn't have the backbone to shoot him.

But she would. She would pull the trigger. Maybe she'd aim at a shoulder or something not life-threatening. A leg would be best so he couldn't run after her, but she wasn't sure her aim was that accurate. Maybe at close range, but she'd only have one chance.

She turned, still trying to make it look like she was attending to personal matters. But she glanced out of the corner of her eye to study the landscape behind them. More clusters of rocks sprang up from the open land, some large enough she and Samuel could hide behind. But there was no way to reach them without being seen.

She really needed to get a horse. The animals were tied partway between her and the camp. If she took Bill down—including his gun hand—she could charge toward the animals and jump on a horse. If she could keep the animals between her and the camp, maybe the others wouldn't get a clear shot. Mounting the animal would be tricky with her wrists tied, but she would accomplish it somehow. Then she could ride back to these trees and swoop Samuel up.

Was she prepared to risk her life for this venture? If she were killed, what would happen to Samuel? Her heart thudded in her throat.

She had to pull this off. *Lord, help me.*

"Hurry up, woman." Bill's voice sounded edgy, and she darted a glance at him. He was staring at her, the pistol held loosely in his right hand, lowered brows showing more than a little suspicion. His gun was pointed in her general direction, but not fully at her.

Inhaling a deep breath, she gripped her revolver in both hands to help her aim, then rose. She pointed the weapon at Bill's chest. "Drop your gun."

His eyes narrowed even more, and the grip on his pistol

tightened. "Where did you get that?" He shifted a little so he could see both her and Nate without turning.

She didn't dare take her eyes from Bill to see what Nate was doing. "Drop that gun or I'll shoot. And my aim is good." She made her voice as menacing as she could. Hopefully he didn't hear the tremor she was trying to hide. If she could just keep her mind on what they planned to do with her, anger would take over, dissolving any nervousness.

A half-grin parted his ugly mouth. "You might know how to aim, but you won't shoot me. Pretty thing like you don't have it in you." His gaze darted to Nate for half a heartbeat. "And I'm assumin' Nate here gave you the pistol, although I'm not sure how he managed to hide it. But if he tries anything, you'll be the first one I shoot. Then the boy." All humor fled from his smile.

She inhaled a steadying breath. "This is your last chance. Drop your gun or I'll put a bullet through your chest." The chest might be the only way to keep him from going after her. Would a pistol shot be enough to kill him?

He took a step forward, every part of his ogre face turning menacing.

She gripped the gun tighter, shifted her aim a little higher to his right shoulder, and pulled the trigger.

Everything exploded at once.

Gunpowder clouded around her. Samuel screamed. The flash of Nate's blue shirt marked the corner of her vision.

Another gunshot.

A blow struck her. A body. Knocking her back and sideways. Pulling her down.

Then all turned silent.

The acrid odor of burnt powder seared her nose. A weight pressed down on her chest, locking her right arm. She'd squeezed her eyes shut, but a pain gradually taking over her left arm meant she had to force her eyes open.

The weight on her chest shifted, and she finally pressed her lids open to see Nate moving off of her. He must have lunged at her, knocking her down and landing partially on her right arm. One of his legs was still hooked in the bush he'd flown over.

A shuffling sounded from the other side of the foliage. A groan. Then crying.

Samuel. She pushed herself upright. If Bill was still alive, he would hurt the boy. Either way, the lad must be terrified.

The pain in her left arm sharpened as she raised that limb, and she couldn't help sucking in a breath at a particularly sharp stab.

"Are you hurt?" Nate now knelt beside her, his voice a whisper at her ear.

She glanced at the arm, where a dark stain was spreading over her sleeve. The limb burned like a torch was being held against the skin, but the bullet must have only creased the outside without embedding in her flesh.

Her stomach churned at the sight, but she couldn't let it slow her down. She had to check Samuel. And if Bill's wound was mortal, she and the boy had to get out of there fast.

But she knew the other two would come running at the gunfire. She may have already lost her chance to get to a horse.

Scrambling up to her knees, she peered over the bush to check Bill before she stood completely.

The sight before her gripped her chest, stilling every part of her. She was vaguely aware of Nate beside her, doing the same.

Bill sat on the ground, legs splayed in front of him. Samuel lay across his lap with Bill's beefy arm wrapped around the boy's neck. The lad's red-rimmed eyes had grown impossibly round, filling half his face.

And she didn't blame him with the barrel of a pistol pressed to his temple.

"Let the boy go, Bill." Nate's voice barely penetrated her shock at first. But then from the corner of her eye, she saw him slowly rise, hands out in front of him.

"You throw that pistol over here." Bill spoke to her. "And any other weapons you both have. Knives, everything." His gaze cut to Nate with clear meaning.

"I don't have anything else." Nate's jaw hardened.

"No knives?" Bill narrowed his gaze.

"Nothing."

Bill studied him another moment, then turned his focus to Laura. "Stand up real slow and throw your gun over there. If you even flinch, I'll end his life here and now. He won't be the first mouthy kid I've put a bullet in, and I doubt he'll be the last."

The lethal expression on Bill's face left her with no doubt he'd do just what he said. Bile churned in her middle, rising into her throat so she could barely keep from casting up her accounts. *Dear God, keep him safe from this madman.*

NINETEEN

*L*aura forced herself to take a breath, then answer so this crazed man would know she planned to comply. "I'll do exactly what you say, just don't hurt the boy." If he injured Samuel because of her actions, she'd never be able to live with herself. And Joanna . . .

Gripping the pistol by its barrel so Bill wouldn't think she planned to use it, she eased up to standing. Then leaned over the bush and tossed it where he'd pointed.

"Now, you two come around and stand over to my right. If you make one move I don't cotton to, you can say good-bye to this brat. And good riddance. Don't know why we had to bring him along to begin with."

She held her hands out, matching Nate's position, as she skirted the bush and stepped toward the place where Bill motioned. Nate stayed close behind her, and something about his presence eased a tiny bit of the strain across her chest.

When they were in place, Bill shifted the boy on his lap.

"Stand up." He barked the words, then rose up to his knees as he hauled Samuel with him.

Laura didn't breathe as the giant of a man struggled to his feet, keeping the barrel of his pistol pressed into the temple of the terrified boy. She raised a desperate prayer upward. *Lord, please don't let that gun go off. Hold in the bullet.* As much as Bill was moving around, his finger could brush the trigger without even meaning to.

And that would spell death for Samuel.

She held her breath until Bill and the boy were both standing. He stepped backward, his arm still wrapped around Samuel's neck and the gun still pressed to the child's head. Bill stopped them at the gun she'd thrown down. "Hand me that pistol, boy. Slowly."

Bill released his hold on the lad, but kept the handgun aimed at him as Samuel bent to pick up the weapon. Had such a young boy even held a pistol before?

She had to credit Samuel for keeping his wits about him, even though he was clearly terrified. He wasn't crying, although his eyes were red. He didn't speak, which most likely would have irritated Bill even more.

Once Bill had the weapon, he gripped a wad of Samuel's hair, securing the gun at the side of his head again. The poor lad swallowed, his face as white as the fluffy clouds above.

Bill jerked his chin toward the camp. "Start walkin'. And I guess I don't need to tell you to keep your hands where I can see 'em."

Turning her back to the madman with the gun took every bit of internal strength she had. She couldn't see what he was doing to Samuel. Nor shield herself before a blow. But she had to obey, so she put one foot in front of the other, holding her hands away from her sides where he'd have a good view.

As they stepped from the trees, Rex's slimy voice called across the distance. "You have things in hand, Carlton?"

"All taken care of." Bill bellowed like a bull parading in front of his cows, and she had to lock her jaw not to cringe at his voice.

Nate walked beside her through the thick summer grass, and she dared a quick glance at his steely profile. Not a bit happy.

And she couldn't blame him. He'd risked himself to help her and Samuel, and now he was being held at gunpoint, too.

But she couldn't worry about that now.

Every bit of her focus had to be on keeping the young boy behind her safe. And when she and Samuel were made to pay for her failed attempt to flee, all the strength she possessed might not be enough to accomplish her goal.

⊷═◉ ◉═⊶

This was the place.

Isaac signaled a halt even as worry pressed harder on his chest. They were still a couple hours out from River Crossing, but the route was simple enough that he could give Joanna directions if she wanted to separate from him after he told her his story.

Lord, soften her heart. Prepare the way.

Somewhere along their travels today, he'd begun to open himself to the possibility that maybe she'd understand that his misdeeds were in the past, far behind him. Maybe she could find forgiveness. If any person could be that gracious, Joanna would be the one.

But he was fooling himself. Deep inside, he knew that. Her fears for her son and friend filled the air between them with a weight that made it hard for him to breathe.

"What's wrong?" Joanna rode up beside him as he wiped a sleeve across his sweaty brow.

He eased his reins to allow his gelding to graze. "Thought this would be a good place to let the animals eat a minute. We can finish off the last of the meat, too. Another couple hours or so and we should reach River Crossing."

She nodded and took the food he handed over from his pack. But the grim line of her mouth and tightness at her eyes said she wasn't happy about the delay. What he had to say would only send her mood lower.

But he had to tell her. Had to push his pride aside, be honest with her. Maybe God could yet make good come out of this situation.

He held his chunk of meat in his hand, for there wasn't any way he'd be able to eat it. Not with his stomach churning. He summoned moisture into his mouth, sent up another prayer, and turned his focus to Joanna.

"There's . . . um . . . something I need to tell you."

Her attention jerked up to him, her expression uncertain, gaze wary. She was certainly on edge, and his tone must have raised all her internal warnings.

He pushed on. "You haven't asked how I know where the men we've been following are headed. But I need to tell you."

Her eyes were too penetrating, too distracting when he was trying to string the right words together. He looked away, toward the last low mountain that stood between them and River Crossing.

"A decade ago . . . no, the story starts a little earlier than that." He should have been more prepared. He'd certainly thought about this conversation enough. "I told you my ma died when I was seven, then Pa and I came west to look for gold. I grew up right alongside him, panning and sluicing and being exposed to all the types of folks that worked the goldfields. I probably saw more than I should have at that young age."

The words were true, but he had to be careful not to cast blame for his actions on anyone else. Only *he* had made the choices he so regretted. "The work was hard. Or maybe I was just lazy. But I started thinking up ways that sounded much easier to make a living.

"When I was eighteen, a couple fellows moved into the gulch where we lived. They were twin brothers, Aaron and Nate Long, and they had the gold fever. We hit it off pretty well, and it wasn't long before I'd convinced Aaron that we could make our money much easier by holding up miners on their way to trade in their hard-earned gold for supplies and such. Nate wasn't so sure about the idea, but those two brothers had a bond stronger than any I've seen. I'm pretty sure Nate just went along to watch out for Aaron."

Isaac's stomach had turned sour enough to cast up what little he'd eaten that day. He never should have put Nate in a situation where he had to choose between doing the right thing and loyalty to his brother. Isaac was responsible for that man's downfall. For both of them.

And so much more.

He didn't have the nerve to look at Joanna. Most of him didn't want to know what she was thinking anyway. It couldn't be good.

It was time to finish his tale. Inhaling another fortifying breath, he pressed on. "Over the next year, we did a lot of petty thievery." He pinched his lips and shook his head. "Petty makes it sound insignificant. We stole gold from more men than I could count. We all agreed we didn't want to hurt anybody. We were just in it for the profits, and the money was good.

"But halfway into that year, the gold lost its shine. I started hating every robbery. Hating myself for getting us all into it—so much so that I loathed even waking up each morning, having to live inside my own skin. Finally, I told the brothers I was done. I didn't even accept my share from the last job we pulled off. Just walked away.

"I thought they would stop, too. Nate and I'd had several conversations about how we wanted to change our line of work. But Aaron had developed a craving for the money and power that came from each robbery.

"I heard later that the boys hooked up with a couple others who were doing more than robbing miners on quiet trails. They robbed saloons and anywhere else they were sure to make a decent profit, and it didn't seem to matter anymore whether people got hurt in the process."

He wanted to lean over his horse and vomit, so strong was

the taste of bile in his throat. Never had he told the story
its entirety. Only in bits and pieces when he'd rejoined hi
father, begging for forgiveness.

His heavenly Father had known every single action in
Isaac's past, so he'd not had to put his sins into words there,
either, only the deep sorrow of what he'd done. His desperate
need for forgiveness. For a new life, washed clean by the work
Jesus had done on the cross over a thousand years before. He
had to keep his focus on that. God's forgiveness, even though
he hadn't deserved it at the time. Still didn't deserve it now.

Through the years since then, any time he'd run into a lawman on his hunting trips, he'd offer to lead the fellow to the
hideout where they were now going. But he'd never shared
the extent of his involvement with the gang. He'd also never
had one of the men take him up on it. This was such a vast
territory with so few men assigned to keep the peace, none
could justify the possibility of a wild-goose chase for thieves
who hadn't actually affected the people in their own town.

Of course, this was the first time the gang had been ac-
cused of murder—and of a sheriff, no less.

"So those men, Aaron and Nate and the other two, they're
the ones who kidnapped my son and Laura?" Joanna's voice
held enough strain that it might snap.

"I think so." He had to look at her. If for no other reason
than to make sure his revelation hadn't made her ill.

When he finally forced his gaze to her face, he couldn't
tell exactly what she was thinking. Between her steely jaw
and the deep lines on her forehead . . .

And her eyes. Those beautiful eyes he loved now held a

tortured look that squeezed his chest so hard that it felt like his heart might cease beating.

Thankfully, she didn't look at him. Her jaw worked. Was she about to speak? Or was that simply an effort to keep from venting her anger on him? He knew she'd held back so far from spewing all the fear and turmoil and anger over what her son must be suffering.

He wished she would release it. Scream and rage at him. He deserved whatever she could dish out, and if unleashing her fury on him took away a little of her pain, all the better.

TWENTY

*I*saac braced himself as Joanna opened her mouth to speak, but the words that came out were clipped, as though she had to force out each one. "What did you do after you left the others?"

He let out a long breath. Not what he expected her to ask. "I used what money I'd saved up to pay back those men I could find, but it wasn't even half of those we'd robbed. After that, I came back to my father's claim. Asked his forgiveness, then buckled down and put in a hard day's work. I'd already begged forgiveness from God, and I was ready to put that wayward year far behind me."

She nodded, a single bob of her determined chin. And she still didn't look at him. "So you know these men well?"

Isaac scrubbed a hand through his hair. "I used to know Nate and Aaron well. Not sure how much they've changed these ten years. I've heard of the others, Rex Stanley and Bill Carlton, by reputation."

"This place you think they're taking Samuel and Laura

to, you've been there?" Each of her questions seemed so intentional, so specific.

"I have. Many times." He'd been the one to discover the cabin tucked tightly among boulders and crags in the mountainside. The place must have been an abandoned hunting shack, but it had worked perfectly as their living quarters when they needed a quiet place to regroup.

Again, a single nod, as though she'd decided something within herself. "Let's ride on." She nudged her horse forward, still not offering him a single glance.

He let his shoulders slump as he guided his gelding in beside the pack mare. At least she hadn't run him off. It appeared she thought she still needed him. *Thank you, Father.*

Any chance he'd had for a lifetime with Joanna was gone now, but maybe the Lord would allow him to help her through to the end of this trial.

⋄⟫═⊙═⟪⋄

Darkness pressed hard as the horses wound up the steep mountainside. Laura had no idea how the men could see to guide their horses around the sharp rocks poking up from the ground and the holes hidden in the deep shadows.

Aaron led the way, with Samuel in his arms and Rex riding close behind. They'd interrogated Aaron about whether he'd given the pistol to his brother, but the man adamantly denied any help in the attempted escape.

She was pretty certain neither Rex nor Bill believed him.

She wasn't sure she did, either. But it didn't seem to matter at this point.

She and Samuel were just as captive as they'd been for days now, and their nightmare was about to get worse when the group reached the cabin in the next few hours.

Nate was also still bound, with his horse tethered behind Rex's mount. What would the men do to him? If they somehow ever managed to get out of this nightmare, what would he do then? End his time as a thief and criminal? If he came out of this alive, would he look for honest work? Maybe God was using this horrific circumstance to call back one of His children from the dangerous road he traveled.

What if God had orchestrated this entire kidnapping just to reach one lost soul? Even though it might be at the sacrifice of her virtue, could she be content with that? *Oh, Lord.*

The now achingly familiar churning in her middle intensified. She had to keep her mind from straying in that ominous direction. This present ride up a treacherous mountain in the thick of night was worry enough. The ache in her side had radiated up to throb in her temples, and the leather cord around her wrists dug into the open wounds already festering there.

And her arm . . . the flesh where the bullet had creased the skin burned like fire had been pressed to it. Which, she supposed, had been the case.

As the horses climbed up the steep incline, Bill's grip around her injured ribs made her breath come in short, jagged intakes. All this pain was almost enough to keep her mind from the night ahead.

Almost.

From the comments she'd overheard, the cabin that was their destination lay somewhere up this mountain. With the night so late, would the men decide to delay her torture until the next day? That would give her a few more hours to find a way out. Maybe in the darkness and activity of reaching the cabin, she'd be able to slip away.

Lord, make a way. Please.

Everything was harder with her hands tied, and getting Samuel free would be five times more challenging.

Something loomed in the darkness ahead, trees maybe. Aaron guided his horse toward them, and it looked like he would ride directly into the woods.

"That's far enough." Rex's voice cut the air, but it didn't ring with the same lethal edge his tone usually held. Maybe human emotion actually did run through his veins, making him susceptible to exhaustion and pain like any other person.

If she didn't know better, she would think the sound that drifted from his direction when he dismounted was a groan. Or maybe a grunt, but definitely laced with pain. She couldn't summon a single bit of sympathy for him, although she didn't try hard.

"Get off that horse and head toward the cabin." Rex refocused his rifle on Nate, who obeyed, his bound hands making his dismount awkward. Maybe he was keeping his actions slow to avoid raising concerns in Rex, or maybe he was as weary as they all seemed to be.

Nate moved quietly into the trees, and Rex took a step to follow him. Over his shoulder, he threw final commands.

"Bill, bring in the chit and the boy. And don't lose them."
His voice dipped in a snarl. "Aaron, put the horses up the
hill to graze and haul the packs in."

Maybe this was her chance. With only one man guarding
both her and Samuel, perhaps she could catch him unawares.

Bill pulled her off the horse as he dismounted, sending
her sprawling with no way to brace herself. His viselike grip
around her waist kept her from tumbling, shooting a knife
through her ribs.

With one beefy arm holding her tight against him, he extracted his rifle. The ominous click of the gun being cocked
filled the air. Then he turned back to where Aaron had dismounted with Samuel. "Bring the boy here."

Little Samuel trudged toward them, exhaustion cloaking
every movement. He'd lost the vigor of the boy she knew
and loved, this awful ordeal stripping away his zest for life,
including the constant talking and wriggling. As much as his
over-activity had tested her patience before, the loss of the
personality God had created in him made her heart ache.

Once she got them free, would he return to his normal,
cheery self? Or would the trauma he was being forced to
endure forever cast a shadow over him?

Why, God? How can this be your plan? Maybe He'd
turned His back on her altogether. But this innocent boy?
Surely God wouldn't leave a defenseless child among such
wickedness. Yet it seemed even harder to believe their kidnapping had been out of His control.

With no warning, Bill released her, thrusting her away
from himself as he grabbed Samuel. She barely kept her feet,

and when she'd righted herself, she turned to see the vile man held his rifle tucked into his shoulder in a shooting position. He held Samuel out in front of him, and the rifle barrel was almost pressed into Samuel's shoulder.

"Now march through those trees, woman." His tone hung low, maybe a little exhausted. But with enough menace to show he wouldn't hesitate to shoot the lad.

If only she could reach for Samuel's hand to help ease the boy's fears, but she couldn't with their hands tied. If she'd thought the darkness was thick in the open, stepping into the trees felt like a blanket closing over her, wrapping her in smothering black. She reached out with both bound hands to grasp each tree she passed, supports to keep her from tumbling if she tripped over roots or saplings.

At last, a bit of faint light appeared ahead, broken by the looming outlines of the trees at the edge of the copse. She moved toward the light, still gripping each tree she passed.

At last, she stepped from the woods. A wall of rock rose up in front of her, blocking them as far as she could tell. Bill and Samuel emerged from the trees behind her, and she turned to make sure the boy hadn't been injured or scared out of his wits by the darkness. Samuel's mouth was clamped shut in a tight line, his pale face almost glowing. But he looked more resigned than terrified. Her chest squeezed tighter, yet he was holding up so much better than she would have expected.

"There's a sideways opening in the rock over there." Bill nodded toward a shadow in the stone. "Go through it."

She shuffled that direction, and when she reached the spot, there was indeed a crack that turned to the left, wide enough for a person to walk through. She stepped into the opening, rock rising high on either side of her for a few strides until it opened into a grassy clearing. The darkness made it hard to tell for sure, but the clearing looked to be guarded by stone walls on either side. Like a hidden garden, tucked away so no one would ever discover it.

"Now into the cabin."

Bill's voice jolted her forward. Through the darkness ahead, she could just make out a form that could be a cabin. And as she neared, the shape became clearer. A smallish structure with no windows, and only a single door in the center of the front. The cabin seemed to be built into the rock behind it, a sheer mountain that rose as far up as she could see in the darkness.

Foreboding settled deeper in her chest as she neared the door. That door would seal her fate. Maybe the men were too exhausted to carry out their plans for her tonight, but it would happen tomorrow. And once she stepped into that cabin, she'd be trapped. With no view of the open air. No chance of slipping away.

She stopped at the door, her throat closing so she could no longer draw breath. Her hands wouldn't lift to push the wood open.

"What are you waiting for? Get in there." Bill's growl had sunk lower. Deeper.

She didn't dare anger him while he had a rifle pointed at Samuel. Especially with the gun cocked and ready to fire, even by accident.

Raising her hands to push the door open took every bit of

her inner strength. A light shone from inside as the partition creaked inward. Not a bright welcoming glow, just a dim pushing back of the darkness.

As she took the first step in, she struggled to make out the jumble of objects laying around the room. On the left wall in front of a small hearth and along the back lay scattered piles of furs and lumps of blankets—or maybe those were clothes.

The lamp sat in a corner on the far right, illuminating Nate's broad shoulders as he worked with his back to them. There were crates stacked in each corner, and he was pulling items from the one on top.

"Put the chit over there on Nate's bed, and the boy in that front corner." Rex's voice jerked her focus back to the left. She'd not seen him stretched out on one of the stacks of furs.

"You heard him, boy. Sit yourself over there." Bill pushed Samuel toward the front corner and sent him sprawling forward with a shove.

She barely held in her cry as the lad toppled over. But a small pile of blankets broke his fall. Samuel scrambled into the corner and turned to sit with his back against the wall, curling into himself as he looked out at them.

When was the last time she'd heard him speak? He hadn't complained through any of the afternoon's events. In fact, she couldn't remember a sound from him since the soft crying when the guns had fired during her failed attempt to escape at midday.

The weight on her chest pressed harder. *Lord, help us. Why would you make such a sweet boy endure this?*

Bill turned on her, pointing his rifle straight at her chest.

"Now you sit on those furs over yonder." He motioned toward the middle of the back wall. She turned and found the stack easily enough, then sank down onto it, holding her breath against the pain in her ribs.

The pile was surprisingly comfortable, pulling her into its softness like warm blankets. Not that she'd curl up and sleep. She didn't even scoot back against the wall, just sat at the edge. She had to be ready for whatever they planned to do next.

She may be at an extreme disadvantage, but she wouldn't go down without a fight.

"Now tie their feet up tight. It's too late to do anything with them tonight. I plan to enjoy my time with her tomorrow. Then I'll let you at her." Rex's languid tone turned sharp. "Nate, where's that food? Don't think dawdling is going to get you out of anything."

Nate turned from his work near the far wall and carried a plate forward to Rex. She couldn't tell what it was in the dim lighting, but just the mention of food raised a growl from her midsection. Would they be fed at all tonight? As content as she'd be if the men forgot she and Samuel existed, the boy was looking gaunt from so many days with limited food. Hunger had a way of stealing her strength, too.

And she would need everything she had to face tomorrow.

TWENTY-ONE

*T*he farther they rode, the more Joanna's anger simmered.

How could she have misjudged Isaac so badly? From the moment she met him six months before, he'd been a pillar of strength, filling her with the sense that she was safe with him. That his integrity was a core part of his nature.

Now to learn that he'd started a gang of thieves?

And not just any gang. The very group who kidnapped her son and friend, and were likely tormenting them even now. Sure, he may not have ever meant for the thievery to turn to kidnapping and harsher crimes, but he was forever connected to them through his past actions. She wouldn't be able to forget that. And only by God's strength would she ever be able to forgive him for it.

Was he helping her now simply to atone for his past? Maybe he didn't truly care about her or Samuel after all. At least, not the way she'd come to believe that he'd cared.

But there was no time to focus on that now. Dusk was

quickly fading into darkness as they rounded the side of the last mountain standing between them and the little town of River Crossing.

A few lights glimmered in the distance, outlined by the shadows of buildings. She nudged her horse faster. *Almost there.* If this rocky ground weren't so dangerous in the dark, she would have pushed the animals into a canter.

There, up ahead, was the help they needed to free her boy and Laura. Did Isaac know anyone here? Or, maybe the better question was, did any of them know him by reputation? The last thing they needed was for the men of the town to imprison him for his past crimes.

Perhaps she needed to ask him that question, or at least ask how he intended to summon help. She couldn't blindly rely on him to handle the situation.

Reining her horse to the side, she motioned for him to ride up next to her. She couldn't bring herself to slow her mount, so he would simply need to catch up.

When he pulled abreast, she glanced over at him, forcing her anger not to sound in her tone. "Do you know people here? Or how do you plan to gather help?"

"I've met the livery owner and the man who runs the mercantile. It's been a while, so I'm not sure they'll remember me. I was planning to start at the barn, tell him what we're up against, then see what he recommends. I remember thinking he seemed like a good sort of man."

"Will he be there this time of night?" As late as the sun set during these summer months, it must be well past nine o'clock.

"Best I remember, he had a little house in the back of the barn. I imagine we can find him. If not, we'll see who else we can roust. It's a small community, so it shouldn't be hard to find people."

All right, then. Lord willing, in just a few hours, they'd be headed up to the gang's hideout to free her son. She sent another prayer heavenward and pushed her gelding faster.

Isaac was right about River Crossing being a small town. As they rode through what looked to be one of only a couple of streets, lights winked from many of the buildings, either through windows or around doorframes. Glass was so hard to come by this far into the mountain country. And the cost to get it here could easily cover food supplies for an entire family for at least half a year.

"There's the livery." Isaac pointed to a building ahead on their right. The wide doors were closed, but he reined in his horse in front of them. "I'll ride around behind the barn and check the house. Be back shortly."

"I'll come with you." She still wasn't ready to leave this mission in his hands. Not even this small part. Besides, what if he couldn't summon the man from atop his horse? She'd need to dismount and knock.

Isaac didn't object, just steered his horse toward a well-worn path leading around the side of the building. Her gelding didn't require much encouragement to follow. These horses had traveled an incredible distance together this past week alone. All three of the animals hung weary heads, but at least they were still able to keep moving. Even the injured mare, although she'd needed prodding these last few hours.

You'll get to rest soon, girl. Joanna would need to make restitution for the mare's wounds once they made it back to the livery in Settler's Fort. Hopefully the owner there would be understanding.

"Hello, in the house," Isaac called out as soon as they rounded the rear of the stable. The "house" didn't stand on its own as she'd expected, but looked to be rooms built onto the back of the stable. Flowers lined either side of the door, a sign there was likely a woman somewhere on the premises.

A muffled voice sounded from inside, then a moment later the door opened. The man was pulling his shoulder braces up over blue shirtsleeves as he stepped out on the stoop. "Lookin' for a meal and a bed for your horses?"

The livery owner's gaze shifted to Joanna and the widening of his eyes was clear even in the darkness. He slipped a hand behind him to tuck in the tail of his shirt, then straightened and squared his shoulders, turning his focus back to Isaac.

"Yes, sir," Isaac answered. "The animals are tired and hungry, and the mare has wounds from a wolf that need tended. But we have a more important matter to take care of first."

As Isaac told their story in a few succinct details, the man's face hardened. He crossed his arms over his chest while he listened, then the moment Isaac finished, he spun and motioned toward the path around to the front of the livery. "Bring your horses around to the front. I'll spread the word first so men can be gathering, then see to your animals." He pivoted to look at them as he continued walking. "Mrs.

Holder lets out rooms, so I'll tell her to make a place ready for you, ma'am."

"No need, sir." As wonderful as a clean room with a real bed sounded, she wasn't about to step back while the men took over the hunt for her son.

"Once you gather some men, we'll all put together a plan." Isaac's voice filled the space between them, its firm tone deciding the matter solidly. And the way he emphasized *all* made her want to hug him.

Not that she would. Ever again.

She pushed back the wayward memories of his arms around her, holding her tight in his protective strength.

They rounded the front of the stable, and the owner stepped to her horse's side, apparently to help her down. She motioned him back. "Help Isaac. His leg is broken. I can see to the animals while you start gathering men."

He backed away uncertainly, but when she dismounted, he seemed to finally decide she was capable.

Isaac had already slid to the ground, and he stood by his gelding's side, holding to the saddle for support. Would he mind this stranger helping him hobble into the barn? He'd been trying to be as independent as possible lately, but there were times he simply needed to accept aid. Everyone needed assistance at one time or another.

She led her gelding and the packhorse into the barn, and the owner called after her. "They can go in the first stalls on the left and right, ma'am."

After Joanna pulled the packsaddle from the mare, the weary horse limped into the small enclosure. It only took a moment for her to find the hay tucked in a corner, and the sounds of contended crunching drifted behind Joanna as she closed the door.

Isaac stood with his horse in the hallway near the front of the barn. The livery owner must have taken her at her word and gone to gather men, for he was nowhere to be seen.

She walked over to Isaac. "Should we leave the geldings saddled? Do you think they'll get enough men together to ride out tonight?"

The lantern hanging by the front doors gave her a shadowed view of Isaac's face. He turned to her, and the weary lines around his eyes were hard to miss. Her chest squeezed at the sight, even though she wanted to feel no sympathy for this man.

"I think we'd be inviting trouble to ride up that mountain in the dark. The gang will hear us coming and we'll lose our chance of surprise, which is our best opportunity. I think the wisest move would be to head out at first light." His voice seemed to sag the more he spoke. "Besides, these boys need a break. I'm sure there are other horses here we can use."

What was she doing, making this man trek even farther up the mountains with her? With his broken leg, he should be in bed under a doctor's care.

But she wasn't sure she could do this without him.

Stepping close enough to see the dark green of his eyes, she lowered her voice. "I know you need sleep, but we should see if there's a doctor who can look at your leg before you get in the saddle again."

He shook his head, not quite meeting her gaze. "I doubt they have a real doctor here. I'll be fine. Don't worry about me."

He was probably right about the doctor part, as small as this settlement seemed. When she had a moment, she'd ask someone to be sure. But there was more she had to say.

She inhaled a breath to gather her courage. "Isaac, you're not responsible for the actions of those outlaws. They've made their own choices. You've done your part to help bring them down. Just tell the men of this town where to find their hideout, and then you can let yourself rest. Recover."

His jaw flexed and his Adam's apple bobbed as he locked his gaze with hers. "I promised I'd get Samuel back, and I won't stop until he's back in your arms."

Her heart ached at his words, at the determination marking his features. She'd wanted a champion like this for so long. Emotion stung her eyes, threatening to overwhelm her defenses.

Yet, as Isaac said, Samuel wasn't back in her arms yet. They still had much to accomplish, and every moment mattered. She turned away to unsaddle the gelding she'd ridden, and she was only partway through the task when the livery owner returned.

"We've a group assembling at Mrs. Holder's to talk through what should be done." He handed two matching poles to Isaac. "She sent these along. Her late husband used them to walk with when he broke his leg." The pair had a cross brace at the top, which looked to be wrapped with fabric. Much better than the painful nub on the stick Isaac had been using.

"Thanks." Isaac took the tools as the man led his gelding to the stall beside where Joanna was working.

Isaac examined the pair, then fit them under his arms and tried to walk forward a step. He was a bit awkward, but after a few strides, seemed to find a rhythm.

She had the horse unsaddled now and released him to find the hay stashed in the corner of his own stall.

Weariness weighed over her like a rain-soaked wool coat, but she couldn't let herself succumb yet.

"Just leave yer saddles and whatever you don't need for the night here. They'll be safe enough." The livery owner stepped out of the stall where he'd been working. "Let's get you both on down to the Holder place so you can eat and rest a bit 'fore you meet the boys."

With the pack that held their food and blankets in hand, she followed him to Isaac's side. "I don't think I caught your name, sir."

He turned with a genial smile. "Sorry about that. Jessup Tillis, ma'am. At your service."

She nodded. "I'm Mrs. Watson."

With Isaac using his new walking sticks, they trekked down the quiet street. Mr. Tillis stopped at the door of one of the few homes that boasted a glass window. He knocked, and seconds later, the door swung open.

"Come in." The voice and skirts belonged to a woman, but with the light behind her, it was impossible to see more than a slim profile. Their hostess stepped aside, and Mr. Tillis motioned for Joanna to enter first.

As she took the two steps into the house, the shift in the lighting allowed her a better look at the woman who must be Mrs. Holder. Graying hair tied in a chignon bespoke neat efficiency, but it was the kindness in the woman's smile that drew Joanna, filling her with a sense of relief so strong that tears sprang to her eyes.

"Come in, my dear." Mrs. Holder reached for Joanna's arm and pulled her farther into the room. "I've stew warming on the stove and a bed all ready for you. I'll put your bag in your room. You must be exhausted."

Her voice rolled with such a gentle cadence, so motherly, that it was all Joanna could do to keep from leaning in. Giving over her cares to this stranger and sinking into the warm bed.

The click of wood on wood sounded behind her, pulling her attention back to where Mr. Tillis was helping Isaac into the room. As the livery owner turned to shut the door, Isaac raised his gaze to Joanna.

His exhaustion showed in his eyes, but there was a determination there, too. A promise. And the realization surged all the way through to her core. She could trust Isaac to rescue her son. He wouldn't stop until he'd accomplished the mission.

She wasn't sure yet if she could trust him with anything more. But this single most important task was enough.

She did her best to telegraph her response through her own gaze. *Thank you.*

TWENTY-TWO

*J*oanna took a seat as Mr. Tillis helped Isaac into a chair at the table, then the man stepped back. "I'm headed to the barn to make your animals a bit more comfortable, but I'll be back when the others come so we can put together a plan." He nodded toward Joanna. "We'll get your boy free, Mrs. Watson. The men around here won't rest until it's done."

"Of course." Mrs. Holder stepped through the open doorway from the kitchen carrying a tray with both hands. "But first these two need to eat. 'Twouldn't surprise me if you haven't had a decent meal in days." She laid bowls of steaming soup in front of Joanna and Isaac, then set a plate of biscuits and a crock of jam between them. It seemed like a lifetime since she'd had biscuits, and it didn't even matter that these were a bit too hard to be fresh from the oven.

The savory aroma of the stew drew her first. Floating in the broth was more than just the meat they'd eaten for the last several days. Chunks of potatoes and onions and several other vegetables rose with her spoon. It was all she could do not to rest her chin on the edge of the bowl so her weary senses could savor the smell. She was almost too tired to eat.

But the food would revive her, so she inhaled one bite after another.

While she and Isaac ate, men began to file quietly into the room. The first one's diminutive size and features made his mustache look like it covered at least half his face. Behind him came two others, whose matching builds and the cleft in both their jaws bespoke a strong family resemblance.

All three shook Isaac's hand and offered respectful head nods to her. "Sorry to hear about your boy, ma'am." The first man offered this condolence. "Those men have been causin' trouble in these parts for years now. We'll do our best to see the matter settled for you."

Before Joanna could get out a thank-you or ask any follow-up questions, Mrs. Holder bustled into the room. "I've got coffee for you all. Sit and be comfortable until the others arrive." She placed five cups around the table and began pouring dark brew from a carafe. "Mrs. Watson and Mr. Bowen, this is Jeremy Knight"—she motioned toward the smaller man—"and the Canton brothers, Adam and Wesley."

The clomp of boots sounded from the front room, and three more men entered. Mrs. Holder's home must be used as a general meeting space often for them not to feel the need to knock. As they entered the dining room, Joanna's eyes quickly scanned the taller man in the front and the middling fellow just behind him. Mr. Tillis from the livery brought up the rear, and the familiar face eased the angst in her chest a tiny bit. She'd met him less than an hour ago, but he'd worked quickly to gather this group to help.

"This looks to be everyone." Mr. Tillis took the open chair opposite Isaac as the others filled the remaining seats. "Samson's down with ague, and Thomas Ruffle's best breeding mare is sick. He said he'll help as soon as the animal pulls through." Then he turned his focus to Isaac. "I think most everyone knows why we're here, but we'd appreciate all the details you can share."

Isaac's deep voice filled the room as he told how they'd discovered the kidnapping and journeyed through the mountains, following the gang's trail. "The farther we traveled, the more certain I became that these are men I knew several years back. At least, I knew two of them. I'm familiar with their hideout, a little cabin tucked around the backside of the largest of the three peaks up there." He pointed northward. "The structure is protected on three sides by the mountain and on the fourth by a rock wall, so I think the only way to get the boy and Miss Hannon out safely is to surprise the men and take them out one by one."

Silence took over the room as the men sent furrowed-brow glances amongst themselves.

Mr. Knight, the smallish man with the large mustache, was the first to speak. "I've been up that mountain a good bit, and I've never seen a cabin there."

Isaac nodded. "That's why it's been such a good hiding hole. The opening through the rock to reach the cabin is so narrow, you think it's just part of the mountainside.

Last I saw it, there were a few trees that helped disguise the entrance, too. But it's there. Unless they've torn the place down since I last saw it a decade ago, the cabin is still there. In front is an open area that could prove dangerous. We'll have to figure out a plan to draw the men out so we don't have to ride into that open area where they can pick us off."

Mr. Knight spoke again. "You're sure the men have taken their captives to this cabin?"

Isaac nodded. "As sure as I can be without going there. The last tracks we saw before we turned off toward town were headed exactly for the trail up that mountain."

Mr. Knight glanced at Mr. Tillis, and Joanna couldn't quite read the look that passed between them.

Then the livery owner turned to Isaac again. "I'm just curious how you're so familiar with this cabin and those men. I think you said you knew two of them?" He posed the question respectfully, but it was hard to miss the undercurrent of accusation in his tone.

She could feel Isaac's tension, even without looking at him. He'd said he never told anyone about his past indiscretions, except for his father. And now her.

How would he answer these men? A part of her wanted to speak up and make an excuse for him. To protect him from the anger the truth would raise.

He didn't have to tell all. They could come up with some whitewashed version that would mollify these men's suspicions and keep Isaac from facing the shame of his past.

A past she knew in her deepest heart he regretted. Hated. Had turned from completely.

"I know two of the men because I used to be part of their gang." Isaac's voice sliced through her thoughts, filling her with a dread that tightened all her nerves. "I was the one who first suggested to Nate and Aaron Long that we take up robbery to earn an easy living. After a year stealing gold from miners, my conscience finally caught up with me and I left the group. I thought the other two would turn to an honest living, as well, but they met Rex Stanley and Bill Carlton, who convinced them to keep going. Through the years, I've heard their crimes have worsened considerably. But they've never come near enough to Settler's Fort for me to do anything about it. The times I've tried to get lawmen to go after them haven't panned out."

She couldn't help but stare at him, the sting of tears pricking her eyes. He was telling all? This sacrifice was more than she would have required from him.

Isaac's voice had maintained an even tone so far, but it dipped with his last words. "Starting that group is my biggest regret." He swallowed hard. "But that's only one of the reasons why I'm determined to free Samuel and Miss Hannon. We need to take down those men. They've done enough damage. It's time to end it, once and for all."

Now the tears welled in her eyes as images of the possible damage flitted through her mind. She locked her jaw and turned to survey the men around them.

Mr. Tillis was the first to speak. "Well, I suppose you do know where they've been hiding, then. And if you're sure you're on our side, your knowledge of the men will likely come in handy."

A weight slipped from Joanna's chest, and she could finally draw breath again.

Isaac nodded. "I'm definitely on the side of right." His gaze slid to her. "I'll do anything and everything to get Samuel back for his mother, and to help Miss Hannon. Maybe if I'd taken this journey sooner, none of this would have happened."

The anguish in his eyes speared through her, and if all these men hadn't been around, she would have rested her hand on his. Her son's kidnapping wasn't his fault, no matter how much part of her wanted someone to blame.

But Isaac wasn't responsible for the heinous actions of these men. She could see that now, with the haze of shock and anger no longer clouding her vision.

The men around the table had already shifted the conversation to forming a plan, so she reined in her focus to their words.

"The first half hour or so of the trail isn't bad, but I think we'll need light for the rest. If they have a lookout stationed, carrying a lantern will give us away. If we leave at first light, how far up the mountain is this cabin?" One of the Canton brothers—she couldn't remember which was Adam and which was Wesley—looked to Isaac for a response.

"At least two hours from the edge of the trees that border the mountain. There's a narrow pass that lets you wind around to the back side of the mountain. We were always careful to take a different route each time so we didn't create an obvious trail. I imagine they're still doing that."

"But you can get us close to the cabin without them hearing?" The other Canton brother leaned back in his chair, arms crossed and brow lowered in a thoughtful expression.

Isaac nodded again. "We'll need to leave the horses farther back. Might be best for me to scout ahead to see their positions before everyone comes."

Mr. Tillis leaned forward. "What about your broken leg? That's gonna make it awfully hard to move closer on foot, especially by yourself, if you go ahead to check things out."

Isaac's jaw tightened. "Those walking sticks Mrs. Holder lent me help a lot. I'll do what I have to do."

A mental picture of Isaac crawling over the rough mountain ground where they'd camped slipped through Joanna's thoughts. She wouldn't put it past him to use that means of travel again if he had to.

And she could only love him for that willingness.

She leaned forward. "I'll scout ahead with Mr. Bowen in case he needs an extra set of legs."

All heads turned to her. Some brows dipped in consternation, while others rose in surprise. All except Mr. Tillis, whom she'd already declared her intentions to when they first met. A glimmer of concern shadowed his eyes, but he said, "Might be best if you wait down the mountain with the rest of the men until we know the situation, Mrs. Watson. I'll be Mr. Bowen's extra limbs if'n he needs them."

She craved a glimpse of her son. A chance to see the despicable men who'd stolen him. To know for herself what condition he was in. But perhaps Mr. Tillis would be more help to Isaac. She couldn't let her own yearnings get in the way of accomplishing their goal.

With a deep inhale for strength, she nodded to Mr. Tillis. "All right." While she waited with the men on the mountainside, she'd be doing her part in prayer, lifting up their mission to God every step of the way.

⋘━◦━⋙

This day would change the rest of his life, although which way it would go, Isaac had no idea.

He tucked both borrowed revolvers in his waistband. He'd fastened a strap to carry his rifle over his shoulder so he could have both hands free to use the walking sticks, but that didn't stop him from hating the restrictions of his injured leg and the bulky splint. Joanna had asked Mrs. Holder to inspect the break, but he'd waved both women away. They could fuss over him all they wanted after their mission was complete and Samuel was back in his mother's arms.

Now was the worst time he could have ever chosen for this weakness.

But he couldn't change it, and the clop of hooves outside meant Tillis had come to help him aboard his borrowed horse. As much as he hated having to rely on others almost every step of the way, the willingness of the men in this town to help take down the kidnappers was a gift from God.

Thank you, Lord.

He positioned the walking sticks under his arms and limped out of the bedchamber. In the main room, Joanna stood by the doorway, a lantern in her hand. As she turned to him, the

222

flickering light illuminated the tight lines of strain across her face.

She watched him approach, maybe waiting to help him down the stoop outside. Or maybe she just needed reassurance that they wouldn't stop until her son and Miss Hannon were returned. That God would guide their efforts today.

He stopped in front of her and reached for her hand. She hesitated. But when she tucked her warm fingers in his palm, he stroked his thumb over the back of her hand as he held her gaze. "Can we pray?"

She exhaled, and some of her strain seemed to slip out as she nodded.

Bowing his head, he raised his heart to the Father, letting that guide his requests for safety, petitions for peace, prayers for strength. As he said "amen," a reverent spirit filled the space around them. An intensity held them in place, in that position of prayer.

At last, the sound of a boot on the stoop outside proclaimed it was time to get moving. He raised his head and gave Joanna's hand a final squeeze. Maybe it was his imagination or the dim sunlight, but her face didn't look as careworn as it had minutes before.

With Tillis's help, they were soon mounted and riding down the street toward a group of other mounted shadows gathered in front of the livery. The men were mostly silent as they rode out of town, and Joanna stayed beside him. She probably still didn't trust him, and surely didn't like him, but at least she knew all his flaws. If she chose his company now, she did so with her eyes wide open.

Light crept over the eastern mountains as they rode, the faint gray of predawn shifting into a fiery red as the sun rose higher in the sky. They'd reached the base of the three peaks that stood together, and Isaac took the lead, aiming for the joint between the center mountain and the one on the right. The rock and a few scrawny trees made the area look like a wall of continuous stone, but he rode toward the break he'd passed through many times.

When the gap opened up, seeing the unique bit of landscape was like returning to another lifetime. This view had once been so familiar, yet he'd thought never to lay eyes on it again.

They rode through the opening single file, and Tillis's horse balked at the narrow entrance. But the man kept steady pressure on the young gelding and spoke in gentle tones, and it wasn't long before the animal moved forward.

As soon as all were through, he halted his borrowed mare and turned to the group. "We'll be on the back side of the mountain soon, just below the cabin, so keep as quiet as you can. Try to stay in soft ground, away from loose rocks. Partway up, I'll signal a halt and we'll have to go the rest of the way on foot."

Most of the men nodded, and Knight said, "Lead on."

As Isaac turned his mount forward and guided her around the slope, he couldn't help feeling he was leading the group into the valley of the shadow of death.

TWENTY-THREE

*T*he walking sticks dug in hard under Isaac's arms, rubbing blisters he had to force himself to ignore. Keeping quiet with these poles over the loose stones of the mountainside required more focus than if he'd been walking on two feet.

But having Tillis by his side brought a steady reassurance he hadn't expected.

When they rounded the boulder to see the patch of trees that guarded the rock wall and the cabin's hiding place, he halted. Tillis stopped beside him, and Isaac worked to not show how hard it was to catch his breath.

He motioned toward a cluster of lodgepole pines and kept his voice to a whisper. "The trees and bushes cover a crevice barely wide enough for a horse to enter. If we were to pass through that crevice, we'd be in clear view of the cabin with about thirty strides of open land in between. I suspect they'll have someone watching that front. It's the only way in since there's vertical mountain slope or a solid rock wall on every other side."

Tillis nodded. "So one of us goes through the trees and peeks around the edge of the crevice? Probably best for the other of us to be stationed behind a bush there, ya reckon?"

Isaac took a deep breath and nodded. "I'll look first, then we can change places so you can see the lay of the land."

They started forward, one cautious step at a time. Any man who lived by his gun would be well trained to pick up on the slightest sounds.

The little cluster of trees and shrubs he remembered had grown taller and wider, with the old pines stretching up to the sky and new growth feathering around the edges. The ground in this section had less of a slope than what they'd been climbing, which made it easier for Isaac to limp forward from one tree to the next.

Tillis stayed behind him like a shadow.

At the edge of the copse, Isaac motioned for him to stay put, then strained to hear any sound. Wind ruffled his hair, an almost constant sensation up on this mountainside. A hawk soared in the distance, searching for prey, no doubt.

No other noise or movement made itself known. What if he was wrong about the gang coming here? He'd seen a few horse tracks coming up the mountain, but maybe those were from Indian mounts. What if the men they sought had changed hideouts? It had been ten years, after all. As well hidden as this cabin was, maybe they thought it would be foolish to keep the same retreat for so long.

These good men from River Crossing probably wouldn't take kindly to being led on a foolish manhunt.

Shifting his gaze from his surroundings to watch the position of each of his steps, he eased forward through the trees one silent step at a time until he'd crossed the short distance to the mountain wall. The crevice was exactly where he remembered it: at a sideways angle so you had to turn into the space between the stones before you could see the opening on the other side.

He peered in first, listening intently. Was that the murmur of a male voice? He couldn't tell for sure. Only a sliver of green grass was visible from the angle he stood. He'd have to step fully into the crevice to see anything more.

One of his walking sticks clicked against the rock underneath him, and he cringed, stilling. If any of the men were standing guard, they may have heard the noise.

No sounds came from the other side of the rock wall, so he took another step forward, careful to place each step of the walking stick quietly. He was at the edge now. Ready to peer around the corner.

With achingly slow movements, he leaned against the rock, just forward enough to see around the edge. The corner of the cabin came into view, then the door in the center. All seemed quiet. They'd cut several slits in the wood to allow whoever stood watch to see outside, so he couldn't know if anyone was watching. Not yet.

With the full cabin in view, he stayed motionless, eyeing the tiny openings and watching for movement. He may not be able to see anything from this distance, but maybe there would be a glimmer of light. The flash of something white. Anything to prove people were in there.

Then he'd need to draw them out.

It must have been at least twenty minutes, or maybe only ten, since time seemed to crawl by, but then the sound of a voice drifted from the cabin. Too deep to be Aaron or Nate, but definitely male.

Then it struck him. Something he should have thought about long before now. Where were the horses?

They used to keep them either in this area in front of the cabin or in a section farther up the mountain. Seeing the horses would help them know with more certainty that the gang was holed up in the cabin. Then again, he'd heard the voice moments before, which meant someone was there.

Easing backward, he turned and stepped out of the crevice, then limped toward Tillis.

The man stepped from behind a tree as he approached. "See anything?"

Isaac shook his head. "I heard a man's voice coming from inside. Just a word or two I couldn't make out. We need to locate their horses, though. There's a little grassy spot up the mountain where we sometimes tied a rope corral to let the horses graze. Do you wanna hike up and see if the animals are there?" Should they cut them loose? If the horses came clambering down the mountain, it might stir the men into a frenzy.

But then . . . maybe that's exactly what they needed. At the right time.

Stepping closer to Tillis, he spoke in low tones. And within a couple minutes, they had developed a plan.

One that would require divine help to carry out.

⋅⊰═◦═⊱⋅

It took everything in Joanna not to pace. Not to call out for Isaac to see what was happening. Not to race up the mountain after him.

What if he fell, and the noise alerted the kidnappers? What if they were a day too late for her son? For Laura? Bile churned in her stomach at the thought of what her friend had likely suffered. Joanna couldn't imagine what that would be like.

Didn't want to imagine.

One of the men—a Mr. Camden—had a pocket watch. He was kind enough not to share the time unless she asked, but as an hour passed, then another fifteen minutes, then five more, his tone said his patience with her requests was waning.

Finally, she turned to the group. "Something must have happened. They were only going to scout out the area, confirm who was there, and come back so we could make a plan. I'm going up to see what's wrong. Is there one man who'd like to accompany me? I think it's best if we stick in pairs."

Mr. Knight straightened and opened his mouth to respond, but before a word could come out, a voice sounded behind her.

"No need."

She spun to face the newcomer, even as the timbre of Isaac's voice settled the raw edges of her nerves. "Isaac."

He was safe, as hale and hearty as he'd been when he and Mr. Tillis walked up the mountain. The livery owner now stood behind him, and both of their expressions looked optimistic.

Or maybe that was wishful thinking on her part.

She strode toward them, as much to do something with herself as to learn what they'd found. "What did you discover?"

Isaac spoke up, his usual confident presence easily taking over the lead role in this mission. "The cabin is mostly quiet, but I heard a man's voice inside. Their horses are in a rope corral a little farther up the mountain. We have a plan, but it will take all of us to pull it off."

"You didn't see Samuel? Or Laura?" She had to stop herself from clutching his arm, squeezing answers from him that would reassure her at least a little.

Isaac met her gaze, pain deepening the green of his eyes. "Not yet. But everyone looked to be holed inside. We'll know soon."

She forced herself to take a breath and nod. She had to trust that between Isaac, these men, and her heavenly Father, her boy and friend would be saved.

And unhurt. *Lord, please.*

As Isaac laid out the plan they'd developed, with a few added comments from Mr. Tillis, the knot in her middle pulled tighter, her chest nearly closing off breath more than once.

It might work. Or it could make things even worse.

Yet as the men around her batted about questions and pondered other options, the truth became painfully clear. This was their best hope to rescue the prisoners *and* take down the gang members.

Both of those goals were of utmost importance. They had to make sure this awful evil was never forced on anyone else.

Isaac stood at the edge of the crevice once again, peeking around the corner to see the cabin. This time his walking sticks lay at his feet and he held his rifle, fully cocked and ready to take down any man who stepped out, firmly against his shoulder.

Knight stood behind him, then Tillis, then the rest of the men. All except Adam Canton, who was helping Joanna with the horses. She'd argued vehemently against being given a job so far away from the main action—or at least from the bulk of the gunfire.

He wanted her as far away from flying bullets as he could get her. *Lord, protect this woman. No matter what, keep her safe. Please.*

He may have lost his chance with her, but he still wanted her to be healthy and happy. And to have her son safe in her arms.

As he studied the slits in the cabin wall, he was fairly certain a flash of white passed in front of one of them. Could that be Miss Hannon? Or one of the men? If only he knew what was happening inside.

A whinny sounded in the distance, then an answering call. He glanced behind him, even though he could see nothing, save the stone wall and a few treetops above it. Enough time had passed that Joanna and Adam were probably releasing the horses up on the hill.

The excitement would start any time now.

A few more painful minutes passed as his nerves bunched tighter and tighter.

Then a shot split the air. That would be Adam shooting to rile the horses. He focused on the cabin, squinting to see any motion, any shift of lighting at those peepholes. His ears strained for sound, both from behind and ahead.

Something shifted at the slit cut into the door. One of the men peering out probably. He raised his rifle and squinted down the barrel. Did he dare shoot without knowing who stood on the other side of that wood? The men probably wouldn't allow the woman or boy near the peepholes, not if they were prisoners.

But he couldn't take that chance.

Especially with Joanna's son.

His ears picked up a distant sound. The clack of hooves on stone, if he wasn't mistaken. Probably not loud enough yet for the men in the cabin to hear.

But as the seconds passed, the noise grew louder. The shrill whinny of a horse sounded again, either in excitement or fright. *Keep the animals safe, Lord.* Isaac didn't want them hurt, just needed them to draw the men out of the cabin.

He kept his gaze sighted down the barrel of his Hawken, and when the door opened, he was ready.

A figure darted out, tall and lean, with a brown shirt and dark trousers that almost hid him against the worn wood of the cabin. Yet it wasn't hard to recognize the set of his shoulders, the way the man carried himself. The fellow sprinted to his left toward the wall, where Isaac would have to expose more of himself to follow the man with his rifle.

But the pain in his chest made him pause. Could he shoot Aaron? Actually kill a man? He had to wound him at least.

Shoot his gun hand? Except the man had been almost as good with his left as his right. Maybe he could hit a leg so he'd stay put.

He had to do it now. Pushing everything from his mind except his focus down the rifle barrel, he leaned around the rock wall. Aaron had run the length of the long stretch and now sprinted down the short wall straight toward Isaac, gripping a rifle in both hands. His legs were moving too fast for an accurate shot, so he raised the gun to aim at the right shoulder. Far enough from the heart it shouldn't do too much damage.

He squeezed the trigger.

TWENTY-FOUR

Through the haze of gun smoke, Isaac watched as Aaron jerked but didn't fall. More relief swept through him than he should have felt. The rifle must have fallen from Aaron's hands when the bullet hit, for he reached down and swooped it up with his left hand, then pressed himself flat against the rock wall.

He turned his gaze to Isaac, but no flash of recognition appeared on Aaron's face. He breathed hard, his shoulders rising in great heaves from the effort he'd spent. And maybe from the pain of the bullet wound, but Aaron showed no sign of it.

Maybe now would be the time to barter for the prisoners' release. He deepened his voice so maybe Aaron wouldn't recognize it. "Turn yourself in and you won't be hurt any further. We want the boy and woman back."

A flash of something crossed Aaron's face—annoyance, maybe? But the expression fled, leaving only pressed lips to show his displeasure. "I'm not the one you need to convince."

Isaac exhaled a breath. So the kidnapping hadn't been Aaron's idea. "Then come this way and we'll keep you from getting shot while we convince the others."

Aaron tipped his head, as though listening for something. Isaac cringed. He'd not disguised his voice that time. Did the man recognize him?

But when Aaron spoke again, his voice didn't carry a hint of suspicion. "Doesn't sound very safe to me. How many of you are there? How do I know you won't shoot me through the chest the minute I hand over my gun?"

Isaac dipped his chin, focusing on changing the tone of his voice. "We have twice as many as you. All seasoned gunhands. Like I said, we came for the woman and the boy. As long as they're turned over unharmed, none of you will be hurt."

Aaron looked straight into Isaac's eyes, and this time there was no doubt in Isaac's bones the man knew who he was. "It wasn't my idea, Bowen. And I didn't hurt either one of them."

Isaac sucked in a breath. A small part of him felt a wash of relief. Then he focused on Aaron's other words: *"I didn't hurt either one of them."* Did that mean the others had? He opened his mouth to ask, but the distant clack of hooves was now a thundering sound. The animals were running down the grassy stretch just above them.

Aaron tipped his head to listen, then raised his brows at Isaac. "It doesn't matter what you try, Rex and Bill aren't going to send them out. And I'm not leaving without my brother."

The determination in the man's eyes was an all-too-familiar sight. Aaron and Nate held an unshakeable loyalty to each other. Isaac had never seen anything break that bond. Not even the weighty guilt brought on by a life of crime.

"Step aside." The low voice came from behind.

Isaac pulled back, grabbing his walking sticks so he could hobble out of the crevice before the horses charged through.

Joanna and Adam appeared through the trees, each riding their own mounts and leading two more horses. The men on the ground swarmed them, taking the ropes of the gang's animals.

A flurry of low comments sounded between the men, and Adam's brother led the first horse forward to the crevice. If the gang kept the routine they'd used years ago, these horses would be used to walking through the narrow opening, over stone that would clatter loudly beneath their hooves.

One by one, the men loosed the four horses into the courtyard area in front of the cabin. Isaac strained to hear anything the gang might be doing on the other side of the wall, but he could hear nothing except the noise of the animals.

He limped forward behind the last horse, closing in the gap in case one of the animals tried to bolt back out. Or if one of the men—like Aaron—tried to leap aboard a mount and use the horse's power to force his way to freedom.

Carefully, he peered around the edge of the rock. The cabin appeared quiet, except for the four horses milling in front. Then he leaned farther to check Aaron's position. That man would have had time to dart back into the building while they were bringing the horses in, but he still stood pressed against the rock wall.

They needed to take him captive, but the thought of using force pressed hard on Isaac's chest. He had to talk Aaron into coming on his own. But maybe the man would share a few details about the situation inside first.

"Are the woman or boy hurt, Aaron?" He tried to keep his voice from sounding too harsh. Too demanding. Aaron was more likely to give information if he didn't feel forced.

"Just a few bruises and scrapes. Mostly from that woman trying to escape. She got in a gunfight with Bill, which didn't help any of us."

A gunfight? He'd only met Miss Hannon a handful of times, but Bill had a reputation for his brawn and ruthlessness. She must have been desperate to take him on.

A shuffling sounded behind him, and he glanced back to see Joanna sitting atop her horse, only an arm's reach behind him. The way her face had blanched, she must have heard Aaron's words.

She met Isaac's gaze with fire in her eyes. "I'm going to ride in. I'll stay low and stir up the other horses so they can't get a good shot at me."

"No." He shook his head hard. "Once you're through the opening in the rock, you'll be fully exposed for anyone to pick you off. I'll fire a shot to stir up the horses, then we'll draw the men out."

Her chin jutted upward. "I doubt they'll come. Even if they do, it'll take too long. Who knows what they're doing to my boy and my friend while we stand here. I'm going in."

The bile in his gut churned like a raging river. Under no condition could he allow Joanna to ride into that courtyard with rifles pointed at her, eager for the clear shot she would give the criminals.

She was right that they needed to take action. His original plan hadn't worked at all the way he'd hoped. He had to come up with something else.

Something better.

He didn't dare fire into the cabin while he had no idea where the two innocents were. He wanted to go in after them himself. He hated sending these men into clear danger, but they had a better chance of coming out alive than Joanna. Once she saw her son, her decisions would likely be tinged by too much emotion.

"I'll do it." Knight's voice rang strong as he stepped up beside Joanna's horse. The determination on his face brooked no argument as he reached for the animal's reins and looked up at Joanna. "Like you said, Mrs. Watson, we don't have a minute to lose. I'll need to ride your horse."

"I'll ride in with you." Adam Canton still sat atop his horse behind Joanna. "Two of us can keep them on their toes."

Isaac eased out a sigh of relief. "I'd go in alone if I could, but I'd have trouble once I was off the horse."

Knight motioned for Joanna to dismount. "Please, Mrs. Watson. We need to hurry."

Her face was a tempest of conflicting emotions, and Isaac almost stepped in to make his case clear. But she finally leaned forward and dismounted. Knight leaped into the saddle and readied his rifle.

"We'll cover you with gunfire on this end." Isaac held the horse's reins as the man finished preparing for the charge.

He turned back to the stone wall and eased around so he could see Aaron. "Drop your rifle, Aaron. This is your last chance to come join us out of the way of gunfire. Otherwise, your life'll end with a stray bullet, likely as not."

Aaron studied him, then shifted his gaze back to the cabin. "Nate's in there, tied up like a prisoner for trying to help the woman and boy. I've done a lot of things I'm not proud of in my life, but I'm not leaving my brother behind." His voice rang firm.

The knot pulled tighter in Isaac's midsection. He'd not been able to imagine the Nate he knew taking part in whatever these men had planned for such innocents. As much as it was a relief to hear he'd not gone along willingly with the plan, this meant they'd need to get Nate out without injury, too.

He turned back to the men behind Knight and Canton. "Make sure your rifles are loaded and ready. We need to keep steady fire toward the cabin to distract them, but don't shoot inside the building unless you see one of the men shooting at us. Aim for the ground or the sky."

Then he looked to the two mounted with rifles at the ready, prepared to charge in the moment he gave the signal. Without wasting words, he relayed the new information about Nate. "I have no idea where he'll be tied or how the cabin is laid out these days. But Rex and Bill shouldn't be hard to miss. They'll be the ones shooting at you." He couldn't help a grimace.

"Let's go, then." Knight straightened in the saddle, clearly raring to get started.

With an ache in his chest, Isaac stepped aside. Sending these men in his place felt wrong in every way possible. *Protect them, Lord. Guard them on every side, and make their mission successful.*

As soon as the horses cleared the rock crevice, Isaac stepped to the edge and fired a shot toward the sky just above and to the right of the cabin.

Rifle fire lit from the building, and the two mounted men ducked low in their saddles. Knight's small stature made it possible for the horse's mane to almost cover him.

They'd closed half the distance by the time Isaac had used up the bullets in all his guns. He stepped back to allow someone else to shoot while he reloaded, but stayed close enough to the edge of the opening so he could see what was happening in the yard.

Canton was the first to reach the cabin door, and he leaped from his horse on the threshold. With rifle ready in both hands, he kicked hard on the door. The wood had to be at least a dozen years old and quite weathered, so it splintered easily enough under his blow.

At that moment, Knight's horse stumbled and went down, somersaulting the man forward on the ground. With a grace not many men could manage, he sprang to his feet, took half a second to get his bearings, then charged toward the cabin door.

Maybe Canton's entrance distracted the men inside enough to keep them from shooting Knight. *Stop any bullets aimed at them, Lord.*

Shots continued inside the structure, and Isaac kept his focus pinned to the open doorway. A bit of gun smoke wafted out, but otherwise, he could see nothing but darkness.

"Should we keep firing?" Joanna stepped back from the shooting position, planting herself just in front of him where she could still see the cabin. She must be out of bullets, too, for Wesley Canton stepped into her place at the wall.

"Hold off for now. Make sure we're all fully loaded for whatever happens next." Best he take his own advice, too. Quickly, he reloaded the rifle and both revolvers, only taking his eyes from the scene ahead when he had to.

The shots had been intense for the first minute or so, but now they'd stopped. Occasional banging sounded inside, like a fight was taking place.

A woman's scream sounded from inside, tightening Isaac's nerves even more. Wesley Canton pushed off from his spot on the wall and sprinted toward the building. "I'm going in."

Joanna snapped the action shut on her rifle. "Me too."

"No." He reached out to snag her arm, but she was too fast, and he stumbled forward, barely catching himself on the rock wall. "Joanna!" He tried to keep his voice low enough it would reach her but not echo all the way to the cabin.

Whether she heard or not, she didn't stop running, rifle in one hand and skirts pulled high in the other.

His heart leapt into his throat as he watched her. He almost missed the men swarming around him, charging forward to help. Gripping his rifle, he stepped forward to follow.

Then almost went down as he put weight on his broken leg.

His frustrated grunt was impossible to hold back, but at least he didn't say the words that tried to spring through his lips. After reaching down for his walking sticks, he fit them under his arms and swung forward.

A movement at the corner of his gaze made him stop short. Aaron still stood against the wall, his face hard as he held his rifle pressed into his shoulder. He wasn't looking down the barrel to aim, though. Just seemed to be prepared. But for what?

To shoot one of the men from town when they came out? But he would have done that when the fellows were running toward the house. Would he turn on Rex or Bill? *Lord, let him be on our side.*

But Isaac couldn't chance it. He had one of the four gang members right here. He couldn't risk him getting away. They'd brought rope he could tie Aaron up with, but something about that didn't sit right. With Isaac's weak leg, it was possible Aaron could overpower him if he wanted, but that wasn't the problem. Maybe his reticence was a lingering softness for the man who'd once been a trusted friend.

Lord, show me what to do. He waited for a feeling of direction to settle in his soul. A clear peace about tying up the man.

"And lest I should be exalted above measure through the abundance of the revelations, there was given to me a thorn in the flesh . . ." That same verse from before, except this time he had a strong inkling the *thorn in the flesh* referred more to his splinted leg, the frustrating injury that held him back from being the first to charge into the cabin.

Maybe he'd not conquered his pride as much as he'd thought. *Forgive me, Lord. Make my motives pure. Use me as you see fit.*

Shouts echoed from the cabin, spinning Isaac's focus in that direction. A man backed out of the doorway, pistol aimed at someone inside. Camden, if he wasn't mistaken over the distance. The fellow stepped to the side to allow the next man to exit.

A hulking frame stepped from the darkness, arms raised as he had to duck to get through the doorway.

Bill.

A thrill surged through him. The men from town must have gained the upper hand. If they all made it through this with the gang captured and the innocents safe, it would be more than a miracle.

For the first time since he'd realized who had kidnapped Joanna's son and friend, he felt a bit of hope rising in his spirit.

TWENTY-FIVE

*A*s two more men from town stepped through the opening, guns trained on Bill's back, it was all Isaac could do not to whoop for joy. *Thank you, Lord.*

Another man exited the cabin with hands held to the side. Not raised high, but far enough from his body that he must be a captive. A begrudging captive. Isaac had never seen Rex Stanley in person, but he'd heard the man was as wily as a snake.

More wily.

From this distance, he couldn't tell much about the man's appearance, but the sullen attitude was clear from the set of his shoulders. When Knight prodded him with his rifle, Rex jerked away, as though he couldn't stand to be tainted by the touch.

Everything in Isaac wanted to sprint forward. To see how Joanna and her son had fared. And Miss Hannon. Nate, too, for that matter.

Isaac glanced over at Aaron. He leaned forward, his focus

clearly on the men leaving the cabin. Looking for his brother, no doubt.

Isaac turned his gaze back to the building. All of the men now marched across the clearing except one of the Canton brothers. Adam, he was pretty sure.

But none of the captives had stepped outside. Nor Joanna.

Lord, what's wrong? His heartbeat thumped loud in his ears. Now was his time to step forward. He could feel the release in his spirit. But he had no choice but to tie Aaron.

Grabbing up the rope, he slipped his rifle strap over his shoulder and tucked the walking sticks under his arms. He limped around the end of the rock wall and headed toward Aaron. "I need to tie you up so I can help free the prisoners. I'll make sure your brother's not hurt."

Aaron slid a sideways look at him, then studied the cabin once more. At last, he let out a loud breath and turned to Isaac. He lowered his rifle to lean against the rock, then extended his hands in front of him. "Mind putting them in front? This aches a good bit." He dipped his chin toward his right shoulder, where a patch of blood the size of a man's hand marred the shirt fabric.

Isaac nodded as he stopped in front of Aaron, then grabbed an end of the rope and made quick work of a strong knot. When he finished, he couldn't help but look up into Aaron's piercing gaze. "Sorry about that. Nothing personal."

Aaron's tight jaw dipped in a single nod.

That was all Isaac had time for. He swung forward toward the men, handing over the rope when he reached Camden. "I've tied up Aaron. He's been shot in the shoulder, and I think he's mostly on our side, so don't be too rough with him." He nodded toward Bill. "These two are the ones you have to watch out for."

Camden dipped his chin in acknowledgement, his gaze and rifle barrel shifting back toward the giant of a man glaring at them. "We'll see to 'em."

As Isaac passed Rex, the man's lethal gaze sent a shiver down his spine. This one was dangerous in every meaning of the word. Anger surged in his chest again.

Lord, why? It seemed so cruel for God to allow an innocent young woman to be taken by force and held captive by a ruthless man like Rex Stanley. The man walked with a strong limp, so perhaps she'd been able to defend herself. Isaac was still struggling to believe Aaron's words about how she'd squared off in a gunfight with Bill.

Leaving Rex behind, he hobbled forward, his gaze set on the cabin. When twenty strides still separated him from the structure, a figure appeared from the darkness inside.

Nate.

The man limped from the building, then stepped aside to wait for the next person to exit.

A woman appeared in the opening, raising a hand to shield her eyes against the bright sunlight. She had to be Miss Hannon, but he didn't remember her being so gaunt. Not much more than a skeleton with clothing draped over her.

As she lowered the hand shielding her face, he could better see how her hair sprang out in wild patches. Was that a bruise blackening her eye?

Rage boiled up inside him, but he forced himself to tamp

it down as he closed the final distance between them. "Miss Hannon?"

She looked at him with eyes a hundred years old. Weary and desolate, like a wasteland with nothing left alive.

"Mr. Bowen." Her voice was flat, and he couldn't help but notice the way Nate stepped closer to her. Not close enough to touch, but the awareness of his presence was impossible to miss.

For now, though, he needed to focus on getting them all back to town. "Are you injured? We'll bring the horses around for you, so rest here for now."

His gaze slipped up to Adam Canton, who'd stepped out behind her. The man nodded and motioned toward the ground beside the doorway. While the man helped her sit, Isaac turned his focus to Nate.

Isaac's long-ago friend met his gaze with an intensity that spoke to the connection they'd once shared. To the lifetime that had passed since then. A glimmer of shame shone in Nate's eyes.

Isaac was the first to extend his hand, and after a second, Nate took it. "I heard you helped Miss Hannon and Samuel. Thank you."

A flash of pain passed through Nate's eyes, and he looked away. With a halfhearted nod, he pulled his hand back and turned to where Miss Hannon sat propped against the cabin wall.

Isaac straightened. They could talk more later. Now, the need to find Joanna and Samuel clawed at him like a wildcat.

He hobbled inside the dark interior of the cabin, blinking

to clear the halos of light from his vision. A soft humming drifted from his left, and he turned that way.

A figure curled in the corner—Joanna. His heart raced as he swung toward her. The men wouldn't have left her here alone if she was injured in the fight, would they?

Then his adjusting eyes caught the tiny body she was curled around. Samuel's bright red hair was hard to miss, even in the dim lighting. He reached the two and laid his walking sticks down, then used the wall to lower himself to sit beside the boy.

"Hey there." He ducked down to see Samuel's face, which was barely visible as he pressed against his mother's side. "How are you, son?"

He reached out and rubbed Samuel's back, just underneath where Joanna's arm held him tight, to feel for himself that the lad was real.

Isaac let his hand wander up to rub Joanna's arm, giving what reassurance he could through a simple touch. She raised her face to his, and the red tingeing her eyes and marking her face made his chest ache.

He brought his hand up to her shoulder, settling it there. He could do so little to help her, but maybe just knowing she wasn't alone in the midst of her swarming emotions would help.

"How is he?" Isaac had to know, and the boy hadn't answered him.

She held his gaze. "He's not saying much, but I don't think his body is injured. At least, nothing broken." She pressed her cheek to her son's hair, snuggling him tighter. The boy pressed into her but still didn't speak.

Every other time he'd spent more than a passing moment with Samuel, the lad had talked incessantly. Now, his silence reverberated through the cabin like a gunshot in a canyon. How much terror had this lad endured? Had he been beaten? Or was the abuse more in his mind and emotions?

Isaac leaned into the pair, holding tight as he sent up a flurry of prayers to the only Father who could heal the wounds inflicted during the past week.

⟶ ⟵

Tears leaked down Joanna's face as she clung to her son. So many times she'd feared she would never hold him like this again. Yet God had brought them both through the ordeal.

She would never again take for granted his little-boy hugs. Never wish away his endless chatter. If only he would speak to her now. His silence frightened her more than she wanted to admit. She'd never seen him go this long without speaking, even in those final minutes before sleep claimed him each night.

Hopefully it was just shock from the men bursting into the cabin so suddenly. Joy from reuniting with her unexpectedly. Emotions he couldn't express with words. Once all the excitement settled, he'd be just like before. Moving and talking incessantly.

And she'd soak in every moment.

She inhaled a breath, releasing as much of her angst as she could. Isaac's warm strength around her made it doubly hard to end these quiet moments. But she needed to get Samuel away from this place, from whatever memories would plague him here. And the raw blisters on his wrists needed doctoring, in addition to any other wounds he'd incurred.

She straightened, and Isaac eased away to give her space. She summoned the closest thing to a smile she could find. "I think we're ready to go back to town."

He stood, with a hand propped against the wall to steady himself, then he reached out to help her up.

But she couldn't quite bring herself to release Samuel. Isaac must have read her mind, for instead he shifted his reach to her son. With him on one side and her on the other, they lifted him up to standing. One of the Canton brothers had already cut loose the ties that had bound Samuel's wrists and ankles, but the boy still seemed unsteady.

Once Joanna had gained her own feet, she tucked Samuel in close to her side. Together, the three of them started toward the open door and the bright light of freedom.

⋯⟡⟡⋯

Something didn't feel right. Isaac hobbled on his walking sticks behind Joanna and her son as they stepped out of the gang's cabin. Though the sun still shone as brightly as before, a chill pricked his arms. Was the danger not yet over?

As much as he wanted to stick close to the woman and boy who'd come to mean so much to him, an urgency in his chest propelled him forward. He caught Joanna's eye as he moved around her. "Take your time. I'll get the horses." He didn't want her to worry about anything more. Maybe this unease was simply leftover nerves from before.

Yet he knew better than to ignore his instincts.

The men were all gathered at the far end of the open area, near the rock wall. Six horses stood among them, all saddled and waiting. A brown skirt was visible at the edge of the group. Miss Hannon must be eager to leave this place.

Rex and Bill had already mounted, with men on either side of them, probably securing them to the saddle. Isaac would check them himself to make sure there was no chance they could escape.

Not alive, at least. The damage these men had done would not go without punishment.

Isaac was halfway across the open area, doing his best to ignore the blisters from the walking sticks under his arms, when a shift in the men caught his focus. Nate and Tillis helped Aaron rise from where he'd been sitting on the ground, and then they walked with him toward one of the horses.

A pang pricked his chest at the reminder that he'd put a bullet in the man's shoulder. He'd had to. At least, he was pretty sure of that at the time. They'd get him back to town, and one of them could patch him up so the wound didn't fester.

Then he could escort Joanna, Samuel, and Miss Hannon back to Settler's Fort. Life could return to normal.

Except he didn't want his life to revert back to the boring existence he'd managed before. Now that he'd come to know Joanna, any picture without her in it seemed dull and colorless.

Samuel, too. Though the time they'd spent together was only a few days combined, he yearned to help the boy. To be a man he could look up to. A father who took him fishing and taught him to whistle and pointed him to the Father who would never leave him, not by death or any other reason.

Lord, if it's not too late, I'd love another chance with them both. God might not see fit to give it to him, but it didn't stop everything in Isaac from yearning for another opportunity.

Shouting ahead raised his focus.

"Gun!" He couldn't tell which man yelled it, but a blast ripped through the air.

TWENTY-SIX

A second shot sounded.

Then a third blast filled the courtyard, this one the deeper boom of a rifle.

Men scrambled about in confusion, and Rex no longer sat atop his horse. Had he been the one to shoot? Maybe he'd pulled a gun that the others hadn't found when they searched him. *Please let them have searched him.*

So much frustration pressed in Isaac's chest as he scrambled forward, trying to see who might be down. Some of the men hovered near the horse Rex had been mounted on. Isaac was about ten strides away when he recognized the broad shoulders of Nate Long among the second grouping of men, leaning over a figure lying prone on the ground.

The knot in his stomach tightened. Not Aaron. He didn't want any of the men to die in this battle, but particularly not his old friend. A man who might finally be ready to leave his life of crime behind.

Two men shifted when Isaac neared, allowing him access

to the injured man. Aaron lay in the grass, his hands gripping his leg. Nate used both hands to press a cloth to the spot beside where Aaron clutched.

Crimson soaked through the fabric, a much brighter red than what was drying on his shoulder. Two bullet wounds this man had suffered—and from the blood spreading over Nate's hand, the leg wound was the worst.

What could he do to help? Stopping the bleeding had to come first, and Nate was working on that. A glance at his face showed his skin had blanched, his lips pursed in a thin line.

"Is the bone broken, too?" If so, they'd need to set it. But that could wait till they made it back to town.

"I don't know for sure. It's bad." The strain in Nate's voice cracked on his last word.

"We need to get him to town. I don't think we can get a wagon up the mountain, but one of us should ride back to River Crossing and bring a buckboard to the base of the hill." Isaac turned his focus to Aaron's tight grimace. "I hate to ask it, but if we get the bleeding stopped, do you think you can ride a horse down the mountain?"

The man gave a single tight nod, his breath coming in tiny gasps.

"Here's my shirt to tie above the wound." Tillis tugged the garment over his head.

The two of them worked together, a couple other men from town assisting. Once they had the job well in hand and someone had been sent back to town to retrieve a wagon, Isaac moved to see what was happening with Rex.

Pulling himself up to his feet with the walking sticks was getting harder each time he pushed his weary body through the action, but his wasn't the worst injury. And he had a great deal more to do.

As he turned toward the other cluster of men, a brown skirt caught his notice. Miss Hannon stood apart from the others, near the rock wall. She had her arms wrapped around herself, and her gaze was locked on the men around Aaron. Her face looked impossibly pale.

He walked toward her. In truth, she looked like she might need someone to catch her in case she swooned.

"Miss Hannon?" His words seemed to break her trance, and she jerked her gaze to him.

"Is he . . . will he die?" Her voice barely sounded above a whisper.

Poor woman. She likely already endured watching Sheriff Zander's death. Now she'd been forced to endure more bloodshed. He couldn't lie to her, but maybe he could soften the seriousness of Aaron's condition.

"He's hurt, but we'll get him to town and do everything we can for him." Isaac still didn't know whether Rex was alive. But Aaron was the one who seemed to be drawing her focus.

Her lips parted like she would speak, then she closed them. Then opened them again. "I didn't mean to shoot him. I looked up and saw Rex with that pistol aimed at me. I got so angry. After everything he'd done . . ." A bit of color crept back into her face and her eyes regained some life.

"I grabbed up a gun someone had dropped and aimed it at him. My finger must have squeezed the trigger too soon.

Aaron was diving toward Rex . . . to stop him, I think. I didn't mean . . ." Her words faded into a whimper as she raised pleading eyes to him.

Lord, help her. He reached out and laid a hand on her arm. "We'll do what we can for him. Why don't you wait with Joanna for now? We'll get you back to town soon."

She nodded and walked woodenly toward Joanna and Samuel, who were making their way across the yard toward them.

Isaac heaved out a sigh. What would happen next?

As he made his way toward Rex, Knight stepped away from the others to meet Isaac, his mouth in a tight line. "He must have had a revolver hidden somewhere we missed. Aaron saw it before anyone else and tried to stop him. That effort must have made his bullet go high. Miss Hannon reacted before I could get my rifle aimed at him. We don't need to worry about him anymore, though." The man looked almost apologetic, and the same kind of remorse slipped through Isaac.

As many crimes as Rex Stanley had committed, maybe he deserved death. But every man's life was precious in God's eyes. Taking that life was no light thing.

Isaac eased out a long breath of the turmoil building in his chest. He scrubbed a hand through his hair, his gaze sliding over to find Joanna.

She stood just outside the gathering of men, one arm around Samuel and the other around Miss Hannon. Joanna's chin was raised as she watched them, her inner strength evident in her regal bearing.

They'd both made it through the battle, through the awful ordeal of the past week. And Samuel was safe.

His gaze wandered around the clearing that held so many memories. Each one added another layer of guilt, sinking like rocks in his belly.

He inhaled a deep breath, then released it. He could put the guilt behind him now. God had forgiven him. And he'd finally helped stop the evil he set in motion all those years ago. Now he could focus on the future.

⁓⊷◉⊶⁓

Joanna cradled her son in the back of the wagon, holding him as close as a second skin. They could have ridden her horse, but Samuel needed every bit of her focus that she could give just now. He sniffled a great deal, and when she asked Laura, her friend said he'd been ill for several days.

Her heart nearly broke at the thought. Her baby, the only family she had left, sleeping tied to a tree. Feverish, shivering, hungry. He was so quiet, and her fingers found the outline of his every rib without seeking them out.

She tucked her chin tighter over his matted red curls. Her gaze found Laura, riding one of the horses alongside the wagon.

Speaking of quiet, her friend hadn't spoken a word unless prompted. Joanna had tried to ask about what had taken place, but Laura hadn't shared many details. Joanna wanted to pull her friend close, to tuck Laura away from anything that could hurt her. It would likely take some time before the woman was ready to talk.

A groan emanated from the man lying on the other side

of the wagon bed, louder than the steady stream of moans that had slipped from him since they'd all piled into the conveyance.

With all the blood soaking his makeshift bandage, he must be in a great deal of pain. In truth, she was struggling to find any sympathy for the man. Maybe for his brother, who Isaac said had helped her son and friend. The brother who now knelt over the wounded man, fear marking his face in a way that reminded her of her own terror this past week, wondering if her son would live or die, and how much pain he'd endured.

Squeezing her eyes shut, she tried to focus on something other than those awful memories. Tried to focus on her joy. *Thank you, Father. I can't thank you enough.* Those were the words echoing through her mind as Mr. Tillis halted the wagon in front of Mrs. Holder's boardinghouse.

The woman pulled open the door and pressed a hand to her mouth as she took in the scene before her. "Bless me. Come inside, all of you. I've a warm meal and everything else you need."

Samuel straightened in her arms, probably at the word *meal*. Maybe all her son needed was plenty of food, a hot bath, and a good night's sleep.

Four of the men had taken Bill to be held in a secure place, along with Rex's body. She wasn't sure what would happen to either of them. She wanted justice, of course, but as long as the men had them in hand, she had more than enough to worry about here.

Mrs. Holder took charge of Laura, guiding her into the house like a mother hen nurturing her chick. Isaac appeared at the back of the wagon, propped on his walking sticks, to help Joanna and her son to the ground. The concern cloaking his face made her want to slip into his arms, to let herself be cared for by this man who was so much bigger and stronger than she was. His shoulders were wide enough to bear the weight of her worries.

But she didn't. Just tried to summon a half-smile to thank him for his help from the wagon. Later, when she had more energy and wasn't so close to tears, she'd thank him for every-thing else.

⇥⟫⟨⇤

Laura forced her puffy eyes open but pulled the quilt tighter around her shoulders. The few hours that had passed since they'd arrived in River Crossing felt like days. If only she could imagine herself back in Settler's Fort, back in her tiny rented room. She'd give anything to be back inside those canvas walls on the thin straw mattress she'd once hated.

If only this past week had never happened.

Even now, as the dim evening light revealed the spotless room around her—the washbasin with embroidered towel, the trunk draped in a spring quilt—this lovely environment didn't seem real. Any moment she might awaken to Bill's booted foot kicking her side. Rex's lecherous gaze sliding over her.

She pulled the blanket tighter around her, then pushed herself up from the bed, biting back a groan at the knife of pain in her ribs. She couldn't let herself sleep. Couldn't let the nightmare come back. Couldn't relive the moment she'd pulled the trigger and watched the horror on Aaron's face as her bullet struck.

With the quilt still draped over her shoulders, she slipped her feet into her filthy, worn boots. Mrs. Holder had found a shirtwaist and skirt she could wear while her clothes were being washed. In truth, she never wanted to see that stained and torn brown material again.

She should lay the blanket back across the bed, leave it exactly as she'd found it. But she couldn't make herself remove it from her shoulders. If anyone asked why she kept it tight around her shoulders, she'd say she'd taken a chill.

Summoning a breath of courage, she pulled open the bedchamber door and stepped into the main room. The place was quiet. Nothing like the flurry of activity when they'd first arrived.

She glanced toward the kitchen. No clanging of pans sounded from that room, nor did she hear Mrs. Holder's gentle voice, the tone she'd used to encourage Laura to finish two plates of dumplings.

A moan drifted from the room to her left. The door stood partway open, making it hard not to catch a glimpse of the man sitting on the side of the bed. She recognized Nate's shoulders, although the defeated slump was a sight she'd never seen before. A pang pressed her chest, a sympathy she'd not thought possible this day.

Stepping through the doorway, her gaze found the man lying in the bed. Aaron's face was twisted with pain, his skin almost as pale as the white pillow behind him.

The knot in her middle tightened. Was he dying? She'd not meant to kill Aaron. When Rex turned that gun on her, all the anger from his ill treatment had spewed up like a geyser. She'd not stopped to think, just picked up the pistol, pointed, and fired.

If only she'd taken an extra second to make sure her aim was true. Her error may end up taking the life of the wrong man.

Her feet drew her nearer, even as part of her begged to turn and flee. There was nothing she could do to help Aaron that hadn't been done already.

She gulped a breath to keep herself steady, even as the room around her began to swim before her eyes.

"Laura?" Nate's voice.

She did her best to focus on him, to still the spinning in her head.

"Are you all right?"

As the words took shape in her mind, a laugh almost slipped out. Would she ever be all right after this past week?

"I'm sorry, Laura. I didn't mean . . ." The sorrow in Nate's tone—the pain—pulled her focus. A welcome relief.

She glanced toward his brother. "How is he?"

Nate followed her gaze. "Not good." His voice cracked. "He lost a lot of blood. I don't know . . ."

She could hear the unspoken . . . *if he'll make it.* It wasn't hard to imagine the pain he must be feeling. Guilt pressed harder on her chest. "Is he your older or younger brother?"

Nate cleared his throat, and his tone dropped as he tried to gain control of himself. "Younger. By a few minutes."

She slid her gaze between them again. "You're twins? No wonder you look so much alike."

Nate nodded. "Not identical. But close in every way that matters."

She could feel the ache. The cry in Nate's spirit that said he wasn't sure he wanted to be left behind if Aaron died. She wanted to reach out, to clutch Nate's arm and tell him he still had his own life to live.

He may have to make restitution or serve a sentence for his crimes, but then he could become a new man—any man he wanted to be.

That's what she had to believe was still possible for her. Even though nothing had worked out the way she'd planned . . .

She inhaled a deep breath to strengthen her shaky legs. They wouldn't support her much longer, so she needed to either sit at the foot of the bed or leave this room. Sitting on a bed occupied by not one but two men was more than she could handle.

So she managed an "I hope he feels better," then turned and fled.

As Laura stepped into the main room, a motion by the hearth caught her focus. Joanna sat in a rocking chair, Samuel tucked in her arms as she quietly swayed forward and back. The serenity of the scene tugged at her, calling to the raw ache inside. Joanna would be safe, not forcing her to talk or relive anything from this week.

Laura approached the grouping of chairs, and Joanna smiled up at her. The sadness lacing her expression seemed befitting, yet there was a peace about her, too. A tranquility Laura so desperately wanted.

A feeling she might never know again.

She took a seat across from her friend. Joanna glanced back toward the bedchamber doors, then returned her gaze to Laura with a soft smile. "Did you sleep any?"

Laura nodded. "A little." No need to mention the nightmare. Something she'd undoubtedly relive many times over. "How is he?" She nodded toward Samuel.

Joanna's smile softened. "I think sleep will help him the most right now. I can't thank you enough, Laura. He came through far better than I feared, and I'm sure that was due to your efforts. Your protection, even at . . ." Pain crossed her face. "Personal cost. You've been injured, and I can only imagine how frightened you must have been through it all."

Laura averted her eyes away from Joanna. The words struck too close to her pain. Too near the raw places she would have to shore up. She could only nod.

Joanna exhaled a breath loud enough to hear across the space between them. "I'm sure you're as eager as I am to get back to Settler's Fort. I haven't had a chance to speak with Isaac yet about our plan to return, but I'll do that soon. Today, if possible."

She raised her brows at Joanna. "Isaac?"

The woman's cheeks turned rosy. "Mr. Bowen. He's been such a help as we tried to catch up with you. I'm not sure I could have done it without him."

It wasn't hard to tell from that blush and the small smile curving Joanna's lips that the week together had accomplished more than a simple journey. Good for them. Joanna needed a worthy man, and what little Laura had seen of Mr. Bowen made her think he would be just what her friend needed.

If the two had found love, she could be happy for Joanna. At least her friend would have what Laura always wanted.

TWENTY-SEVEN

*W*ould you like to take a walk with me outside? We could go visit the horses." Joanna dropped to her knees to wipe Samuel's face after their evening meal. He'd clutched her hand or skirt every moment since he woke from a long nap that afternoon. While she relished every contact, he probably needed something to distract his mind. Something that would pull forth a verbal reaction.

He nodded in answer to her question, his little hand gripping her upper arm as she finished wiping the last of the gravy from his chin.

At least he was responding, though not yet with words. *Restore my son, Lord. Wipe this awful week from his mind and bring back the happy lad he was before.* Not even his father's death had affected her boy this completely.

But they would recover. Together with God, she and Samuel would find their rhythm again.

A face slipped into her mind. The strong, chiseled lines of a mountain man, confident in his own skin. The man who had been her strength for much of the journey to find Samuel. Who had taken part of her load, made her feel as though she didn't have to shoulder the full weight of the worries.

The man who'd come to mean so much more to her than she ever imagined.

As she and Samuel stepped from the boardinghouse onto the street, her mind strayed back to Isaac. She'd only seen him once since they returned from the shootout on the mountain. He'd been talking in low tones with several others, probably about what to do with the prisoners, and she'd been snuggling Samuel tight in the rocking chair.

Isaac had left with those men, but not before he'd come to her side. He knelt where he could see Samuel's face and rested his hand on the boy's back. "We're real glad to have you back, son."

Samuel had nodded, one of his first physical reactions since they'd rescued him. When Isaac's eyes had lifted to meet hers, the sheen of moisture in them brought forth a matching response in her own eyes. Her soul felt both his anguish and his relief in its very core.

If she'd questioned before whether Isaac cared, she need wonder no longer. Yet, what would they ever do about that? He'd kept an emotional distance between them due to his history with the gang who kidnapped Samuel. He probably thought any chance the two of them had for a permanent connection was destroyed by his revelation.

At first, she would have agreed with him.

But now, after all he'd done for her and Samuel and Laura, all he'd sacrificed to make things right, how could she not see the man he was now? Wasn't there a verse in Corinthians that talked about a man becoming a new creation when he turned to Christ? Isaac had to be the perfect example of that.

She hadn't known him before, during his crime-ridden days. But she knew Isaac Bowen now, and her respect for the man grew with each hour they spent together.

If she were honest with herself, what she felt for him was more than respect. She'd known the intensity of love before, yet this time the emotion felt more mature. Richer.

The question was, what did she plan to do about it?

Thankfully, the livery came into view, offering the perfect distraction to her thoughts. Later, she could ponder what she would do, when her emotions weren't churning so wildly.

Just now, the whinny of a horse made her son raise his head. The inside of the stable was lit by the warm glow of a lantern hanging on the doorpost. Gentle sounds of hooves rustling in hay drifted from within, but no human noises mingled with them. It was possible Mr. Tillis may be working quietly, though.

She approached the first stall on the right and received a welcoming nicker from the mare she and Isaac had brought from the livery in Settler's Fort. "This is the horse Mama rode part of the way to find you." Should she mention the wolf attack? Normally Samuel would love that type of story, so fraught with danger. But maybe he needed to feel safe just now.

Best to settle for a simple explanation. "She got hurt, so then I rode this horse over here." Turning across the aisle, she led her son to one of the geldings.

The horse reached its head over the wall and snuffled Samuel's outstretched hand. Her son made a sound that sent a spurt of hope through Joanna. Was that a chuckle? She couldn't help her own smile as she rubbed the boy's back. "I think he likes you."

The sound of a boot thud and thumping on the hard-packed floor made her spin, her pulse surging. But the outline of Isaac's broad shoulders, framed by the lantern light behind him as he limped toward them with the walking sticks, eased the racing in her heart. "I thought that was you two I saw walking down the street." His voice was light and inviting as he came to stand beside them.

"We decided to come see the horses." She matched her tone to his.

Samuel stared up at the man, but the dim light from the lantern wasn't enough to see the expression in his eyes.

Isaac brushed a hand through the boy's wild curls. "Did you see the burros down at the end?"

Joanna held her tongue, waiting to see if the lad would respond. He shook his head.

"Well, then. You don't wanna miss 'em. Let me get the lantern." After retrieving the light, Isaac led them down the aisle. With the three of them walking side by side, as though they were a family, a feeling of rightness seeped through her.

They weren't, though, and she'd do better not to let her mind wander down that vein until she knew Isaac's thoughts on the matter.

He stopped at a stall with a solid wall around it and hung

the lantern on a nail, then turned to Samuel. "I'll pick you up so you can see inside."

Joanna peered in first, and the sight took her breath. A little donkey stood against one wall, as she'd expected to find. But tucked up against it was a miniature version of the already-small adult burro. The tiny one couldn't be even as tall as her arm was long. Maybe just the distance from her fingers to her elbow.

"How precious." She breathed the words as Isaac hoisted Samuel up beside her.

"Look." Her son's voice held a wonder that matched her own. "It's a big baby and a little baby."

A thrill slipped through her. *He was speaking.*

Isaac chuckled, the rumble rolling over her like a warm cloak. "Actually, that's a mama and her baby. Mr. Tillis said the young'un is about a month old. He also said we can go in if we move really slow."

"I want to." Samuel squirmed to get down, and Isaac lowered him to the ground. As he led the boy to the stall door, he slid a look toward Joanna with raised eyebrows. If she wasn't mistaken, he was asking whether the boy had already started talking again before now.

She shook her head, unable to keep the smile from her face. Clearly, Isaac was good for them both.

As she watched from outside the stall, man and boy approached the animals, first petting the mother, who soaked up the attention. Then Isaac held the foal while Samuel stroked its fuzzy neck and shoulder.

After a moment, Isaac stepped back, leaving the boy to

move back and forth between jenny and foal, stroking their backs and smiling when either of them nuzzled his hand or arm.

Isaac slipped from the stall and joined her beside the wall.

She leaned closer so her voice wouldn't disturb Samuel and the animals. "Thank you. This is the first time he's spoken without being prompted all day."

"I'm glad we found a distraction for him." Isaac's voice was near enough to her ear that his breath brushed her skin.

She could lean a tiny bit more and her shoulder would touch his, absorbing his warmth. His strength. Everything in her wanted to.

But she gripped the stall wall. Maybe changing to a less tender subject would distract her. "So . . . what happens next?"

She could tell by the way he stiffened that he understood exactly what she meant. He let out a long breath. "Well, there's no lawman here in River Crossing, and no telegraph to wire for one, so we need to get the men back to Settler's Fort. Lanton will know what needs to be done with them, and Aaron needs the doctor there pretty quick."

Her stomach tightened at the thought of moving the men, transporting them for over a week. How many chances would Bill have for escape? At least the one who seemed to be the worst of the lot was no longer alive for her to worry about.

Guilt pricked her chest. That wasn't the right attitude. A man's life had been taken. But what was the difference in being shot during capture or hung at the command of a judge? There was no doubt he was guilty of kidnapping, but probably a great many more crimes, also.

Isaac spoke again, so she forced her focus back to him. "A few of the men here have offered to take them, heading out tomorrow morning so they can get Aaron to the doctor as soon as possible."

She turned her face up to his. "That's good."

He was so close that she could see every nuance of his expression. The way the flickering lantern illuminated the dark green of his eyes. The faint lines feathering out from his eyes and mouth. A mouth she could still remember kissing, like a memory she could pull out on lonely nights.

He must have read her mind—or maybe her eyes betrayed her—for his gaze grew even more intense, as though he wanted to kiss her as much as she longed for him to.

But then a little-boy voice broke through her daze. Samuel was chattering to the donkey and her foal, as though they'd been his best friends all his life.

She sucked in a steadying breath and pulled back enough for the cool night air to clear her senses. What had they been discussing? Isaac's words came back in a flood, including the worry they'd summoned. Her gaze found his face again. "Are you riding with the wagon taking the men?" She could barely breathe as she waited for his reply.

He searched her eyes. "I plan to go with you, whenever you, Samuel, and Miss Hannon are ready. Do you want to ride along with the wagon?"

Laura's pale face flashed through her mind. "I don't think Laura could handle being around them again. Samuel, either." And if Bill found a way to free himself, she didn't want her son and friend to be anywhere near.

Isaac nodded. "I bought supplies today, so we can travel on our own and set whatever pace we need to." He paused, and something about the way he was looking at her made her think he was debating whether he should say what was on his mind. Thankfully, he spoke before she had to press him. "I need to ride up to the cabin with Tillis and help bring back everything the men had stored there. If we find any stolen goods, maybe we can return them to the proper owners." He eased out a breath. "Once everything is squared away, I'll come back for you. That'll give the three of you time to recover a little more before we start the journey home."

Something tugged in her chest. A mixture of emotion that was hard to sort out. "How long will you be gone?"

"A day, maybe two if this broken leg slows me down. We'll take packhorses with us, so hopefully we can carry everything."

Fear washed through her. A completely unreasonable emotion, but still the anxious thoughts churned. What if he ran into Indians? Dangerous animals? Other criminals? This land was filled with possible perils.

Isaac must have read her thoughts, for he stepped closer and cupped his hands around her upper arms. "I'll come back for you. With God as my protection, I'll return as soon as I can."

He was right. She had to trust God to keep him safe. If the Father had a future for them together, not even a mountain wilderness full of dangers could stop Him from accomplishing that plan.

TWENTY-SEVEN

*J*oanna, enough of that."

Joanna ignored Laura's words as she dipped the cloth in the wash water and wrung it out again, then set to work wiping the molding around the base of the main room. She only allowed herself one glance out the window. But the street was empty, just like almost every other time she'd looked out. Today was the second day since Isaac left to purge the outlaws' cabin. Should she be worried yet? Whether she should or not, she couldn't seem to suppress the angst swelling in her chest.

"There's nothing left to clean. Come and sit with us. My voice is tired, so you can take over reading." Laura sat in the rocker with Samuel tucked in her lap, entranced in one of the McGuffey Readers that Mrs. Holder had found for them.

The words struck a chord of guilt. Yes, she should definitely be focusing her attention on Samuel. Even though she suspected the distraction was good for Laura, too. All this restful quiet in Mrs. Holder's home seemed to be more disturbing to her friend than helpful.

The sooner they were on the trail to Settler's Fort, the better.

She rinsed out her rag and hung it to dry, then wiped her hands on her borrowed apron as she moved toward her son. A dog barked in the distance, stilling her as she strained to listen.

It was probably the hound that usually sat outside the dry goods store, basking in any sunlight it could find. Sometimes the animal even stretched out in the middle of the street to soak in the last rays.

Its baying bark sounded again. Someone must have come into town.

She shifted direction toward the door and pulled it open. On the stoop, she raised a hand to shield her eyes.

A figure on horseback rode down the center of the street, two packhorses trailing him. She'd recognize those geldings anywhere, but it was the man's confident bearing and the unique way he sat atop his horse that made her heart sing.

She barely remembered to close the door behind her before vaulting from the step and striding down the road. She needed to maintain a shred of self-control, which was the only thing that kept her from sprinting toward him.

Isaac had returned. Finally. *Thank you, Lord.*

They met in the middle of the street, and he slid from his horse, balancing against the animal's side. When he opened his arms to her, she threw her self-control to the wind, stepping into his embrace as tears slipped past her defenses.

His arms were home, pulling her from the fears and worries that had cloaked her these past days and leaving only a joy that made her want to laugh and cry and never let him go.

After long moments, he loosened his hold, pulling back enough so he could see her face. Her tear-streaked, runny-nosed face.

She ran her fingers under both eyes and let her smile shine through them. "I'm sorry. I was just . . . worried."

His own face pulled into a smile, and his gaze dipped to her lips.

Just as her middle did that flip she was becoming so familiar with, a little-boy voice called from behind them. "Isaac! You're back."

She pushed down the spurt of disappointment as she turned. The sight of her son running as fast as his little legs could carry him cleared away any lingering disappointment from the missed kiss. Her heart soaked in the picture Samuel made, with his red locks and freckles bursting in the sunlight.

"Hey there, fella." Isaac gripped his saddle with one hand and bent low to swoop up the boy, pulling him into a hug that looked every bit as strong as the embrace she'd just experienced.

Samuel leaned back within seconds, though, resting one hand on Isaac's shoulder and the other on his beard. "Did you find anything? Where's Mr. Tillis? Those bad men didn't hurt him, did they?"

Her heart clutched at the fear that slipped back in her son's tone.

Isaac met the boy's gaze with a firm expression. "Those

bad men aren't going to hurt anyone again. Mr. Tillis stopped to check on a friend at the edge of town, then he'll be along to eat with us at Mrs. Holder's. And, yes, I think we found everything they had."

Samuel wrinkled his nose. "Can I go with you to give the stuff back? I'm sure people will be awful happy."

Samuel looked to her, and she was already shaking her head. Not under any condition would her boy be leaving her side for a long time.

Before she could answer, Samuel turned his attention to something much more interesting—the horses. "Can I sit in your saddle?" He was already leaning toward the leather seat with his arms outstretched, so much like the Samuel she knew and loved.

"I reckon so." Isaac placed the boy on the seat, then extracted his walking sticks and tucked them under his arms.

As soon as Samuel was in the saddle, he bounced up and down. "Are we gonna go home soon? Mama said when you got here, we'd start back."

Isaac looked to her, the warmth in his smoky green eyes stirring her middle again. "Whenever your mama says it's time."

She met his gaze. "We're ready. We want to go home." And she could hope he understood she meant more than the little house she'd rented in Settler's Fort.

The corners of his eyes crinkled. "Tomorrow morning, then. Home."

Seven days on the trail.

Though they traveled familiar terrain, nothing about this stretch of the journey felt like the first fretful time they'd maneuvered this trail. For one thing, Joanna's person was much more accustomed to long days in the saddle. Maybe the lessening of her aches was due to them not pushing so hard.

But it seemed more likely to be from the lightening in her soul.

Thankfully, their travels had been less eventful than before as they wound their way eastward through the mountains toward Settler's Fort. Of course, Samuel had never been able to go long without some kind of mishap. His pattern held true when he contracted a rash from poison weed during their first eve on the trail. Keeping him from scratching was an impossible feat, but at least the rest of them hadn't contracted the irritating bumps.

If only she could stop the nightmares that had plagued him almost every night. She could only love him through each reliving of his terror and pray the lingering fear passed quickly.

The sweet bay mare kept up well with nothing to slow her except her healing injuries, and Mr. Tillis had sent two gentle mounts for Laura and Samuel to ride. One of them threw a shoe as they traveled a rocky section, but Isaac had purchased supplies to handle that circumstance, so he was able to reattach the shoe in half an hour. Hopefully, they'd arrive at Settler's Fort in time to send the borrowed horses back with the men who'd escorted the gang.

Now, as a thick dusk fell upon their camp on their last

night on the trail, she couldn't help but wonder what would happen when they made it back to Settler's Fort tomorrow evening.

As much as she craved normalcy, she couldn't imagine going back to the mundane, exhausting life of slaving over the laundry pot all day. Would Isaac go back to his home, his books, and his life, where she would see him rarely, if ever?

He'd not done anything to show affection since they left River Crossing. Nothing like that fierce embrace when he rode back into town. His eyes seemed to take on a longing when they landed on her, but that could well be her imagination.

Did he no longer care for her? Maybe he'd chosen to part ways when they reached town and was preparing her for the farewell. Or perhaps he was simply waiting for her to show a sign that she would welcome his touch.

She'd stepped into his arms on the street in River Crossing, but before that, she'd pulled away from each tender moment ever since he told her the full story of his background. Her own reticence might well have sealed her fate—permanently.

"Why don't you go gather water to clean the dishes after we eat? You've stirred those beans enough." Laura's voice held the tiniest hint of teasing, something Joanna hadn't heard since they rescued her from the cabin. Her friend must be sending her down to the creek because Isaac was there watering the horses. Was her pining so obvious?

Joanna's gaze slipped to Samuel, who was playing with a carved horse Mrs. Holder had given him. "Would you like to walk with me, Samuel?"

"He's going to help me lay out the bedrolls." Laura spoke before the boy had a chance to answer. "Then we'll make up a story about his new horse."

Samuel's brows had lowered at the word *help*, but they now spread in a grin as he bobbed his head. "My horse can jump higher than an eagle." He illustrated the claim by launching the toy from a rock and making it soar into the air.

Joanna couldn't help but chuckle as she stood. Laura knew just how to speak her son's language. They seemed good for each other. A bond had grown between them during the awful week they'd endured. And now they appeared to be helping each other heal from the memories. A mutual distraction, perhaps.

Joanna picked up the extra pot. "I'll be back soon."

"Take your time. These beans have a while to cook yet. Maybe you can find berries near the water." Laura's mouth held a hint of a smile as she motioned for Joanna to leave.

Her friend was definitely matchmaking, but maybe this was the chance to take that first step she'd just been thinking about.

Isaac was there by the water, sitting on a wide boulder, staring up at the mountain peaks that lined either side of the valley. The horses grazed around him, munching the grass they'd been longing for all day.

He must have heard her approach, but he didn't look over until she came to stand beside him. His face held a pensiveness that tightened something in her chest.

He patted the rock beside him. "I was just thinking how

these mountains have become a part of me. I don't think I could ever leave this country."

She took the seat he offered, allowing just enough space between them that their shoulders didn't touch. "I know what you mean. There's something about the wild splendor that takes root in your soul." She breathed in the cool air, laced with the scent of pine. "I was thinking I might bring Samuel out for camping trips once things settle down."

He glanced over at her, brow creased in a line of concern. "Just the two of you?"

She'd planned to bring plenty of protection on their trips, but he was right to worry. She couldn't tell him of her secret wish that he would be with them, too.

So she simply turned her gaze back to the mountains rising before them. "We'll see."

She couldn't observe his reaction. Couldn't tell if he read anything into her words or not.

A silence settled over them. Not a relaxed quiet, at least not on her part. Now was her chance, but how did she bring up the topic? She'd never been good at speaking of matters of the heart, not even with Robert during their marriage.

But if she didn't share her mind now, she may never have the chance again. Especially not once they reached Settler's Fort and everyone slipped back into their normal lives.

Turning to face him, she drew in a steadying breath. But a glance at his strong profile centered her even more than the fresh air. This man made her better through his presence alone.

"Isaac?" The word came out shakier than she meant for it to, so she swallowed to bring moisture into her mouth.

He turned to her, concern cloaking his eyes.

She pushed on. "I've had a lot of time to think. About what you said. About your past." She paused to gather her thoughts. Her words weren't coming the way she meant for them to. "I know it was hard to tell me everything, but I'm glad you did."

Her hand longed to reach over and take his, to slip her fingers into his reassuring grip. But she needed to get the words out first. "I see how different you are now from the young man who was looking for an easy living. You've had a wisdom about you as long as I've known you. A wisdom that maybe wouldn't be there without the choices you made early on—and the consequences you faced."

His eyes never wavered from her face, but his expression was impossible to read. Maybe the dim light concealed his thoughts now that night had almost settled on them.

She forced herself to keep talking. "There's a verse in the Bible that talks about when a man follows Christ, he becomes a new creation. I didn't know you before, but I see the man you are now. A man seeking to honor God. A man I can respect."

His gaze took on a shimmer, and his throat worked. Those had to be good reactions. Signs her words meant something to him. But his face was still so hard to read.

He moved his hand to hers, wrapping his warm grip around her tiny one. "I didn't think I'd ever hear you say that." His voice cracked on the last words, and he paused.

"I'm so grateful." He raised their joined hands to his lips and kissed her knuckles.

Tears sprang to her eyes at the emotion that now radiated from him. Could her forgiveness, her respect, truly mean this much to him?

He cleared his throat as he seemed to be gathering himself back together. "This might be too soon to ask, but I don't think I can wait. Finding a wife has never been a focus for me. In truth, I never met a woman who I wanted to be more than a passing acquaintance." His thumb brushed the back of her hand. "But all that changed these past weeks."

She couldn't breathe as his words soaked through her. Could she be hearing him right?

But he wasn't finished. "The better I know you, the more I love you." He raised his free hand to brush the pads of his fingers across her cheek. The sensation sent a tingle all the way down her back, and she leaned into his touch. "I want to be your husband. To be by your side through everything, the good and the bad. To provide for you and make your life better in every way I can. It won't be a wealthy living, but between trapping and what the mountains give, I know God will provide what we need."

His thumb stroked the back of her hand. "I want to take you and Samuel on journeys into the mountains, where we watch the beavers play in lakes and lie under the night sky to count the stars. I want to help teach Samuel how to become a man. A man who looks to his heavenly Father for guidance." His eyes searched hers. "Will you marry me, and let me do those things?"

Tears fell in steady streams down her face. Joyful tears. A release of the emotion overflowing from her heart.

They must have worried Isaac, though, for he spoke again. "I know I can't replace your husband who passed away. I can only be there for you now, to love you and Samuel with everything in me."

She squeezed his hand that still cradled hers. "Yes. Of course, yes." She sniffed, trying to stem the tears. "I'm only crying because I'm so happy. You're a good man, Isaac Bowen. The best I know. I'd be honored to be your wife."

He released her hand and slipped his arm behind her back, pulling her closer. Deliciously close, as he lowered his mouth to hover over hers. "I love you, Joanna Watson." The husky gravel in his voice sent another tingle through her, but it was only a precursor to the power of his lips as they finally met hers.

Oh, Lord. You've blessed me more than I deserve. It was her final thought before Isaac's kiss overtook every one of her senses.

Epilogue

Joanna stared into the oval mirror over the washstand in this room that would soon be hers. A nicer place than she'd lived in since leaving St. Louis a lifetime ago. She'd known love then, a youthful emotion. Maybe even infatuation.

Nothing like the fullness swelling inside her now. The absolute certainty—the peace in her spirit—every time she thought of the life she and Isaac were about to step into.

It helped that Samuel took to the man like a duckling to the water, following him through all of Isaac's chores when she and the boy had come to visit the quiet farm outside of town these past weeks.

And Isaac didn't even appear to mind Samuel's constant chatter. She inhaled a deep breath, even as that same chatter sounded just on the other side of the wall. He was giving someone all the details of the kittens born in the barn earlier that week. The smile that hadn't left her face all day widened a bit more. She could listen to that little-boy voice forever.

Even Isaac's pa seemed to relish her son's company. He'd already been taking him fishing and teaching him to whittle with an old, dull penknife—all the things a grandfather would do.

A burn crept up her throat, filling her eyes. It seemed too much for God to bless them with. After every loss she'd endured, every stripping away of the people and things she loved, to be blessed with this new family. She could scarcely believe it was real.

A knock sounded on the bedchamber door. She dabbed at her eyes and sniffed to clear the knot of emotion from her throat. "Enter."

The door opened, and Ingrid Bradley stepped in, the good friend who'd first brought her and Samuel to Settler's Fort after Robert's death. Ingrid's face glowed with the smile lighting all her features. "I came to see how I can help."

After closing the door, she took three long strides across the room and pulled Joanna into a hug. "I'm so happy for you, I can't find the words."

Joanna squeezed her friend, sinking into the warmth of the embrace. Even though they'd not had nearly enough time to spend together in the months since arriving in town, there was something about Ingrid that spoke to her soul, like the sister she'd loved and lost.

Having Ingrid here to help her on this most special of days was one more gift from her heavenly Father.

Ingrid pulled back, sliding her hands down to take in Joanna's appearance.

Joanna's face flushed under her friend's scrutiny.

"You're so beautiful, Joanna. You always have been, but today—" a happy sigh slipped through Ingrid's lips—"you are perfect."

Joanna turned away. She certainly wasn't used to such attention. "Is the food set up? Anything I can do out there?"

Ingrid chuckled. "Laura has it all well in hand. And you're not to step out of this door until I say."

At their friend's name, she turned around, her heart pinching. "How is Laura? I haven't been able to check on her all week."

A shadow passed over Ingrid's face. "Her healing will be slow. Especially since she insists on helping tend to Aaron Long's injuries. I'm glad to have her under our roof where we can help her, but I can't imagine it's easy to see the man who took part in her kidnapping every day. I'm not sure which is worse for her—memories from her time as a captive or guilt over shooting him when he was trying to save her life."

Joanna nodded. She'd been so thankful when Ingrid and her doctor husband invited Laura to work for them in their clinic, room and board included. Having a safe place to heal from both her physical injuries and the emotional scars of her ordeal was such a blessing.

But Ingrid had a point. How helpful could it be for her to face Aaron during his convalescence? Nate, too, as he was a regular visitor at his brother's bedside when he wasn't working in his new job at the mines. He'd agreed to make restitution for any stolen goods not recovered at the hideout. He would likely be working off that debt for a long time to come.

Ingrid squeezed her hands. "Laura's handling it remarkably well, and she doesn't want you worrying over her on this of all days." Her eyes twinkled, then she released her hold and reached for something in her pocket. "I wasn't sure if you had gloves, so I brought these just in case."

Joanna's breath caught at the bright white of the delicate embroidered cloth. "Ingrid, they're lovely." With tiny flowers covering the fabric and seed pearls lining the hem, the pair was more beautiful than any bit of clothing she'd seen in this wilderness country. Certainly more expensive than anything she'd worn since St. Louis. The burn of tears crept up to her eyes again.

"If you'd rather not wear them, please don't feel obligated. I only brought them in case you wanted a pair."

She sniffed, willing the tears back once again, then found a smile for her friend. "I would love to wear them, Ingrid. Thank you." She took the soft cloth and worked her fingers into each space. "A perfect fit."

Another rap sounded on the door, this one the hurried drumming of a little boy who had no time to waste with niceties like knocking. "Mama, can I come in? I got something for you."

Her smile spread wide. "Yes, honey. Come in."

Samuel pushed open the door and darted in, both hands tucked behind his back. His little body couldn't conceal the plethora of color that poked out from either side.

Ingrid pushed the door closed as Joanna bent down in front of her son. "What do you have?"

His face beamed from one ear to the other, highlighting the freckles that always brightened on his face when he'd been outside. "They're actually from me and Isaac both. We picked 'em together, but he tied it so none would fall out."

He pulled the bouquet from behind his back, hanging it upside down at first as he clutched the end of the leather tie. "I picked the pink ones 'cause I knew that was your favorite color."

The bright variety of wildflowers filled her senses as she took the bouquet, another rush of joy washing over her. "They're beautiful, Samuel. Every flower is perfect." She reached for her son and pulled him into a one-armed hug. She barely had time to smell his mostly clean little-boy scent before he pulled away.

"The paper tied on there's from Isaac. He said once I'm old enough to read, I can know what it says. He also told me to find out if you're about ready. I'm supposed to report back. You better hurry, Mama. He's already starting to melt, and the sun's not even hot yet."

Ingrid chuckled, then extended a hand to Samuel. "Come on, little man. Let's go make sure everything's in place, then I'll bring your mama out." As the boy turned to obey, Ingrid raised her eyebrows questioningly to Joanna.

She nodded. Yes, it was time. She was more than ready to become Mrs. Isaac Bowen.

Isaac had been pacing so much all morning, it was hard to hold himself still as he waited for Joanna to step from the house. Their house.

For so long, this had been merely the quiet farm where he and Pa lived. He'd never realized how lonely their existence was until these past three weeks since arriving back from their journey to rescue Samuel and Miss Hannon.

Whenever Joanna and Samuel came to visit, the yard echoed with chatter and laughter, the kitchen filling with aromas better than anything he'd thought possible. And her smile . . . when she looked at him the way she was looking now, as she stepped down the stairs, moving toward him with her graceful elegance . . . her smile lit everything around her. Righting his world in a way that made him never want to step away from her.

She was stunning as always, taking his breath and pushing away everyone else so there was only the two of them.

And Samuel. The boy walked beside his mother, holding her hand as he led her toward Isaac and the reverend. At least, that's what the boy was supposed to be doing. Really, he marched slightly ahead of Joanna, almost pulling her forward, taking his job of escorting her quite seriously.

A smile tugged at Isaac's lips. Helping to guide this lad through his growing-up years was going to be an adventure. One he was ready for, as long as Joanna was by his side.

She seemed to radiate joy as she reached him, and Isaac had trouble pulling his gaze from her face to accept her hand from her son—soon to be *their* son.

The thought brought his focus down to the lad. Samuel

looked up at him with such a cute wrinkle to his freckled nose, it was all Isaac could do not to ruffle the boy's hair. He clearly wanted to move along with the ceremony.

Isaac took Joanna's hand in his, then reached his other hand out to shake Samuel's. The boy's face turned solemn as he performed the man-sized action. Then Isaac winked, just before the lad turned and trotted back to stand with Pa.

He took one more second to meet his father's eyes, to soak in the love and pride there. He had to swallow down the lump in his throat as he nodded his thanks. Hopefully, his father knew how grateful Isaac was for him, for all his father had been to him throughout his life. But when he and Joanna returned from their overnight wedding trip into the mountains, he'd make sure he communicated his respect and gratitude for Pa with words.

But just now, it was time to turn his focus to his bride.

Joanna's eyes shone with kindness as she looked at him, as though she knew what had just passed through his mind. He adjusted his grip on her hand so he could give her fingers a gentle squeeze. A silent thank-you.

Then together, they turned to face the minister.

It wasn't hard to pledge his love, comfort, honor, and protection. Let any man try to stop him from fulfilling those promises and so many more. Joanna was the wife he never knew he wanted, but now that God had brought her to him, he would care for her and love her with his dying breath.

When the time came to seal their vows with a kiss, she turned to him, a bit of sheepishness touching her eyes. Maybe she didn't want a display of their fiery kisses in front of an audience, and he would respect that.

He used his free hand to reach up and cradle her face, then leaned closer and brushed her lips with his, tasting the sweetness unique to her alone and leaving behind a promise of what was to come. The love he would share with her to the end of their days.

USA Today bestselling author **Misty M. Beller** writes romantic mountain stories set on the 1800s frontier and woven with the truth of God's love.

She was raised on a farm in South Carolina, so her Southern roots run deep. Growing up, her family was close, and they continue to maintain those ties today. Her husband and children now add another dimension to her life, keeping her both grounded and crazy.

God has placed a desire in Misty's heart to combine her love for Christian fiction and the simpler ranch life, writing historical novels that display God's abundant love through the twists and turns in the lives of her characters. Learn more and see Misty's other books at www.MistyMBeller.com.

Sign Up for Misty's Newsletter!

Keep up to date with Misty's news on book releases and events by signing up for her email list at mistymbeller.com.

More from Misty M. Beller

On her way to deliver vaccines to a mining town in the Montana Territory, Ingrid Chastain never anticipated a terrible accident would leave her alone and badly injured in the wilderness. When rescue comes in the form of a mysterious mountain man, she's hesitant to trust him, but the journey ahead will change their lives more than they could have known.

Hope's Highest Mountain
HEARTS OF MONTANA #1

You May Also Like . . .

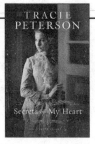

Reunited with childhood friend and lawyer Seth Carpenter, recently widowed Nancy Pritchard must search through the pieces of her loveless marriage for the truth behind her husband's death after his schemes come to light. But as they pursue answers, their attraction to each other creates complications, and dark secrets reveal themselves.

Secrets of My Heart by Tracie Peterson
WILLAMETTE BRIDES #1
traciepeterson.com

When her grandfather's health begins to decline, Havyn is determined to keep her family together. But everyone has secrets—including John, the hired stranger who recently arrived on their farm. To help out, Havyn starts singing at a local roadhouse—but dangerous eyes grow jealous as she and John grow closer. Will they realize the peril before it is too late?

Forever Hidden by Tracie Peterson and Kimberley Woodhouse
THE TREASURES OF NOME #1
traciepeterson.com; kimberleywoodhouse.com

Ex-cavalry officer Matthew Hanger leads a band of mercenaries who defend the innocent, but when a rustler's bullet leaves one of them at death's door, they seek out help from Dr. Josephine Burkett. When Josephine's brother is abducted and she is caught in the crossfire, Matthew may have to sacrifice everything—even his team—to save her.

At Love's Command by Karen Witemeyer
HANGER'S HORSEMEN #1
karenwitemeyer.com

BETHANYHOUSE

More from Bethany House

Years of hard work enabled Douglas Shaw to escape a life of desperate poverty—and now he's determined to marry into high society to prevent reliving his old circumstances. But when Alice McNeil, an unconventional telegrapher at his firm, raises the ire of a vindictive co-worker, he must choose between rescuing her reputation and the future he's always planned.

Line by Line by Jennifer Delamere
Love along the Wires #1
jenniferdelamere.com

Wanting to do her part in the Civil War effort, Clara McBride goes to work in the cartridge room at the Washington Arsenal. Her supervisor, Lieutenant Joseph Brady, is drawn to Clara but must focus on preventing explosions in the factory. When multiple shipments of cartridges fail to fire and everyone is suspect, can the spark of love between them survive?

A Single Spark by Judith Miller
judithmccoymiller.com

Determined to uphold her father's legacy, newly graduated Nora Shipley joins an entomology research expedition to India to prove herself in the field. In this spellbinding new land, Nora is faced with impossible choices—between saving a young Indian girl and saving her career, and between what she's always thought she wanted and the man she's come to love.

A Mosaic of Wings by Kimberly Duffy
kimberlyduffy.com